BROKEN

PEOPLE

Also by Sam Lansky

The Gilded Razor: A Memoir

BROKEN PEOPLE

A NOVEL

SAM LANSKY

HANOVER
SQUARE
PRESS

HANOVER
SQUARE
PRESS™

ISBN-13: 978-1-335-01393-4

Broken People

This edition published by arrangement with Harlequin Books S.A.

Hanover Square Press
22 Adelaide St. West, 40th Floor
Toronto, Ontario M5H 4E3, Canada
HanoverSqPress.com
BookClubbish.com

Printed in U.S.A.

For Dave, who is a part of this story, too

If you were lonely
and you saw the earth
you'd think *here is*
the end of loneliness
and I have reached it by myself.

—Mary Ruefle

BEFORE

Part One

1

An Invitation

*"**H**e fixes everything that's wrong with you in three days."*
This was how it began: casually, not as a grand pronouncement framed as a life-changing event, but just an off-the-cuff remark, and later Sam would wonder how his life might have gone if he hadn't overheard it, or if he'd never been there at all, at this dinner party at the home of an architect somewhere in the Hollywood Hills. There were so many alternate realities in which Sam had made other plans, or failed to look at his calendar and forgotten about it, or just decided not to go and canceled at the last minute—after all, not going to things was one of the few great pleasures of adult life—and then what would have happened? Everything would have been different.

But he had gone to the dinner party. It was a breezy winter night during that hopeful string of days in January just before everyone fully scraps their New Year's resolutions, the cheer of the holidays a recent enough memory to sustain a few more days of good-naturedness, and the dinner party had the feel, as so many things in Los Angeles did, of having been cast, populated with colorful characters from different backgrounds and industries who the host had hoped would find some conversational common ground at the seams of their interests. There was the heir apparent to a casino empire; a character actress Sam recognized from a guest arc on a Netflix show; the architect's ex-lover, an interior designer who had done a capsule collection for West Elm or something; and then Sam, a writer—and probably, he had sussed out, the least fancy person in the room. None of the guests really knew one another, only the host, which made the evening feel a little disjointed, nobody being certain where they fit.

Or maybe, Sam thought, everyone else was actually having a perfectly lovely time and it was just him forever lingering on the fringes of connection, unable to belong—who could say? That wasn't the point.

The point was: at the moment Sam heard it, this odd comment cutting through the din of silverware scraping against dishes and the hum of jazz from an overhead speaker, something shifted almost imperceptibly in the room, like a lens refocusing on its subject.

"What do you mean?" Sam asked, in a high, strange voice that didn't sound like him. He had been quiet for most of the evening, sitting stick-straight with his belly sucked in and his chest puffed out to try to make himself look thinner, picking at the grilled chicken breast and asparagus on his plate as conversations bloomed around him, amiable chatter about misspent winter holidays and the Republican sweep of the recent election, which was worrying to the people at the party because they were liberal but not too worrying because they were all, as far as Sam could tell, rich. Now suddenly he was fully engaged, enough so to interrupt what had previously been a private dialogue between the architect and a pretty but brittle older woman, a stack of Cartier love bracelets clanking on her thin wrists, who was seated between the two of them.

Sam dropped his voice down an octave. "I'm so sorry, that was rude of me—I just totally inserted myself into your conversation," he said. "But what does that mean—he fixes everything that's wrong with you in three days?"

The architect extended his hands outward as if to say, *Who knows?* His name was Buck, and he was handsome in a gently creased, effortless way: ruggedly built, with salt-and-pepper hair and a puckish smile, and eyes that hinted at magic, and that particular tendency Sam loved in other gay men, the ability to code-switch from masculine to luxuriously queeny depending on who he was speaking to, his gruff tenor turning suddenly velvety.

"He's some healer," Buck said. "A master shaman. A client in Marin County spent a weekend with him and said it was the most extraordinary experience of her life."

Sam blinked a couple times. "Right, but what does he do? I mean, fixing everything that's wrong with people! Does he claim to, like, cure terminal illnesses?"

"No, no," Buck said. "Maybe I said it wrong." He dabbed at the corner of his mouth with a napkin. "My client said that the shaman heals other conditions. Depression, anxiety, addiction, trauma—that sort of thing. Emotional stuff. She was in the absolute grips of postpartum depression and after three days with the shaman she was cured. Like ten years of therapy in a single weekend, she said. He works in small groups, doing private retreats. I was thinking about hiring him for my fiftieth next month." He laughed. "I probably shouldn't go into fifty like this."

"But how?" Sam said, a little desperately. He looked around at the other guests, who were now watching this exchange, rapt, as it assumed a new intensity that verged on impolite. "I mean, if you could do ten years of therapy in a single weekend, wouldn't everyone be doing that with this shaman instead of, like, going to therapy?"

"Five stars on Yelp," someone said.

Quickly the conversation turned back to easier subjects, and for a moment Sam considered trying to keep the discussion going, but he didn't know how to do so elegantly, and so he just dropped it, and this felt deeply weird to him—that no one was even remotely curious about getting more details about this mysterious master shaman who could fix everything that was wrong with you in three days.

But then, a few minutes later, the woman next to Sam brought it up again. "You sounded very curious about the shaman," she said. Maybe she'd read it on him that he wanted to keep talking about it.

"It's just not the sort of thing you hear every day," Sam said. "And I'm interested in…how people change, I guess. If people can change."

"What would you change about yourself if you could?"

Sam took in the question. *Everything*, he thought. "I don't know," he said instead.

"Buck said you're a writer," she said. "That you published a novel."

"Yes. Well, no. Not a novel," Sam said. "A memoir."

"What's the difference?"

"A novel is fiction," Sam said. "A memoir is an autobiography, but it reads more like fiction. It's a person telling a story from their life."

She studied him appraisingly. "You look a little young to have written a *memoir*," she said, pronouncing the word in an affected Francophone style, *mem-wah*. "Famous parents? Or did you fall into a ravine mountain-climbing and claw your way to safety or something?"

"No," he said, feeling his face grow warm. "Just a colorful account of all the dumb things I did when I was a teenager in New York." This was usually how he explained it when it came up in these situations. He balled his hands into little fists under the table.

"I knew you weren't a mountain climber," she said, satisfied. "Well, I'll read it anyway." She took a sip of her wine. "Will you write more books?"

"Yes," Sam said. "I mean—I'd like to. I should be so lucky."

"What's the next one about?"

"Love and sex. That kind of thing."

She shook her head. "When I was young, we just talked with our girlfriends about who we were sleeping with—not the whole world. You millennials make everything so public!" She looked off at nothing. "I did always want to write a book, though. It seems so romantic." Then she turned back to Sam. "My friend Danielle Steel writes books. Do you know her?"

Sam shook his head slowly. "No," he said. "No, I don't know Danielle Steel."

"Oh."

"So what would you change about yourself, if you could?" he asked.

She considered it for a moment. "My neck." She pulled back the vaguely crepe-like skin beneath her jawline until it was taut, the stacks of bracelets sliding noisily down her forearms. "But I'll go to Dr. Markowitz for that." She released it and laughed hoarsely. "Not some medium or whatever."

"Your neck looks great," Sam said gently. "You don't need to do anything to your neck."

"You're sweet," she said, pulling at her neck again. "I wish I'd been more grateful for my youth when I was young. But so it goes, right?"

When she said this, it occurred to Sam that he should appreciate his own youth now while he still had it; and then this, the next thought, that there was a very real possibility that he would still be pathologically self-conscious and anxious when he was this woman's age, and that idea, of the years sprawling out before him, of never being able to quiet the chorus of self-obsessed insecurity, of it just going on like this for decades, filled Sam with a dread so black that it was nauseating.

It would be better to be dead, he thought, and the feeling was potent in a way that made him want to say it out loud, to stand up from the dinner table and announce, "I want to be dead!" He did not want to die, in a practical sense—the corporeal permanence of death terrified him—but rather, to already be dead, to skip the death process and coast into a static condition of un-being, was something he fantasized about often. Certainly that had to be better than sustained consciousness.

Does everyone feel that way?

Say something.

"So it goes," Sam said loudly, and he took a bite of chicken breast and chewed it very slowly.

At the end of the night, Sam put on his jacket and said goodbye to the other guests. Buck was in the kitchen, filing dishes into the sink. It smelled like olive oil and lavender, and Sam thought, for a moment, about how nice it would be to have a home like this.

"Thank you for having me," Sam said. "It was great to get to know your friends." This was a lie. He had been uncomfortable for the entire night, anxiety gnawing at him, that sense of being uneasy wherever he was ratcheting up in intensity the longer he'd stayed. He felt ambiently guilty, as he often did. Maybe it was because he hadn't brought a bottle of wine, as everyone else had, even though he was sober and so he would not have been able to drink it; but, as he had considered it, a recovering alcoholic showing up to a dinner party carrying a bottle of wine was likelier to cause concern than the rudeness of showing up empty-handed.

A Diptyque candle, he thought. *You should have brought a Diptyque candle.*

Buck turned to face him. In some animal part of Sam's brain he wondered whether Buck wanted to sleep with him, and whether that was something that Sam himself would like, too. Sam thought that he would. He didn't know Buck well but the older man seemed interested in Sam, although Sam couldn't quite divine what the nature of that interest was— if it was friendly or flirtatious, driven by lust or curiosity. For a moment he imagined himself wrapped in Buck's arms, Buck's stubble on Sam's face—how good it would feel to be held, rough or tender—and then, just as quickly, that desire browned to loneliness, like fruit oxidizing, and Sam felt stupid and greedy for wanting it in the first place.

"I'm glad you came," Buck said. His voice was softer now, more liquid. The two men stood for a moment, hips squared toward one another, and again Sam noticed the way the atmosphere thinned slightly. "If you're curious about the shaman," Buck said, "I'm flying up to have dinner with him in a couple weeks. You should come with." He said this so coolly it sounded unremarkable. Maybe for Buck it was.

"Where does he live?" Sam said. "The shaman."

"Oregon," Buck said. "Portland."

"Oh, that's where I'm from," Sam said, surprised.

"Kismet."

"I think you basically have to be a shaman to live in Portland," Sam said. "Or a vegan chef. Or a scrappy, fiercely opinionated writer at an alt-weekly. Or you work at a coffee shop but pay your rent by selling restored vintage clothes on Etsy. Those are the only four jobs in Portland. Everyone does one of those four things."

Buck didn't laugh. "Right," he said. "You should come."

"It's really nice of you to invite me."

Now Buck smiled, but it was at how Sam had sidestepped the offer. "Think about it," he said.

Outside Buck's house on the street, in the cool still night, a siren wailing somewhere distantly, Sam hugged his arms around his shoulders and walked toward his car. At certain moments it still felt implausible that he actually lived here, in Los Angeles, after having spent so many years in New York, like at any moment he might wake up to find that he had just dozed off on the F train early one morning and dreamed up the last two years of his life. He liked silent, empty nights like this—not the crowded anonymity of being one of a thousand bodies weaving their way up and down congested Manhattan sidewalks but an open sky, a sleepy residential neighborhood, his feet padding soundlessly down the hill. In New York, Sam had been lonely but never alone. Here his solitude was verifiable, externalized; it existed out in the world, shadowed by streetlight.

He was twenty-eight now. Time only moved forward. He was old enough to feel ashamed of not having accomplished more, though people liked to remind him, in a way that irritated him, that he had accomplished quite a lot, but when he went to things like a rich guy's dinner party he still felt like a little kid playing dress-up, miming out the behaviors of his parents but never quite getting it right—a laugh that went on a little too long, fumbling with the dinnerware, standing on the edge of a circle of people chatting congenially and swirling their drinks as he waited for a point of entry that never materialized.

Maybe it was because he was sober that he always felt out of place. Still, he kept getting invited to things, which was curious to him—that his discomfort was felt but not seen, that he had developed enough of a mask over years of enduring awkward social situations that people couldn't instantly intuit how he felt all the time. What a thing, he thought—to be well liked by everyone but yourself.

Sam unlocked his car, watching the headlights illuminate the darkened street. At night you couldn't see the scuffs and scrapes on the rear bumper and driver-side door of the car, a black Audi sedan that he had leased the week he had come to California, still buzzing from the high of having picked up his entire life and left New York. He hadn't even considered whether or not he could actually afford it on his modest salary, hadn't researched whether it was a good car, even. He had lived in New York since he was a teenager and had never had a car of his own before, though he did know how to drive, sort of, and the Audi, with its sleek contours and luxury finishes, looked like the kind of car that would be driven by someone who had made it, someone who really had their life together.

The car was a big long boat of a thing that barely fit into the cramped parking spot in the garage of his West Hollywood apartment complex, and it was nearly impossible to wedge into the compact spaces that filled most lots in Los Angeles. Within the first month Sam had already crashed it twice, backing carelessly into medians and scraping it against a wall trying to park at Whole Foods when he urgently needed to pee. And then driving down Melrose, a woman had rear-ended him, and when they pulled over around the block she got out of her car crying, waving her phone around with Instagram still open on the screen, begging him not to go through insurance because if she got in one more accident she'd get her license revoked, and Sam felt so bad for her that he just took down her phone number and never called her or bothered getting it fixed, since the damage was all cosmetic and the car was already beat-up enough anyway. He had grown to hate the car, this expensive symbol of his impracticality.

Never mind that after a few weeks driving it around Los Angeles, on streets clotted with Range Rovers and Bentleys, it no longer seemed like that nice of a car. An Audi sedan came in the West Hollywood gay guy starter pack, along with an Equinox membership and those Gucci mules everyone seemed to be wearing. (Neither of which Sam could really afford after his lease payments.) Sometimes it felt as though everyone in Los Angeles was rich and yet nobody ever seemed to work.

Sam did work and he was not rich. He was the entertainment editor at a magazine in the twilight years of old media, in an economy where the internet was threatening jobs like his into obsolescence; all it would take, he thought, was one pivot to video and he'd be out of a job. He had failed to recoup the advance on the book he'd released a year earlier, about his troubled adolescence spent strung out on drugs and in rehab, although its underperformance was a secret, or so he told himself, something only he and his publisher really had to know. His whole life looked good on paper, but it didn't actually net out to much.

Privately Sam wondered when he was included in things like this, the dinner party at Buck's house, how much his résumé was responsible for the invitation, because it made him

seem interesting by default, especially because he was still rel-
atively young. So few people in Los Angeles even read books
that to write one seemed to strike people as very special,
though of course, Sam reasoned, there was a time when writing a book was only a wild dream to him, too, but then, most
things become unremarkable as soon as you have done them.

On some level he remained certain that he had stumbled
into this career through sheer dumb luck and someday, un-
avoidably, he would be exposed for the fraud he was and the
whole house of cards he'd built from these accomplishments
would come tumbling down, leaving him with nothing. People talked so casually about "imposter syndrome," like it was
just a nagging occasional anxiety to be rationalized away.
But Sam found that each morning the constriction around
his throat had grown a little bit tighter, even while he continued to try to project an image of confidence and success,
meeting friends at SoulCycle and picking up the tab for dinners out—"No, no, I got this," he'd say as he swiftly grabbed
the check, trying to ignore the guilt that clawed at his throat
about how unaffordable it all really was, to stay in the warm
bright swell of beautiful spaces and beautiful things for one
more moment until reality kicked back in.

Where did that come from, he wondered? Was that a gay
thing? An upwardly mobile middle-class thing? Was it a mental health thing? Or maybe it was just a symptom of modern
life, when there were so many different ways for Sam to have
his own inadequacy reflected back to him, every time he
opened Instagram, where, it seemed, everyone was always in
Mykonos or Tulum in their designer clothes and white teeth
and abs, always the abs.

Yet the thing that depressed him the most was that he had
no traction on the second book. The book was his albatross.
Once he finished it, he imagined, things would get easier—an

influx of cash, even a modest one; a sense of forward momentum, something to point to as proof that he wasn't actually that much of a flop; and maybe when it came out, he would finally be content. But contentment—every time he thought he was approaching it, the finish line jumped to just beyond his grasp. That wouldn't happen after this book was done, he told himself as he got into the Audi. This sense of unbelonging would actually leave him, for good.

It must have been his résumé, Sam thought as he made switchbacks down Laurel Canyon—the reason Buck had asked him to dinner in the first place, to fill a vacancy in the cast. Surely Buck didn't see Sam as a romantic prospect. He probably just wanted Sam around as a new and interesting thing to show off, like the Aston Martin parked in Buck's driveway—which, Sam noticed, did not have a single scuff.

At the base of the canyon, Sam called his best friend, Kat.

"How are you?" he said.

"Emotionally exhausted," Kat said. "Just leaving therapy." She said something to this effect every time they spoke, which they did nearly every day, and this was comforting to Sam, both the predictability of it and the intimacy that came with having known someone for so long you could completely drop the veil and say exactly what was on your mind without fear of being misunderstood. They had become friends when they were in high school and had somehow managed to remain close through all the turns of early adulthood, and were so connected now that when they spoke, Sam could intuit the meaning behind the slightest modulations in the tone of her voice, knew exactly what she was about to say before she said it.

Kat lived in Portland, their hometown, so they only saw each other a few times a year now, but in his mind's eye he could see her as vividly as if he were watching her on a closed circuit camera—driving across a bridge through the rain, windshield wipers working furiously, a curvy blonde in yoga pants and a hoodie, forever running late to a workout class, sucking six-dollar cold brew through a straw. People underestimated Kat because she was pretty and voluble, but she was flintier, and more perceptive, than she seemed.

"What's going on?"

"Oh, the usual," she said. "Existential dread and environmental despair. Did you see this new report out today about the sea level rising? I spent all afternoon spiraling."

"No. What did it say?"

"Sam," she said emphatically. "We have, like, twenty years left before we're all basically underwater." Kat talked about the end of the world like it was an inevitability. Maybe it was.

"I don't know if I can take that in," Sam said. "My anxiety is already so bad just scraping through my life as it is. If I truly engage the possibility that the planet is dying, it will incapacitate me and I'll end up just completely withdrawing from the world and never leaving my apartment again. You know?"

"But isn't that exact attitude how we ended up here?" Kat said. "None of us can accept how fucked the earth is so we just keep, like, busying ourselves with work and life, pretending like it's going to be fine! I just keep thinking, like, why is my boss sending me 9:00 p.m. emails about this new business pitch tomorrow when we're in the middle of a mass extinction event? And when can I tell him to fuck off and just move to a commune in Southeast Asia or something to live in peace until the Big One hits?"

"I'll meet you there," Sam said. "I'm ready to go analog." He thought about it. "Although you know they won't have pressed juices or a spin studio on the commune."

"But I only need those things in the first place to distract myself from the fact that the world is ending," Kat said. "Which is probably why my credit card is maxed out. And did I tell you two new stretch marks on my thigh popped overnight? Literally overnight, Sam."

"Having a body is the worst."

"The worst," she echoed, like it was a chant. "My New Year's resolution was to be more gentle with mine, so I've been following all these body-positivity activists on Instagram, right? And I'm dying to believe that they've found a way to truly accept themselves and embrace their curves and find health at every size, but I just don't understand how it's possible." Her voice dropped. "Like, am I really just supposed to look at some pictures of bigger-bodied women and read a Rupi Kaur poem and undo a literal fucking lifetime of having it messaged to me by society that my value as a woman is contingent on the size and shape of my body?"

"I don't know," Sam said. "I don't think gay men are told that by society so much as we're told that by each other. Which is fucking harrowing, too." He sighed. "And part of me just wants to pull the rip cord and stop habitually undereating to maintain a body weight that's within the bounds of gay-acceptable, but if I do that, will I ever find a husband? But will I ever find a husband anyway? So wouldn't it be better to just be fat and happy?"

"More important," Kat said, "does any of this even matter when everything is on fire all the time?"

"I wish I had never been born into a body," Sam said. "My soul should have been born into a haunted painting, or a cursed pendant that torments a family for generations."

"A haunted painting!" Kat said, like it was a bright idea. "I'd be so much better at that than I am at being a human woman."

Sam paused. "I went to this fancy dinner party tonight and this guy was talking about some shaman who fixes all of your emotional problems in three days."

"Dude," Kat said. "How do we get in to see him?"

"It gets spookier," Sam said. "He lives in Portland."

"No shit. Do you think I've seen him at my barre class?"

Sam laughed. "But do you think it's possible? To just, like, fix people?"

"Of course not. If it was, rich people would just, like, hire a shaman and be happy," Kat said. "And all the rich people I know are miserable." A horn honked in the background. "Learn to drive!" she yelled. "Sorry. Not you."

Sam pulled into his garage. "The guy invited me to go up to Portland and meet the shaman. Should I do it?"

"Absolutely," Kat said. "Like, what if you do it and you're just, like, one of those people who floats through life on a cloud? What if he makes you, like, not neurotic and self-destructive and body-image-dysmorphic and burdened and you just, like, love your body and feel good about yourself and shit?"

"I think if my anxiety and depression were going anywhere, they would have gone there by now, right?" Sam said. "Like, I'm pretty sure this is just how I am." He drummed his fingers on the dashboard. "You know. That sweet spot between normal and completely fucking losing it all the time."

"'Normal' is bullshit," Kat said. "It's, like, something Big Pharma invented in the '60s to make consumers feel bad about themselves. You sound exactly like everybody else who's at least semiconscious as we collectively speed toward the cliff with our brakes cut— Fuck, there's never anywhere to park." He could hear the murmur of rain splashing on the windows, her car pulling to a stop. "I'm late for my yin class. Let me call you back."

★ ★ ★

Sam sat in the car for a long moment after the call ended, staring ahead, lost in thought. It wasn't possible, this idea that you could completely change in a single weekend.

He knew that.

2

Hummingbird

The second sign came the very next morning, when Sam awakened to find something unusual in his bedroom.

The window by his bed, slatted and casement-style, with a rusty old crank that groaned when he turned it, had been open all through the mild Los Angeles winter, which had allowed the bougainvillea that crept up the facade of his apartment building to wrap its tendrils around the narrow glass panes. This produced the illusion of waking up each morning in a garden, the floor littered with a few pale pink petals. Some months earlier he'd opened the window to let a little fresh air in and had just never closed it. He liked feeling both outdoors and in, liked the smells of lavender and smoke that drifted into the room.

But now there was something in his room, a form furiously beating its wings and slapping against his window from the inside. When Sam first stirred, disoriented and still half asleep, he wasn't sure what it was, but he could see its frantic motions. Was it an enormous flying cockroach? Were those a thing in California?

Yet when he sat up, reaching for his glasses, he realized it wasn't an insect at all. It was a hummingbird, iridescent blue with a long pincerlike beak. She was frightened, insensibly smacking against the glass and bougainvillea with startling force. It would not have shocked Sam if the window frame had cracked from the thrust of her movements. She was just an inch or so from the opening in the window, but the spiny fingers of the bougainvillea's vines and leaves had obscured her exit route, leaving her trapped.

Sam moved closer to her and her movements grew more panicked. He reached out with one hand as if to whisk her outside, but she flew out into the room, circling frantically over his bed, then making a run for the other window, which was closed. She whipped against the glass helplessly, urgently, as if possessed.

Him being there was probably just stressing her out more, Sam thought. Maybe if he left the room, she would find her way outside. This was how he preferred to deal with most problems—ignore it and hope it goes away on its own.

He backed out into the hallway, closing the door so he could no longer hear that frenzied slapping noise. In his living room, Sam caught a glimpse of himself in the mirror. His close-cropped brown hair was pushed to one side from sleeping with his head buried in the pillow, and his face was ruddy. He walked closer to the mirror and studied his reflection as he did so many times a day, pushing out his belly and sucking it back in again so his rib cage protruded over his stomach, pulling at the flesh around his midsection, as if the motion might shrink it.

He was tall and broad, with a frame that could carry a deceptive heaviness, but after a lifetime of losing and gaining weight, he'd reached a sort of equilibrium where, he thought, he was neither objectionably fat nor did he have the kind of body that he ever wanted anyone to see. In a preening, health-conscious place like Los Angeles where everyone talked about their bodies constantly, he spoke of his hardly ever, only to Kat, who understood the way he felt; it was as if he hoped by not mentioning his body, people might not notice that he had one. He fantasized about having the sort of physique where he could post thirst-trap selfies and have his inbox fill up with fawning messages, the kind of body that would make men cruise him at the gym, but he had settled here instead, and as he looked at himself for a long moment he felt silly for caring so much about the way he looked.

Noah had liked his body, Sam thought, and some distant loss pinched him in the form of a memory; he wished he had a partner still, someone to provide backup in the fight against quotidian challenges like a hummingbird invasion.

How would Noah have handled it, Sam wondered, if they were still seeing each other—or, rather, if they were still spending every night together, as they had done until fairly recently? It had never been a real relationship, exactly—more like a fling that had spiraled out of control. They had decided to see other people, but Sam knew that was the beginning of the end: a phasing out of one another, as hourly texts turned to daily check-ins, and soon weeks would pass without them speaking at all.

It wasn't surprising that it had flamed out. They were both addicts in recovery, which had given the beginning the texture of something laced with a speedy euphoria, all crackling electricity and empty promises about tomorrows that felt so real in the whirl and spill of the moment. But after they had built up a tolerance to one another, they stopped making each other high; they had seen too much of one another's darkness, in ways Sam was loath to relive now, the way last night's hangover can poison tonight's revelry. Addicts, even sober ones, are always using something. If you are lucky, you will realize it when the thing they are using is you.

But Noah would have been handy here. He would have taken charge of the situation with the hummingbird, found some way to fix it, like that's just a thing that you reflexively know when you are a certain type of man. A basic life skill, like changing a tire or catching a football: evacuating a bird from a bedroom.

As with all the guys Sam dated, Noah was half man and half boy; in his late thirties, he wavered between the infectious excitability of a little kid and a very grown-up seriousness—which was earned, Sam knew, since his life had been hard. Sam had been spared many of the graver consequences of his own using years, scraping by with no lasting material repercussions, although whether that was the product of dumb luck or good hustle or divine intervention he couldn't say; he'd even gotten a book out of it. Noah had paid a heavier price. Like Sam, he had been an intravenous drug user before getting clean, but unlike Sam, Noah had spent time homeless, living on the streets of London until a nasty overdose brought him to his knees. Now five years sober, he was an advertising executive who had come to Los Angeles to work on a project for a client. Looking at him now, so polished, you would never have guessed that his history had been so tortured.

They'd met at a twelve-step meeting in Silverlake, where Sam went swoony over his loose, slackerish charm. He was tall and lean and the night they'd met he'd worn a hoodie and sneakers that made him look like an implausibly handsome Brooklyn dad, or the guy that the protagonist of a sitcom dates for an episode or two. He was Paul Rudd sun, Mark Ruffalo moon—all scruff and the right amount of smarm. On their first date, over a long, lazy dinner at Soho House— Noah was a member and actually hung out there, which was douchey, but also hot—Sam was so enamored with him, his warm, unaffected amiability and the frank way he recounted the horrors of his past, which in the retelling seemed some- how breezy, less hellish than instructive. Years of sharing his story in meetings had made him a nimble orator, deft at tempering the dark with the light. He didn't overtell the story, the way Sam always did; he was clear and concise and true, and his accent, to Sam's susceptible American ears, made him seem automatically important. "Crystal meth gave me wings," Noah said.

"Then what happened?" Sam asked, even though he al- ready knew the answer.

Noah's eyes went dark. "It took away the sky," he said.

"There's something different about this guy," Sam told Kat on the phone that night.

"What's his deal?" she asked.

"I don't know, dude," Sam said. "He's really sparkly. Like someone who knows he's getting a second chance and isn't gonna waste it."

But the thing with Noah had imploded in the most ter- rible of ways. Sam should have known better. He always got snookered by charisma. It was his favorite drug.

Gingerly he cracked open his bedroom door, hoping to find stillness, but instead, there the hummingbird was again, humming like a radiator in a New York winter. At the sight of Sam, she began to beat her wings even faster, pounding against the glass again, of the wrong window—the one that was entirely closed. Sam stared at her, or perhaps they were staring at each other—it was hard to say.

He retrieved a broom from the hallway closet and returned to his bedroom, brandishing it like a weapon. Gently he lifted its bristled end toward the bird, pushing it in her direction, and she skipped along the surface of the glass like an ice skater on a rink, searching for an exit that wasn't there. He pushed it closer to her and off she went, back to the half-opened window, her little claws scuttling and scraping. The sun beamed cheerfully onto his face, haloing the bird in light. Once more he pushed the broom toward her, until she found the opening and flew away.

And just like that, he was alone again.

But all morning, Sam was haunted by her—the hummingbird. Sitting in his living room, he heard the slapping of wings somewhere in the periphery; when he turned to look, though, there was nothing there. By midafternoon, he felt unsoothed enough to call his mother.

His mother was a wise woman, learned and fierce. When Sam was growing up, she had been expansive in her interests: she researched the life of Jesus, then the holy wells of Ireland, then Native American animal medicine, then the pagan rituals of her Scandinavian ancestors, from which a passion for genealogy had sprung, and so she mapped both sides of the family back centuries deep, making pilgrimages to Norway to meet anyone with whom she shared a scrap of genetic material. After Sam's parents divorced when he was a teenager, and Sam left Portland with his father to finish his last few years of high school in New York, she settled into her traditions, or maybe they settled into her. She moved to an A-frame cottage in the woods of Oregon, where a rosary hung from the door and a carved wooden scepter adorned with the tail of a fox rested against the kitchen table; she said it was her animal totem. Now on Thursday afternoons she volunteered at a nearby women's prison, teaching spirituality workshops.

Sam loved this about his mother, loved the way she saw the world even if he didn't always buy in. When he was visiting her, there was nothing that felt better than untangling the symbolism of a bewitching dream over the morning's coffee, his performance of begrudgingly discussing it, pretending to be too cynical but sort of believing whatever she said. If he told her he had seen a coyote while driving back to her house that night, her eyes went saucerlike with wonder.

"Oh, man," she would say, standing to retrieve a book from the shelf, then returning to her overstuffed armchair by the fireplace, tucking the voluminous folds of her bathrobe underneath her. "That is a powerful omen." She was a village mystic without a tribe who might benefit from her wisdom, and so Sam tried to, whenever possible, as much for her satisfaction as for his own.

He told her what had happened with the hummingbird. "Wow," she said emphatically. Then, again: *"Wow."*

"What does it mean?" Sam asked.

"Was the bird agitated?"

"I mean, it was a hummingbird," Sam said. "I kinda feel like agitation is their natural state. And like, honestly, same."

"I should really consult some texts before I give you my take on this," she said. "Let me call you back."

A few minutes later, Sam's phone rang. "Okay," his mother said. "The hummingbird has great significance in many different traditions. The indigenous peoples of the Andes Mountains believe that the hummingbird dies on cold nights but comes back to life when the sun rises, so it represents resurrection and rebirth. Its wings actually move in a figure eight—

like the infinity symbol—which make it a powerful marker of eternity and continuity. And because it can fly backward, the hummingbird teaches us that we can look back on our past. But in Native American cultures, they believe that the hummingbird represents a spirit being who helps those in need—like a shaman."

"It's a symbol of a shaman?" he said. The back of his head went numb and that thing happened again, like the air in his apartment was changing in its composition, the light filtering in through his blinds growing a little brighter.

"Yes," she said. "Why?"

"That's—that's just weird," he stammered. "I was at this thing last night and people were talking about a shaman." He considered it, talking himself out of it. "Then again, it's LA, so people talking about a shaman probably isn't that surprising, right? Only this guy is up in Portland, which is another weird coincidence, I guess." He paused. "What does a shaman do?"

"Oh, a lot of things," his mother said. "Healing people using ancient wisdom. Plant and animal medicine. Mediating between the realms." In her steady tone, it sounded unimpeachable.

"So what's the difference between a healer and a shaman?" Sam asked, biting his nails.

"Healers work with energy," she said. "And a lot of people work with energy, in different ways. But a shaman is more about the spirit world—connecting with the divine realm and harnessing that power to do good in this one—in the material world."

"Right."

"Why are you asking me about this?" she said.

Sam rubbed his eyes. "I don't know," he said. "This conversation last night, and the hummingbird this morning—it feels like something. It's sticky. I can't explain it."

"Maybe it's the call," she said.

"What call?"

"You know," she said. "The call of the spirit world. The call of what's beyond."

There was a long pause. Sam looked again at his reflection in the mirror that rested in a diagonal angle in one corner of the living room. The mirror was over six feet tall and four feet wide and made of hammered steel—an artifact from his life in New York, from a much fancier apartment than this one. Like everything in his apartment, including Sam himself, he thought, it was so solid, so heavy, so unmistakably of this world.

"Or maybe a hummingbird just flew into your room," she said to his silence.

A few hours later, Sam drove to lunch, the leafy streets of West Hollywood giving way to the scrubby strip malls that dotted Santa Monica Boulevard heading east, an airless skyline, midday bumper-to-bumper traffic for no apparent reason. He parked on Larchmont just south of Melrose, putting two hours on the meter.

Elijah was waiting for him on a bench outside Café Gratitude, wearing a rumpled blazer and leather loafers, like a walking advertisement that he'd come from New York, studying a menu as if it was written in a foreign language. Which, for all intents and purposes, it was.

"Elijah," Sam said, and Elijah looked up and smiled, pulling him into a bro hug, the kind of half handshake, half embrace Sam had never been able to execute right.

"Sammy," Elijah said. He squeezed Sam's shoulder. "What the fuck is this place, huh? You've really gone full LA on me."

"We're all eating plant-based now. Has that not made it back to the East Coast?"

"Christ," Elijah said, sizing him up. "Look at you. You look so healthy."

"I don't want to look healthy, Elijah. I want to look thin."

Elijah waved a hand dismissively. "Shut up," he said. "Let's get a table."

Elijah was Sam's book agent, and he was a good one, or so Sam hoped, although to be fair he was the only one Sam had ever had. He had signed Sam as a client when he was just a year out of college and had only a few freelance clips under his belt. Together they'd shaped the proposal for what became Sam's first book, the memoir about his troubled adolescence and efforts to get clean. Elijah had rightly identified that Sam's story fit tidily into an existing genre: addiction memoir was a reliable bet, and the book had sold to a major publisher. But they hadn't seen eye to eye in their subsequent conversations about Sam's next book. When Elijah had written him to say that he would be in town for a few meetings, Sam had seized the opportunity to meet with him in person. He would sell him on this book. And if not that, at least it would be a free lunch.

"So," Sam said after they sat down. "Did you read the pages I sent you?"

Elijah made a humming noise with his mouth. "I did, yeah," he said. "I'm just not entirely sure you have it yet, Sammy. I don't know the story you're trying to tell. I don't really see you on the page."

Sam felt his shoulders arch reflexively. He forced them down his back. "What does that mean? It's my story. How can I not be on the page?"

"I mean—listen, part of the problem is the form, right? I know we've had this conversation a handful of times already but I really have to caution you against trying to write another memoir. It's such a hard genre. Especially for men. I mean, it's a women's genre, frankly—and I just think it's very limiting for you—and if you're going to do it, well, it has to be extremely focused, with a very strong and marketable hook, and I just don't think you have that yet. I'm not even really sure what it's about."

"It's about finding myself in my twenties," Sam said defensively. He looked over Elijah's shoulder, where a girl in a fringed suede crop top was posing for a photo with her turmeric latte, its saffron foam clinging to her lip. Her friend passed her the phone to review the pictures. *Story or grid?* the girl asked.

"But you haven't found yourself," Elijah was saying. "If you want me to be honest, it feels like you don't really have the distance to tell this story yet. Like you haven't learned all the lessons. I see this problem, this lack of self-awareness, so often in confessional writing."

Sam hated that word—*confessional.* How diminishing it was. "Oh, I think I'm self-aware," he said. "I know my problems intimately. I just have no idea how to solve them."

"And that's it! That's the gap between self-knowledge and wisdom. You don't have the wisdom yet," Elijah said. "And if you're going to write a memoir, you need that. This might be therapeutic to write, or even necessary, but it isn't satisfying to read, and your misery makes you unlikable on the page." He raised his hands. "Now, maybe if you wanted to write a novel, or a reported work of nonfiction, that might make more sense for you, but I just don't see a commercial path forward with this."

The girl in the fringe was taking pictures of her avocado toast now. *Am I basic?* she asked her friend, who laughed. *Yes!*

"But this is the only thing I know how to do," Sam said.

"Memoir is just—" Elijah sighed. "Listen, don't get me wrong—I'll sell it if it's sellable—but it feels like we're raising a generation of narcissists who believe that their experience is important enough to justify broadcasting to the world. And most of them just…aren't. Everyone's a memoirist. Social media is just one big memoir."

"No, we're a generation of public diarists," Sam said. "Your Throwback Thursday—that's a memoir. There's a difference."

"What's a Throwback Thursday?" Elijah said.

"Never mind," Sam said. "Elijah, I really believe in this story."

"I'm sure you do," Elijah said. "But not all stories demand to be told."

"So is that what you're saying?" Sam said. Something inside him twisted. "Elijah, I've been working on this for over a year. You're saying this story isn't worth telling?"

"No, I just mean…" Elijah sighed. "Maybe there just isn't a book here." He rested his hands on the table as if he were about to deliver some bad news, and now his voice sounded kinder, even if what he had to say was brutal. "You know your problem? Because you are young, you think everything that happens to you is interesting."

Sam slammed the door hard as he got back into the car. He fumbled in the center console for the in-case-of-emergency pack of cigarettes he had stashed away. He lit one, rolling down the windows as plumes of smoke surrounded him, then sped away.

He knew Elijah had been fair in his assessment, that he had identified the thing Sam was most afraid of anyone seeing—which was that he really didn't know what he had spent the last year writing. He had begun out of necessity, telling the story of everything that had precipitated his departure from New York, and then had attempted to fashion something resembling a narrative out of that cathartic outpouring, trying to discern why it had all happened the way it did, a Rorschach test with the blood on the page. But this was the maddening paradox of writing about your life: in order for it to be any good, you had to know what it all meant, and in order to know what it all meant, you had to write about it, and there he was, a snake eating its own tail, scouring his past for answers he didn't have.

And then, stopped at a traffic light on Fairfax, the thought flashed through Sam. *What if the shaman could fix it?* It was impossible. But what a seductive fantasy, this notion that he could have all his issues resolved overnight. Imagine the book he could write then, with all that profound self-knowledge.

Except life did not work that way. People did not heal in a weekend through some mystical experience. It did not matter how much money you had to try to buy it. It was not possible.

Sam reminded himself of this as he drove back to West Hollywood, past the juice bars and yoga studios and walk-in psychics, and past a crystal store, where a slab of raw amethyst sparkled, smugly, from inside a glass case.

3

Symptoms

Sam paced around his apartment as the sun set. He read and reread the pages he'd been working on, the ones Elijah had found lacking. Furiously, he ordered takeout, a bowl of seaweed and vegetables from a vegan restaurant; if he was going to be a professional failure, he told himself, at least he would not be fat. But by the time it arrived, he had worked himself back up into a frenzy and was no longer interested in wellness. He just wanted to feel secure and heavy. He wanted to eat the feeling, to eat at the feeling, to eat in a way that would both harm the feeling and harm himself for having the audacity to feel it.

He threw the bowl away without opening it. Waste of money. *This is why you're broke.* He ordered two burgers from Shake Shack and did not eat them so much as he inhaled them, tearing at the chewy bun with his teeth, tasting the way the salt made his mouth go at once dry and gummy. He smoked three cigarettes on his fire escape, one after the other, sending text messages to all the guys he'd had casual sex with in the last year. Just thinking about you. How have you been? He opened Grindr and began to scroll through the rows of toned torsos, squeezing the flesh on his stomach anxiously.

But then, mercifully, one of the guys he'd texted responded—Martin. Come over, Sam said. He brushed his teeth and punched the remnants of the takeout trash deep into the garbage, lighting a candle to mask the stale aroma of the binge. There was nothing to be done about how queasy he now felt, but this—this need to act out—was like an override switch that would keep his nausea at bay, at least until after this was over.

Sam wasn't even that attracted to Martin, who was boyishly handsome but a sloppy, overeager kisser, yet being with him was preferable to spending the evening alone, spiraling. Mostly Sam was irked that Martin was, as far as he knew, happily married; Sam knew they had an open relationship, to which he had no philosophical objections, but Sam hated the idea that Martin could sleep with him and then go home to a stable partner. It was so gluttonous, to seek sex on top of love. Sam followed Martin on Instagram and resented him profoundly. Every time he posted a photo of his husband with some affectionate caption—"So lucky to have found this guy!" followed by a string of heart-eyed emoji—Sam felt that rage bubbling up inside him, all those spiteful tides of envy and want rising like bile in the back of his throat. *This guy*. Sam hated that.

But when Martin arrived at his door twenty minutes later, wearing a guilty smile, it didn't matter that he was him. As far as Sam was concerned, it could have been anyone. In fact, Martin had put on some weight around his midsection in the months since they'd last seen each other, which was welcome for Sam; it meant that he would feel less self-conscious, less ashamed of his body, reasoning that, on some level, he couldn't be rejected by a guy who was fatter than he was—and the ugliness of that thought, and the security it gave him, made Sam feel even darker—but still, he was safer here than with any of the strong-jawed guys with trim physiques who crowded Santa Monica Boulevard just east of Robertson on weekends, spilling out of gay bars, their foreheads dewy with sweat, liquor-tipsy and free in their bodies. And as Sam tugged Martin into bed, he had the sensation of sinking, into his basest impulses and into that uneasy crevice that existed between desire and disgust, junk-food sex, his chest heaving, his worst self, soft bellies, all that hunger.

After it was over, they lay next to each other, panting. Then Sam turned over on his side. "Do you think people can change?" he asked.

"Oh God," Martin said. He scrunched his eyes closed, then opened them again. "Do we have to do the deep pillow talk thing? I get enough of that at home."

"Just answer the question."

"Of course people can change," Martin said. "People are always changing. Like rivers or whatever. We never stay the same. Personally, I'm getting worse all the time." He side-eyed Sam. "Why are you asking?"

"I was at this thing last night and people were talking about a shaman who can fix everything that's wrong with you in three days," Sam said.

"Well, that sounds like a stretch. Unless you're already pretty close to perfect."

"What would you change about yourself?" Sam asked.

"I dunno," Martin said. "I could probably be a better hus-

band. I should be more grateful for everything I have, I guess."
He rubbed his eyes. "You?"

"I'd probably hate myself less, if I could," Sam said, and as
soon as he'd said it, he realized it was too unvarnished a thing
to say, but it was too late.

"Why would you say that?" Martin asked. "Why do you
hate yourself?" He rested his hand on Sam's head, in a way
that was more intimate than they really were; Sam jerked
away.

"Oh, fuck, I don't know," Sam said. "I just do. I always
have. Doesn't everyone?"

"No, I don't think so. Not to make you feel worse."

"Really? I think of self-loathing as being so universal. We
all have so many symptoms."

"What do you mean by symptoms?" Martin said.

"You know," Sam said. "*Symptoms.* You drink or you take
drugs or you smoke or you fuck strangers or you don't fuck
anyone or you codependently entangle with people or you
overeat or you starve yourself or you binge and purge or you
compulsively exercise or you spend money you don't have
or you gamble or you self-harm or you throw yourself into
work so you don't have to bother with having a personal life
or you binge-watch shit on Netflix because fictional characters are just so much easier than actual people with all their
very real faults and shortcomings or you stay in bed all day
trying to blot out the world on those days when it's all just
too much to bear." He stared up at the ceiling. "But all those
behaviors, even though they look so different, are symptoms
of the same problem—you can't be with yourself. Because
you don't like yourself."

"But why don't you like yourself?" Martin said impatiently.
"You're a good person." He cocked his head. "I think. There
could be bodies under your bed."

It was a good question. Sam thought maybe there was no why. Maybe some people are just born self-hating and self-destructive and we die that way. And so we go to therapy and twelve-step groups and we take antidepressants and anxiety meds and we journal and go to yoga and exercise and take baths and drink pressed juices and repeat affirmations to ourselves in the mirror and listen to Brené Brown podcasts. But we're just swimming against the tide, because the darkness always comes back. All we ever do is learn to manage the symptoms.

"I'm not sure," Sam said. "I wish it didn't feel this way."

Martin fumbled in the bedsheets for his underwear, like he was uncomfortable. He stood and pulled his shirt over his body, as if suddenly realizing that he was exposed, and Sam felt a brief flash of tenderness, and then, just as quickly, it dissipated.

"I'm sorry that it's so dark for you right now," Martin said. "Maybe you're depressed. Have you ever been to therapy?"

Sam fumed silently. Tears sprang into his eyes. He blinked them back. He would not cry—not here. Not with this guy. "Yes," he said. "I've had a lot of therapy. Therapy can be great. But it can also be so...*diagnostic*." He said the word like it was a slur. "What about when you already know how and why you're fucked up, but you can't seem to fix it, no matter how hard you try? What then?"

"My therapist helped me see how much my unhappiness was a choice," Martin said. "It was really useful."

"So you think people choose misery over happiness because, what—they prefer self-hatred?"

"I think you might be attached to it," Martin said. "I mean, I don't know you that well."

"You were inside me five minutes ago," Sam said. "That's like a gay handshake."

"Oh," Sam said, "now who's being dark?"

Martin raised his hands as if to say, *I surrender.* "I'm gonna go." He stood and kissed Sam on the forehead. "I hope you find a way to be nicer to yourself," he said. "You don't have to be unhappy."

"I'm not unhappy," Sam said. "I'm trying."

"Right," Martin said, and he shut the door behind him.

The third sign came later that night in the form of a dream. At first, Sam was falling through an inky sky. He moved his arms, but they weren't arms—they were wings, only they didn't work. As he descended into the darkness he heard something that sounded like an ancient hum, a long buzzing. His plumage was spectacular but he was broken. He knew exactly what he was, this sad and mangled thing. Thin spindly bones. Webbing as sinuous as lace. When he opened his mouth, no noise came out. Just a gust of feathers, cobalt as a tropical sea.

He landed at the surface of a window, or maybe it was a mirror. He stared back at himself, the long stem of a pincer obscuring his face. And then he was beating at his reflection, so violently. There was a spray of blood. Finally it cracked open and there were shards of glass everywhere, like diamonds in the soft down of his bloody feathers.

He opened his eyes. It was morning, but still early. His phone, charging on the nightstand, was ringing. It was Kat, her contact photo a picture of the two of them from some New Year's they'd spent together years earlier, both grinning goofily, and for a moment Sam was struck by how young they looked. Then he picked up.

"Hello?" he said blearily. He knew she was upset before she spoke, just from the way she inhaled. "What's wrong?" he said.

"I just had the worst panic attack," she said. Her breath was shallow.

"What happened?"

"I don't know—I just—I woke up early with this horrible weight on my chest and I couldn't stop thinking about that climate change report and how, like, incredibly fucked up the world has become, and then I started thinking about my own ticking clock and how much pressure I'm under from everyone—from my mom, from society, from all the girls at my agency—to have babies when, like, what kind of future would I really be giving them, you know? I mean, kids are getting gunned down in their schools, like, every week." She groaned, like it was too much to take in. "If you even make it through childhood, you're inheriting a planet that we've already destroyed. Everything is just so bad right now. Everything is bad and I have to go to Melissa Schuman's fucking wedding this weekend and pack my tits into a truly heinous bridesmaid's dress and pretend like the world isn't falling apart, and it's just like, why? For what?"

"You don't have to have kids," Sam said. "So many women—so many people—don't have kids. That's okay."

"But I do want them. I just don't want them to have to live in this world."

"I'm so sorry, Kat," he said. "I really am." He wanted to offer a solution of some kind—to tell her to stop reading the news, to be in nature, to meditate—but he knew it would be trite and unhelpful. Being a friend didn't always mean solving the problem. Sometimes it just meant bearing witness.

"Don't you get stressed out about this shit?" she said, like an accusation.

Sam closed his eyes. "Most of the time it all feels like it's happening really far away from me. Like the world is something that's happening to other people, but not to me. Maybe it's just that there's so much clutter already in my brain that I can't take in anything else. As if all of my anxieties are a barrier between me and all the things I should be worried about." He felt selfish and small. "Sometimes I wonder if this is just what being a person feels like. I thought it would be different."

Kat took a long beat with this. "I am definitely not a model of mental health but you sound super depressed," she finally said. "Maybe you should go back on the Wellbutrin."

"Oh, no. It made my anxiety even worse. I was *twitching*."

"Lexapro?"

"My dick completely stopped working."

"You're having sex? With America more divided than ever?"

"That's not the point."

"What does your therapist say?"

"I stopped going a few months ago."

"Why? You didn't tell me that."

"It just wasn't productive anymore."

"Are you sure?"

"Yes," he said. "Kat, I don't want to talk about my problems anymore. I'm so tired of listening to myself complain." He took a deep breath. "I don't know how to fix it for you, but at least know that you're not alone. I feel like I'm coming apart most of the time, too."

"What do we do?"

"I don't know," Sam said. "I really don't want to be like this."

After he got off the phone with Kat, he fell back asleep. When he awakened a few hours later, sunlight beaming into the bedroom, petals on the floor again, he saw a message from Buck on his phone.

Going to meet the shaman next Monday, it read. Want to

come? He'd sent it early that morning, while Sam had been on the phone with Kat. How funny. It made him feel like there must have been some electricity in the air in that moment, some energetic field that they were tapped into, an invisible current of hope and need. The problem; the answer.

For once, Sam didn't overthink it. There was nothing to think about, really. He just replied.

Yes, he wrote, and as he typed, his fingers didn't feel like they belonged to him—as if something was moving them, something that was not him but wasn't not him, either, and when he looked down at the screen to see what he had written, it was so plaintive it actually surprised him.

It said, Take me with you.

4

Magical Thinking

The shaman wore khakis.

And a collared shirt. And a V-neck sweater. And round eyeglasses. He had close-cropped hair and white teeth. He could have been a substitute teacher, or a suburban dad on a rare night out, or the new boyfriend your divorced aunt brings to Thanksgiving dinner. He was nondescript, unmemorable, square.

His name was Jacob.

They were at an upscale farm-to-table restaurant in Portland, crowded with good-looking young people. The shaman had suggested the place, and now that they were there, the whole thing felt so bougie, much more so than Sam had anticipated, although given Buck's income bracket it probably shouldn't have come as a surprise that even his shaman would pick a restaurant that had Aesop hand soap in the bathroom.

"So, Jacob," Buck said. "Tell us about your work."

"Sure," Jacob said. He wiped his mouth and leaned in closer. Like puppets on strings, Sam and Buck both leaned in, too. Jacob's voice dropped an octave.

"I operate a clinical practice in the field of transdimensional intercession," Jacob said.

Buck and Sam looked at each other, then back at Jacob. "Right," Sam said. "What does that mean?"

"Well, let's start with the first part—transdimensional," Jacob said. "If you think about the world we live in, the physical world, that's one dimension. So—I don't know what you believe, and frankly, it doesn't matter—but since you're here, you probably believe that there's stuff happening, sometimes, that you can't necessarily see or manipulate in the real world, in this dimension. So maybe you call that God. Maybe it's many gods. Maybe you call it energy. Maybe for you it's memory or emotion—subtler things, that everyone agrees exist. But whatever it is, not everything that feels real is right at our fingertips all the time, right? There are things that exist outside of real-world experience, but just because you don't see them doesn't mean they aren't real."

Sam nodded. "Okay," he said. He was curious where all of this was leading.

"So you might ask yourself, what is the place where all that stuff exists? Let's call that another dimension. Maybe it's a lot of other dimensions. But it's out there, somewhere." Jacob motioned at nothing. "Or maybe it's in here." He pointed at his chest. "Or maybe it's both. But what you have to understand is that the universe, in its totality, is a multidimensional cosmic energy field, comprised of many worlds, which include infinite realms of nonmaterial, transtemporal and transspatial consciousness. Whether we acknowledge it or not, we are part of this interdependent field system. And under certain circumstances, it becomes possible for us to communicate with other life forms, objects and beings. Is that clear?"

The way he spoke was slightly tense. It was as if he was tracking the movements of everyone in the room behind him—not distractedly, but as though he could sense their energy shift as a server bent down to remove a plate or light a candle. He wasn't timid; there was something forceful and a little bit steely about him. Sam could tell this was a man who cared little about being liked, and he was both envious of and intimidated by this quality.

"Absolutely not, but keep going," Buck said. He looked spellbound. "This is fascinating."

"Okay, let me put it more simply," Jacob said. "When I say 'transdimensional,' what I'm talking about is opening the gate between this dimension, that we're in right now, and other ones, and allowing travel between the two. Does that follow?"

"Sort of," Sam said.

"That brings me to the second part—intercession."

"And what is that?" Buck asked.

"It means I'm intervening on your behalf," Jacob said. "To call in the great power of the spirits that live in those other dimensions into this one to heal you. You also may end up crossing dimensions, traveling into others and inviting what lives there into yours. But the bulk of the work is done by me, as the intercessor, working with the spirits that are out there in other dimensions to remove whatever is causing suffering. We clear it out. I call it a clinical practice because that's really what it is—it's like surgery. And like surgery, it's very intense. It can be quite painful. But it is extremely effective."

"And where, Jacob," Buck said, "did you learn to do all this?"

"I've trained with cultures around the world," he said. "And my practice synthesizes teachings from many different traditions. With the Tungus of Siberia, in the birthplace of shamanism. With the holy swords of the Hmong tribe in Laos. With Bwiti practitioners in Gabon, working with the Tabernanthe iboga. And I lived in the Amazon with the curanderos of the Shipibo tribe, who taught me how to work with the healing properties of *la medicina*." He said this as untheatrically as if he was listing any other kind of educational or professional history: *Wharton, then two years at Goldman.*

"I've heard Laos is beautiful," Buck said. "There's an Aman there, right?"

"Okay," Sam said. "Can I zoom out for a second?"

"Certainly," Jacob said.

"I get that all of this is mysterious and mystical and I don't need you to give me a blow-by-blow of exactly how it all works. But on a practical level, what exactly do you do?"

"I work over the course of three evenings," Jacob said. "And on each evening, I hold a ceremony. Although in many ways the three-day experience is its own sort of extended ceremony."

"What happens in the ceremony?" Buck asked.

"A number of things," Jacob said. "There's an energy clearing. Some prayers. Songs. And I administer plant medicine."

"Plant medicine?" Sam said.

"I work with a number of different medicines," Jacob said. "Tobacco. Sage. Cacao. But primarily I work with ayahuasca."

"Oh," Sam said.

Buck looked at Sam, registering the disappointment on Sam's face. "What's ayahuasca?" he said.

"It's a psychedelic, right? You trip?" Sam sighed. "Yeah, I don't think I can do that." He'd heard a little bit about ayahuasca, which seemed to be a thing trendy, wellness-minded people were doing in private but rarely discussed in polite company, like cocaine for the self-improvement set. Sam had been sober for so long that he had stopped trying to keep up with the latest in mind-altering substances. The sheer fact that he had to double-check whether hors d'oeuvres at parties in Los Angeles contained cannabis or not was irritating enough. That he'd come all this way—and put a plane ticket on his nearly maxed-out credit card to get a pitch for an ayahuasca trip—was just demoralizing.

"Why do you say that?" Jacob asked.

"I'm in recovery," Sam said. "I mean, I've taken hallucinogens—I did mushrooms and acid when I was a teenager—but I've been completely clean for over eight years. I don't do anything anymore."

"Sorry—what is ayahuasca?" Buck said, a little louder than was necessary. The waiter set their appetizers down on the table. Jacob waited until he was gone to answer the question.

"It's a very powerful plant," Jacob said. "A medicine from the jungle of the Amazon that helps heal the body, mind and spirit. When used responsibly, in ceremony, its effects can be profound. I have used it as part of my practice for many years now."

"So what does it do?" Buck asked. Sam shot him a look. He was jealous of Buck, suddenly—jealous like he'd never been watching anyone drink a glass of wine over dinner, which was something Sam had explored comprehensively enough to know that it didn't work for him. But this was different: ayahuasca was something Sam had never tried, had never even considered, and it was maddening that Buck could have this conversation in a way that was so open and curious when Sam could not.

"Well, it's very misunderstood," Jacob said. "On a cosmic level, ayahuasca is a living intelligence from the plant kingdom that opens you up to the spirit dimension. But as I mentioned, this is a clinical practice. Think of it like anesthesia. It makes the transformation possible, but it is not the transformation. In this analogy, I'm the doctor. And the spirit that ayahuasca allows for connection to—that's the scalpel."

"But don't people just, like, go drink it in Peru and have crazy visions?" Sam said. "That's all I've ever heard about it."

"People use ayahuasca in that way, yes," Jacob said. "But most Westerners are given so much medicine right off the bat that they just get blasted out into space with no ability to navigate it. That's like asking everyone to be their own sha- man, which is impossible to do without any training. In my practice, I am working *on* you. That's why I only work in very small groups, tailoring the experience for each individ- ual, gradually opening you up to the medicine."

"So," Sam said. "How you're explaining this is, people drink the ayahuasca, you open the door for the spirit, and then the spirit comes in and fixes people?" It already sounded suspect— like all he really did was get people intoxicated enough they would believe anything.

"There's a little more to it than that, but yes," Jacob said.

"And what do you heal?" Sam asked. "Or, the spirit, I guess? The spirit as it acts through you?" It wasn't totally clear.

"It is possible to heal many things with this work," Jacob said. "Physical maladies. Broken hearts. Autoimmune disor- ders. Addictions. Ancestral trauma." He sounded melancholy as he said this, like he had tended to too many of these con- ditions before.

"Okay, I have another question," Sam said. "Is this, like, a magical thinking thing, where you have to believe in spir- its and stuff? Or does this work on, like, miserable, cynical people, too?" He realized that he had sounded a little too breathless and tried to backpedal. "Not that I can do it. Or am going to do it. I'm just curious."

"The spirit doesn't care whether you believe in her or not," Jacob said.

"Her?" Sam said. "It's a her?"

"Yes," Jacob said. "Her. The mother. Or grandmother. The great spirit of the medicine. She will show you what you need to see."

"Like, with visions?" Buck said.

"Maybe," Jacob said. "And then there are times when it's not what she shows you but what she removes. She burns away that which you no longer need, so you can truly understand all the stuff that's ordinarily protected by unconscious defense mechanisms. There's so much that's running below the threshold of regular consciousness that's toxic or limiting. She gets rid of that. Often through various forms of purging."

"You throw up a lot, right?" Sam asked.

"Sometimes," Jacob said. "Not necessarily. It's whatever you need to let go of. Sometimes it's vomit. Sometimes it's laughter. Sometimes it's tears. Sometimes it's shit. We all have things we need to release. This medicine just helps with that."

Sam wondered which form his release would take, if he were to do this. He hoped it would be laughter or tears. The others sounded not quite worth it, especially in front of Buck, who was now, to Sam's relief, signing the check for their very expensive dinner.

"But, to be clear," Sam said, "there's really no way to know if any of this works until the person gets in there with you, right?"

"It works," Jacob said simply. "But if you want to understand more, I can show you."

"What—you want to drug us with ayahuasca right now?" Sam said.

Jacob laughed. "No," he said. "But I can give you a preview."

Sam had met Buck for the first time the summer he had arrived in California; they had been seated next to each other at a dinner theater show, some campy thing at the Rockwell in Los Feliz that a friend had invited Sam to. Sam was taken with Buck instantly. He was good-looking, with silvery hair and a slightly manic quality, one of those people who radiated success. They exchanged phone numbers. Later, Sam asked his friend, a well-connected Instagram gay, if he knew who Buck was.

"Oh, sure," the friend said. "He's in the gay mafia. I'm pretty sure he only dates, like, underwear models he meets at yacht parties."

Sam briefly considered his pathological fear of being shirtless in public and decided to let this one go. It was easier to assume men wouldn't be interested in him than to run the risk of being rejected. Soon he had forgotten all about Buck.

But about a year later, on a dreary winter night, Sam was leaving a holiday party at Tower Bar, standing at the valet waiting for his car, when he saw Buck by the door, studying his phone. "Buck," he said. Buck looked up, not recognizing him. "Sam," he said, introducing himself. "We met last year at that—"

"Oh, right!" Buck said. "At that show. How have you been?"

"Great," Sam lied. "Are you on your way out?"

"Yeah, just leaving dinner," Buck said. "Calling an Uber."

"I'll give you a ride," Sam said, almost without thinking about it. It was a strange offer for him to make, but the impulse overtook him before he had a moment to reconsider.

"Don't be silly," Buck said.

"No, I'm happy to," Sam said.

Buck shrugged. "If you say so," he said, and Sam's car pulled up at the valet.

They made their way down Sunset, past Saddle Ranch, where tourists in cowboy hats and what looked like a bedraggled bachelorette party stood outside, smoking cigarettes, and past the Chateau, where a clutch of paparazzi was gathered at the mouth of Marmont Lane, waiting for a glimpse of some starlet stumbling out of the back of a chauffeured Suburban, when Buck spoke. "So what's been going on?" he asked.

"Same old," Sam said. "Working. Writing. You're an architect, right?" He remembered, of course, but he didn't want Buck to know that he recalled their first interaction that closely.

"Yeah," Buck said. "That's all fine. Working on a big project out in Santa Barbara. It was a rough year, though."

"Why?" Sam asked. He pulled into the left-turn lane at Crescent Heights, the drone of his turn signal hypnotic as a metronome. Most of life in LA was just waiting to turn left.

"I had a really bad breakup," Buck said. "It was—it was kind of traumatic, actually." He laughed, more to cut the tension than because it was funny. "I'm seeing this kid, right? And yeah, he was a lot younger than me—I mean, listen, I remember the Carter administration—but I thought he was different, you know? He was really smart. And ambitious. Seemed like he had his head screwed on straight."

"How old was he?" Sam asked.

"Nineteen," Buck said. He raised his hands defensively. "I know, I know."

"It happens to the best of us," Sam said. But it didn't. Sam couldn't imagine wanting to be with someone that young. He wondered if he'd crave it when he was Buck's age, whether the years he'd spent searching for a father figure in a partner would invert.

"So he wanted me to come with him to Coachella," Buck was saying, "which was probably my first mistake. And then we got there and he…" He laughed. "He ditched me for his friends! Just left me there, like such a fuckin' idiot. Took all the molly I'd bought, too. It was so humiliating."

"I'm sorry," Sam said. "That's shitty."

"I don't know if it was even about him so much as it was about—you know, really having to look at myself," Buck said. "Like, why I keep picking the wrong people. Why I keep dating these boys who are half my age, or younger, even. What am I trying to connect with? Why can't I just, you know, act my age? I'm just so stuck."

"Being gay is a nightmare," Sam said.

"It is!" Buck said.

"And this kind of thing makes you doubt yourself," Sam said. "Right? That's the thing about heartbreak. You can grieve the loss of the person you cared about. But you grieve yourself, too. The version of you that was naive enough to trust. And then you second-guess yourself. Because if your intuition led you to him, how good can it really be?"

"Yes," Buck said. "That's exactly it." He looked over at Sam. "And, you know, I'm lonely, I guess. So I've just been drinking—all the time. I'm sorry. I know you're sober. I know you wrote that book about it."

"Thanks," Sam said, not quite sure what to say.

"Was it hard?"

"To write the book?" Sam thought about it. "Of course. I think writing about yourself is probably the easiest thing to do and the hardest thing to do well. Do you know the writer Vivian Gornick?"

Buck shook his head.

"She talks about how in a memoir, there's two separate forces on the page, both called 'I'—the character 'I' and the narrator 'I.' The character 'I' is the one in the story, the one everything is happening to. But the narrator 'I' is the one controlling how the story is told, and what new understanding you impart in the telling of it. It's not a memoir because something happened to you. It's a memoir because you learned

BROKEN PEOPLE

something from it. Because you found a narrative persona—that 'I'—who is the parts of you that can best tell the story."

"So you must have found that," Buck said. "If you were able to write the book."

Sam shrugged. "I don't know," he said. "Sometimes I feel like I did. I had a writing teacher who told me, it's not about what you remember—it's about why you remember it *that way*. But that version of you stays frozen in time forever in this thing that sits on a bookshelf. It's weird." He felt suddenly self-conscious. "Sorry," he said. "I never get to talk about this stuff."

"I think we all do that, don't we?" Buck said. "We all, you know, tell stories about ourselves and get attached to the version of us that we think we are. You just made yours public."

They pulled up in front of a ranch-style house. "Thanks for the ride," Buck said. "I like talking to you." It was so simple, the way he said it. There was something boyish about it, something vulnerable.

"I like talking to you, too," Sam said. "You know, with the drinking..." He hesitated, not sure whether to go further. "If you ever want to go to a meeting sometime, or need someone to talk to, I'm here."

"Thanks," Buck said. "I appreciate that. Really." He opened the door. Then, almost like an afterthought, he said, "I'm traveling over the holidays but let's get together in the new year. You should come for dinner."

"I'd love that," Sam said.

And then Sam had gone to that dinner party where all this had begun. How odd it was. If there had been a shorter line at the valet at Tower Bar; if he'd stopped to use the restroom before leaving; he might never have seen Buck, and he wouldn't be here at all.

★ ★ ★

The men had stopped at an office building. Jacob stepped forward, fumbling with the keys, and they followed down a dimly lit corridor. At an unmarked door halfway down the hall, Jacob retrieved his keys once more.

"This is my office," he said, opening the door. He switched on a table lamp, illuminating the room.

Buck and Sam stepped inside after him, surveying the space. There was a massage table, covered with a plain white sheet, and a set of overstuffed chairs in either corner of the room, a window looking out at a side yard. A shelf was adorned with a few trinkets: a cylindrical tower of clear white crystal, perhaps a foot high, and a stone hand with prayer beads draped between its fingers, and a small pot containing a round tab of charcoal and some loose incense, and a tarot card lying faceup—the Knight of Cups—with its remaining deck facedown. Sam inhaled and caught a whiff of some aroma—sage, maybe, tinged with juniper.

Jacob turned to face them. "Now," he said. "Which one of you shall I demonstrate on?"

Sam turned to Buck, trying to mask his panic. "You do it," Sam said. "This was your idea."

"Absolutely not," Buck said. "I want to see what happens. You go."

"Does it hurt?" Sam said to Jacob.

"No," Jacob said. "I mean, it depends on what we find. But it shouldn't."

"All right," Sam said. "I'll be the guinea pig."

"Great," Jacob said. He cleared his throat. "You can sit there," he said to Buck, who sat down on one of the chairs in the corner. "And you can sit here," he said to Sam, pointing to the massage table.

Sam took a perch on the edge of the table and folded his hands in his lap. He felt a flurry of nerves.

Jacob fixed his gaze on Sam. His eyes were not unkind but they were unyielding in a way that was disconcerting, as if he already knew everything that Sam wasn't ready to share.

"So what is it?" Jacob said softly.

"What do you mean?" Sam said. He laughed anxiously, looking at Buck for support. Buck lifted his hands as if to say, *I don't know.*

"Don't look at him," Jacob said. "Look at me. What is it?" His gaze was penetrating.

"I don't know," Sam said. He didn't want to do this in front of Buck. He couldn't be this exposed. He stood up to leave, not knowing where he would go. Then he sat back down again.

"It's okay," Jacob said soothingly, like he was casting a spell.

"Oh," Sam said heavily. *What is it?* "I'm just fucked," he said.

"Can you be more specific?" Jacob said.

"I don't know," Sam said. He couldn't look at Buck. "I guess I've had enough therapy to know that I don't like myself very much."

"What does that feel like?" Jacob said.

"It feels like…" Sam trailed off. "I have this loud internal narrator who tells me that I'm a piece of shit, that I don't deserve anything I have, that any day now the whole thing will come crashing down. It's delusional, but I can't stop it. And I have this sense of not being right in my skin. Like I don't belong in this." He tugged at his flanks. "I don't know how to be a person."

"That's why you took drugs," Jacob said. "To numb." Sam nodded. "Was it always that way?" Jacob asked.

"I don't know," Sam said. "I can't remember. It feels like it's gotten worse."

"After he left," Jacob said, his eyes knowing.

"Yes," Sam said. It flashed through him then, knife-quick, that this was how these people operated—in ways that were just vague enough that they could probably resonate. Everyone had a "he" who left. It didn't mean anything. It didn't mean that this guy had any special powers. All it meant was that he'd done this before. He knew how to target people's vulnerable places and how to say the right thing at the right time. This wasn't some big mystical revelation. It was just a new business pitch.

"I'm going to ask you to lie faceup," Jacob said. Sam glanced at Buck, who looked mesmerized by this strange tableau.

"Okay," Sam said. He arranged himself supine, staring up at the white ceiling.

Jacob was hovering his hands a few inches over Sam, moving them across the length of his body, circling the table. His hands were above his legs, then over the crown of his head, then above his stomach. Gently Jacob laid his hands there, on Sam's belly, over his T-shirt.

"Is this okay?" he asked.

Sam nodded.

Slowly Jacob began to knead the soft flesh of Sam's belly with his hands, working it in circular motions. The sensation wasn't soothing or disruptive, but it was foreign. Sam had never been touched like that before, and certainly not there, on his core, the most vulnerable part of him, which remained squishy no matter how little he ate or how vigorously he exercised. It wasn't a place where he wanted anyone's attention, and with only the thin cotton barrier of his shirt it felt so intimate.

Sam opened his eyes, then closed them again. On the inside

of his eyelids were kaleidoscopes of tiny rainbow pinpricks of light and he allowed himself to get lost in their luminescence, to let them carry him into the dark space of his mind. Like a siren on the wind, he could hear a humming and chanting with no discernible words, a song that sounded ancient. It didn't sound like Jacob, whose speaking voice was low and gruff, because the voice was high and clear, but it had to be him, Sam thought. Then there was a round of whistling and sharp inhalations, like Jacob was trying to suck in air through a straw.

And then, sharply, Sam became aware of a black mass in his belly, sore and tumescent, the color and texture of lava rock; he could see it almost, but mostly he felt it, and it struck him as odd that he'd never felt it before since he knew intuitively that it had been there for a long time. It was tough as stone and its weight was enormous inside of him.

How strange, he thought. But it felt as though Jacob's hands were eroding it. Sam could feel it happening, the edges of it being sanded down, small chunks of it breaking off like pebbles, and those bits of detritus were flowing up through him— Sam felt them, coursing through his bloodstream, could feel it as they skipped and pinged along the insides of his body like a pinball machine—and he knew that anatomically this was impossible but he felt it nonetheless, physically.

And then as these bits of detritus rushed through him while Jacob's hands worked over the black mass, Sam's attention turned, suddenly, to the sensation in his head, a buzzing and churning. Or maybe it was in his skull, like his head was a washing machine, and there was something moving in a rapid spin cycle quickly in clockwise motions around the inside of his head. It felt as if his skull itself was made of glass instead of bone, and his glass skull was hollow like a fishbowl, and inside the glass skull was a fluid that contained many fish, swimming very rapidly in the same circles.

The buzz grew to a roar until it was almost deafening. He opened his mouth to speak but he could not. Jacob's hands were on his belly still, pushing and twisting and kneading, and the debris was still flooding through his system. Sam could feel it in every limb of his body, shifting through his shoulders and pulsating down his arms, down into his hands, and tears streamed out of the corners of his eyes. He wasn't sad; the feeling was deeper than emotion. His jaw was quaking. With great effort, he touched his hand to his mouth and his lips were vibrating, so quickly that he couldn't even feel the individual strokes, like it was one continuous motion. His chest burned.

"Can you feel it?" Jacob said. "That's where it lives in the body."

Sam nodded his head. Tears streamed down the sides of his face.

"It's really stuck," Jacob said.

Sam could barely speak. "Get it out," he finally said. "Please. Get it out."

"I can't," Jacob said. "I can shift its position but I can't remove it. Not on my own."

He lifted his hands off Sam's stomach for the first time in several minutes. *No*, Sam wanted to cry. *Don't stop.* His mouth was sticky with mucus. His stomach growled. Why was he hungry? They'd just eaten. His mouth stopped vibrating. That circular motion in his head slowed to a crawl, then went still. He took a deep breath.

After a moment, he sat up. Buck stared at him, agape.

"You did great," Jacob said.

Sam wiped away his tears. He closed his eyes and opened them a few times. The room stopped shaking.

"What was that?" Sam asked. He gripped the sides of the massage table. He looked over at Buck, who had an odd look on his face, like he was trying to puzzle out what had just happened, and suddenly it struck Sam that the entire episode had only taken place inside of him, that Buck hadn't experienced any of it—like an earthquake only he had felt.

"It's what you're carrying," Jacob said. "A lot of people store their pain in their abdomen. That's why they call it your core, right? Yours is very deep and very old. It's going to be hard to get rid of. But we can do it. The medicine will help. And the spirits will do their work."

"And that's it?" Sam said. "We just have to get it out?"

"Not quite," Jacob said. "You have a lot of work to do. There's something in your lungs, too."

"My lungs?" Sam said. He shivered.

Jacob nodded. "Do you get sick often?"

"Not really," Sam said. Something flickered inside him, like a quick knock on the door of a lightless room.

"The crown of your head is also blocked," Jacob said. "We need to open that up. Energetically."

"I don't understand," Sam said, swinging his legs over the side of the massage table. "I mean, anatomically, it doesn't make any sense. This stuff is in my head, not in different body parts. It's all synapses firing in my brain, right? Neural pathways or whatever."

"How do you know?" Jacob said.

"I mean, I just do," Sam said. He crossed his arms. "It's, like, science."

"And how's science been working out for you?" Jacob said, a little snidely. He shook his head, looking disappointed; his expression made Sam feel like a disobedient pupil. "Of course we always think the newest technology is the best. But what you have to understand is that people across the world have been using the tools of shamanic healing to fix what ails them for millennia. There's no patent, no marketing, no clinical trial. And many of these traditions are endangered. But they have survived for a reason. Because they work. I mean…" He backed away from Sam a few paces, and suddenly Sam felt like he had offended Jacob. "I don't need any more clients. At this point, you know what I can do." He smiled coldly. "It's really up to you whether you want it or not."

Sam didn't know what he wanted. He looked back at the altar and focused his attention on the Knight of Cups, which showed a lone man on a horse, dressed in armor, holding a golden chalice in his outstretched arm. It looked as if he was waiting to be served.

5

The Call

When Sam's mother was eighteen, she was working at a diner on the outskirts of Seattle, where she was raised. Late in the mornings, fishermen came in from the bay, their faces ruddy and their hands chapped, ordering chicken fried steak and drinking acrid black coffee. It was the summer she graduated from high school, before she went off to college, to adulthood and all the unknown beyonds of her life.

She had felt different for as long as she could remember, apart-from, some nagging sense of unbelonging. She knew she was intuitive and empathic—that she could sense things might happen before they did, that she could locate the secret in someone before they knew it themselves, that she could feel the private reserve of pain in a stranger and that her own heart would ache. But she considered it a burden. Never a tool.

Until the day a young man came into the diner. She served him coffee and brought him French toast, a pat of butter pooling on its browned skin. When she set the plate down and he looked at her, his bright blue eyes bore through her. She had never been seen like that before.

She ran into the kitchen to catch her breath amid the steam and boiling grease. Her whole body shook. Her pulse raced.

When she returned to the table, the young man was gone. But he had left her a note.

It said, I KNOW WHAT YOU ARE.

He haunted her. He came to her in dreams. His eyes were cool and penetrating. His hand was outstretched as if he might pull her away. In the mornings, she woke up to find her sheets soaked with sweat. She wondered if she would ever see him again.

A few weeks later, there he was, standing on the street outside a movie theater. The sky was heavy with clouds. He smiled when he saw her. Her hands were quivering. He asked if she would join him and his friends on a camping trip up north that weekend. She said yes. She could not have said anything other than yes. Not to him.

The first night, alone in her tent, she shot up out of sleep. The woods were silent, but he was calling her. Not with his voice. Another way.

She unzipped herself from her sleeping bag and left her tent. The wind sang softly in the trees, but there was no other sound, except her footsteps, deliberate through the grass. And still, he called to her. Her name reverberated through her mind in the sound of his voice. She crossed the campsite and continued through the woods, down a long trail that led to a lake. It was summer and the air was sultry. The moon hung low in the sky, white and lucent.

She reached a dock. The lake was still. He was already

standing there at the edge of the water. He turned and they looked at one another. He had been waiting for her.

This, she said, was how it began.

"How what began?" Sam asked. They were standing in the kitchen of his mother's house, tucked in the trees in the hills overlooking Portland, a pot of tea steeping on the stove, a fire snapping in the furnace.

She smiled. "The call," she said. "My call. My invitation to the spirit realm." She wore a long, draped cardigan in an earthy tan and her blond hair was tucked behind her ears. "It's the spirit world's way of telling you that your work is to begin."

"And my work is to do ayahuasca with this guy?"

"Do you think that you should?" she said. When Sam was a child, his mother had been a therapist. Though she had long since closed her practice, she still had a tendency to probe, to return a question with a question. Sometimes he wondered if that was why he'd had such a hard time breaking ground in therapy. It was like trying to learn a language that was already his mother tongue.

"Before tonight, I would have said no," he said. Sobriety's greatest mercy was that, in a grayscale world, it was utterly black-and-white. The idea of tarnishing it for any reason, no matter how compelling, was worrisome to him.

She looked out the window, into the night. Sam wondered what she was thinking. Maybe she was thinking about the passage of time, birthday parties and family vacations, and how Sam had soured from a precocious, eager kid to an angry, withdrawn teenager. Maybe she was thinking about rehabs and hospital rooms, and the way the light looked in the trees on the spring day, nearly a decade earlier, when Sam had come home to her little house in the woods, nineteen years old and newly clean from a last bender that shook him so deeply he swore he would stop using, and he really meant it. Or maybe she was thinking about something else entirely, memories that belonged to all the other lives she'd lived before becoming his mother. Sam could feel what she was feeling, sometimes, but that was it.

"So what do you think I should do?" Sam asked.

"I can't tell you what to do," she said. "But I don't think you've arrived here by mistake." She hesitated. "Sam, you spend an awful lot of time in the material world. Maybe it's time to think about the other worlds you should be tending to."

She stood and walked to a long, thin table in the entryway of her home. Sam had seen it a thousand times, but he had never quite registered it until just now. There was a tower of white stone, a few ancient coins, a picture of the Virgin Mary and several other little artifacts. It was an altar, not unlike the one in Jacob's office. She picked up a small red velvet pouch, cinched with a drawstring, and handed it to Sam. He opened it and emptied its contents into his hand. It was a tooth, porcelain white and marbled with gray streaks, about as long as his index finger and curved with a pointed tip.

"It's a bear tooth," she said. "I acquired it on my travels many years ago. It was found in a cave in the Carpathian Mountains in present-day Romania. It's probably thirty thousand years old."

"Why are you giving this to me?"

"In the Lakota tradition," she said, "the cave bear is one of the symbols of the West Gate—the looking-within place of introspection and inner knowing. I've used this tooth on my altar for years to call upon the power of the West Gate when I have needed to go inward. Perhaps it will help you, too." She was serious. Sacred.

Sam tried to remember if she had been like this when he was younger. He thought she probably had, but she had been more parent than person, and now he regretted the years he'd wasted missing it.

"Thank you," Sam said. He closed his fist around the tooth. "Why did you tell me about him? About the guy you met?"

She smiled, like she had a secret. "Because sometimes spirits take human form to show us what we need to see."

"Don't do it," Kat said. They were having breakfast in the hotel lobby the next morning. Sam had woken up early and thrown on an oversize sweater and baseball hat, creeping out of the hotel room so as not to wake Buck, who was still sleeping. Kat had come from yoga and her hair was still damp, a flush in her cheeks.

"Really?" Sam said. "You don't think?"

She sipped her latte. "I don't know," she said. "It seems dangerous. You don't know anything about this guy. You want to open a portal to another dimension? What if he draws in demons by accident?" She set down her cup. "Or what if you're one of those people who, like, visits the other side and never really comes back?"

"I thought you would be into this," Sam said. "Self-care is your religion."

"That was before I knew he was going to be drugging you," she said. "The ayahuasca thing feels like a slippery slope."

"How so?"

"I'm one of the only people in your life who remembers what you were like before you got sober," she said. "I was there. I was with you. It was really bad. You don't remember because you were always fucked up. But I do. And I don't want to come visit you in rehab again." She shook her head. "This feels like a step backward."

Sam did remember, but only snatches of it: a bloody nose in a gas station bathroom, Kat holding the tissue to his face. Her slapping him awake when he took too much and nodded out on her couch.

"It's been years, Kat. In therapy. Doing twelve-step stuff. Going on and off antidepressants. And I'm still miserable."

"Maybe things aren't perfect but at least you're basically safe being sober," she said. "This could be so destabilizing for you."

"I already feel destabilized," Sam said. He felt suddenly defensive.

"We're all anxious and depressed," she said. "You know that, right? You don't feel good about yourself? Nobody feels good about themselves! Welcome to being a person in the world."

"Did you read all those studies I sent you? About how they're using ayahuasca experimentally with alcoholics and people with eating disorders?"

"Yes, I read them," Kat said. "Well, I scanned them. But those people are, like, in crisis. Are you?"

"I felt it," Sam said. "I felt where the thing lived inside me. In my belly. Do you get how significant that is? It was like being pinched or punched. It was real."

"Are you sure it wasn't a gluten thing?" she asked. Sam bit his lip. She pulled back in her chair.

"I guess I just always thought that people are the way we are," he said. "Like, we grow and evolve, to a certain extent, and maybe our behavior changes, but so much of what makes us ourselves is innate, or intractable. But what if the bad stuff is like a parasite? What if it's something you can actually isolate and remove, like—I don't know, spiritual surgery?"

"Oh," she said. "You've already made your mind up, haven't you?"

"No," he said. "I'm still thinking about it."

She shook her head. "No, you're saying that's what you're doing, but you've already decided." She pointed at him. "I know you."

She was right, he realized. He had known as soon as Jacob had laid his hands on his body the night before. Or maybe he had known as soon as he saw the hummingbird. Or earlier still, that first night at Buck's house. Something was happening, the ground shifting underfoot, and all the things that used to feel steady were volatile now.

"Are you mad?" he said.

"No," she said. "I just hope you know what you're doing."

"Is it problematic to work with a white shaman who's, like, appropriating the teachings and practices of indigenous cultures for personal gain?"

"Definitely," Kat said. Then she shrugged. "But life is a late-capitalist hellscape, so your mystical journey might as well be one, too."

Sam returned to the hotel room to find Buck already up, standing at the vanity. For a moment, he looked at Buck's reflection in the mirror. The musculature of his tanned back, the swell of his chest, the shock of silvery brown hair. The Louis Vuitton duffel on the ottoman.

It reminded him of something, some faraway memory. Another man, another hotel room, another piece of expensive luggage. Another crossroads. The memory of it hung over this morning like a shadow. Or maybe it hung over every day, and that was the elemental wrongness he always felt.

Buck was applying moisturizer to his forehead, a little primly. Beautiful, broken Buck, who couldn't grow up. Then Sam looked past him, toward his own face in the mirror.

For a moment it seemed completely preposterous. The idea

that they could open a doorway to another dimension to usher in some great and ancient spirit to bring them healing. How wild a thought, and how stupid. Not just for anyone, but especially for them, preening modern gays who had so much and appreciated so little.

Gullible, superstitious Angelenos with baggage to spare.

Damaged people, vain and self-seeking, just trying to change.

"Buck," Sam said. They looked at each other.

"Are we doing this?" Buck said.

"Yeah," Sam said. "We are." In that instant it felt like the easiest thing in the world, as if there was nothing to lose and everything to gain, the joyous surprise of a clear blue sky. And this: the idea, so rare and so seductive, that absolutely anything was possible.

6

The Four Commitments

"Shall we discuss what's going to happen tonight?" Jacob said. Buck and Sam both nodded.

They were at Buck's house. A month had passed since the trip up to Portland. Jacob had sent over detailed instructions for the weeks leading up to the retreat, including a rigorous diet: no alcohol or drugs; no meat; no sugar; no salt. Sam had followed it carefully, although this was more in the hopes of losing some weight than out of respect for the process. Jacob had also advised against sexual contact of any kind, including masturbation, for two weeks leading up to the ceremony. Sam had hoped that the combination of being deprived of both food and sex would elevate him into a state of ascetic transcendence; instead it had made him irritable and tightly wound.

For the ceremony itself, Buck had ordered several days'

worth of catered meals dropped off, preportioned containers of unsalted, unseasoned vegetables, quinoa and chicken, all of which were now stacked neatly in Buck's refrigerator. "Is it normal to have your transdimensional journey catered?" Sam asked Buck, who had shrugged.

Buck had also planned to set up what he called "a fabulous yurt moment" in his backyard for their home during the ceremony. "That way," he explained, "we'll have all the resources of the house close by but we can still benefit from the experience of communing with the earth."

"I love this," Sam said, egging him on. "Ranch-hand glamour."

"Rugged. Evocative of the great American West."

"Masc seeking masc," Sam said. "Flannel shirts. Suede boots. Pendleton blankets!"

"That's perfect," Buck said. "Is there a Pendleton store in LA? We need to find machine-washable blankets, in case we barf on them."

Sam was responsible for picking up buckets for vomiting, and a few other last-minute items. Buck called him the morning of the ceremony with a shopping list.

"Did you get the buckets yet? I would try the Container Store at the Grove, maybe—I bet they'll have the best selection of stylish buckets that will fit our aesthetic. And it would probably be good to have a few more green juices—maybe pop by Moon Juice in Melrose Alley and see if they have something nice and alkalizing, maybe a chard blend? And I'm wondering if a few snacks might be good to have on hand—if you go to Erewhon, I'd pick up some activated cashews and dried mango slices, just in case we need it, and anything else that looks appealing that fits within the *dieta*. I also meant to stop at Candle Delirium on Santa Monica by Laurel Hardware and pick up—let's see—oh, twelve six-inch cylindrical white or off-white unscented candles, one and a half inch in diameter? And I *was* thinking, just to really boost the energy of the space, it might be nice to anchor us with a few selenite towers—just four or five, really—so if you wanted to swing past House of Intuition and grab a few, not the enormous ones or the travel-size pieces but the medium ones, a little less than a foot tall, I'd feel so much more secure just knowing that we had them nearby. You know selenite, right? The clear white luminescent crystal."

But when he arrived at the house, Jacob took one look inside the yurt—big cushions lining the perimeter of it, Pendleton blankets in tones of sand and ecru, and the selenite towers now scattered artfully throughout the space—and nixed it. "You're going to want something sturdy to lean up against," he said, pushing against the thin canvas of the yurt's walls. "Trust me." Buck looked disappointed.

Same with all the snacks they'd bought from Moon Juice— chocolate truffles rolled from raw cacao and cinnamon, and sprouted grain crackers made with sunflower seeds, and little bags of goji berries and dried mango slices dusted with cayenne pepper and lime, sorted into little wicker baskets on the dining room table—all of which, it turned out, contained Himalayan pink salt. "What did I say?" Jacob said reproachfully. "No salt."

Most of all, he was unimpressed by the small gray teacups and kettle that Buck had set out on a long wooden table for them to use for serving the ayahuasca.

"What is this?" Jacob said, pointing at it.

"Oh—I bought them at auction," Buck said. "It's this extraordinary artist out of Düsseldorf. They're made from concrete taken from the Berlin Wall!"

"No," Jacob said, and he shook his head. "No. That's not energetically appropriate for this work."

"But—"

"Buck," Jacob said sharply. "I need you to stop trying to produce this experience and just trust me."

Buck looked up, surprised. "I'm sorry," he said. "I didn't mean to—"

Jacob looked out the window at the sky. "It's going to be sundown soon," he said. "We should find our gathering place."

They settled in the den off the side of the great room. It was lined by bookshelves, with an oversize sectional, cozy but not claustrophobic. The three men stood and surveyed it.

"This will work," Jacob said. "You can sit on the floor and lean up against the side of the couch." They laid out cushions on the floor in front of the frame of the sofa and spread out blankets over them, so they would be soft and padded underneath their bodies but could still lean back against a sturdy surface.

Jacob spread out opposite them, with his back to the wall, so he was facing Buck and Sam with a few feet of distance separating them. Carefully he rolled out a faded orange serape in front of him and spread out a number of objects on it. There were two bottles of a dark, viscous-looking liquid—one larger, one smaller—and a wooden tobacco pipe, several bundles of sage, a few sticks of palo santo, two large feathers and a small plastic bucket, which, Sam noted, was much less stylish than the teacup-shaped wastebaskets he had picked out for ceremony.

The sun was starting to dip down below the mountains. It was dusk. They sat in front of him in silence as Jacob laid out his kit, organizing these items.

Sam looked around the room, already feeling slightly dazed. It was as if there was already something happening, even though they hadn't ingested anything yet. Some invisible ripple of energy, some calming balm. He felt peaceful but somber.

"This first night is just about opening you up to the medicine," Jacob said. "It's very common to not experience any effects. It's also very possible that you'll experience full effects. This isn't an exact science. But you can consider this first evening as more of a statement of intent. You're telling the spirit of the medicine that you're available to her—inviting her to come do her work with you. And the work does begin tonight, whether you feel it or not."

Sam felt a little more tension release from his body.

"I want to lay down some ground rules," Jacob continued. "I call these the four commitments. The first commitment is that in this circle we will observe a code of noble silence. That means that the two of you don't talk to each other. You don't touch each other. If one of you is experiencing strong effects or struggling, you don't comfort the other. You stay in your own experience. Is that clear?"

Buck and Sam both nodded.

"Please say yes," Jacob said.

"Yes," they both said.

"Thank you. The second commitment is that we don't leave the circle before the ceremony has closed," Jacob said. "Of course you can get up to use the bathroom if you need to. But you don't get up and go to bed halfway through. You don't go outside. We stay in ceremony until it's over. No matter what happens. I need you to commit, verbally, that you'll see through the night. Please say yes if you can make that commitment."

"Yes," Buck and Sam said in unison.

"Good," Jacob said. "The third commitment is that you do not leave the sacred space I am holding for this ceremony, which extends as far as the gate at the base of the driveway and the end of the yard. Everything that happens within that domain is under my protection. I can leave that enclosure—and I probably will, tomorrow, during the day. But you need to stay within those bounds until we close this ceremony on the third morning. Please say yes if you can agree to that."

"Yes," they both said.

"The fourth commitment is that you don't die during ceremony."

Sam's tranquil mood broke. He looked at Buck, then back at Jacob.

"At least not in your physical body," Jacob continued. "Other parts of you may die. Your ego. Your sense of self. Your consciousness. You may release things that needed to die a long time ago. All of that is fine. But not in your body. Please agree that you will not die during ceremony."

Sam raised his hand.

"The medicine is very safe," Jacob said in response to Sam's raised hand. "You won't die. I just need you to agree to that."

"I'll do my best," Sam said, and he thought briefly about how nice it would be if he died in ceremony—how convenient it would be to not have to deal with his credit card debt or work inbox, to just never have to go back to real life. *Stop*, he thought. *You choose life.*

"Me, too," Buck said.

Jacob breathed in deeply. "Things will happen here over the next three nights," he said. "Wild things, and sacred things. Your responsibility is to stay in it, no matter how frightening or uncomfortable. I will do everything in my power to keep you safe. But it's up to you." His eyelashes fluttered. "The mother is a teacher," he said. "She is not always gentle. But she is always loving. As much as possible, try to trust that she's taking you where you need to go. Ask her to show you what you need to see. Be humble."

Sam reached over for Buck's hand, then remembered he wasn't supposed to touch him. They looked at each other for a long moment. *Please, God, let this work*, Sam thought.

Then Sam felt around under his blanket until he found what he was looking for: the bear tooth his mother had given him. He gripped it in his hand, feeling its pointed edges smooth and cold against his palm. Then he took one long, deep breath and squeezed it tightly.

"Are you ready?" Jacob said.

Sam and Buck both nodded.

"Good," he said. "Let's begin."

DURING

Part Two

7

Rich Gays

First.
   Jacob filled his pipe with tobacco and lit it. He puffed on it, making fragrant plumes of smoke rise through the den. Sam watched through half-lidded eyes, the smoke prickling his nostrils.

Then. Jacob stood and left the room, walking silently through the house until the smoke was everywhere, in and around them, the air thick with it.

He returned to his seat. He picked up both bottles and held them to his forehead, murmuring what sounded like a low, sibilant prayer, hissing and whistling through his teeth. Buck and Sam watched him as he prayed over the medicine, or into it. Then he opened one of the bottles and poured it into a small measuring cup. He held the cup, full of liquid, to his forehead and repeated the prayer. Then he downed it in one gulp.

He sat for a moment, as if letting it settle in his body, then began the ritual over again. He held the bottles to his forehead; he poured a shot; he held that to his forehead; and then he motioned silently to Buck.

Buck crawled on all fours across the floor to sit in front of Jacob. Sam heard some indecipherable whispers and watched as Buck slung his head back, taking the shot. Then Buck returned to his nest.

After a pause, Jacob motioned Sam up to the mat, and like Buck, Sam crawled awkwardly toward him. Jacob held the bottles to his forehead again and Sam sat cross-legged in front of him. Sam could hear the prayer more clearly now— it wasn't in English. Instead it was in some kind of ancient tongue that Sam couldn't identify. Jacob poured a cup for Sam and handed it to him.

Now Sam held the cup full of ayahuasca to his forehead, and as he did, closing his eyes, some electricity shot from the glass into his head through the skin, and chills descended down his back like a shudder. *Show me what I need to see,* Sam thought. The glass was cold against his third eye, the ridges of it pressing into his flesh.

Sam opened his eyes. Jacob's gaze was fierce. Sam wanted to look away, but he couldn't. He held the glass in his hands and took a deep breath. Then he slugged it back in one shot. It was sweeter than he had expected, with the consistency of molasses, thick and gelatinous with a briny aftertaste that made his lips feel numb, and Sam felt it descend down his throat, felt it coat the roof of his mouth and stick to his teeth, swishing saliva around and swallowing it, trying to clear this taste from his mouth, but it was indelible, and it didn't feel holy.

"Thank you," Sam said. He returned to his nest and all three men lay in silence for a moment.

"How long does it take to kick in?" Buck said.

"That's up to her," Jacob said.

He stood and switched off the lamp and the room was cast into darkness.

Sam stretched his body out long. He closed his eyes and breathed slowly and deliberately. *In. Out. In. Out.* His mind was busy, as usual. He wondered what was going to happen. He wondered if anything was going to happen.

He opened his eyes. It was so dark in the room that it looked exactly like the undersides of his eyelids. He turned his head and he couldn't see anything—no shapes, no outlines. He blinked a few times and saw the faintest shape to his right—the form of Buck's body. Then, in front of where Jacob was sitting, Sam could make out the still-glowing cherry of his pipe. It was eerily quiet. Sam closed his eyes again. He could feel his heartbeat in his ears.

Then one loud thought rocketed through him like a thunderbolt: *Did you just fucking relapse? Is that what this is?* Sam's heart raced. *Stop it*, he commanded his brain. *Stop.*

But the thought echoed in his mind, a warning. How many nights had Sam spent in high school waiting for drugs to kick in, waiting for some promised effect to take him out of his reality into another one? Now here he was, back again.

Sam rolled over onto one side. He sighed loudly.

As if Jacob could read his mind—or at the very least, sense his agitation—he spoke. "Clear your mind," Jacob said. "And try to relax."

Relax. The command was absurd. How could he relax when he was about to go traveling off into another dimension? What was supposed to be relaxing about that?

He had never expected to end up here, on the floor of

somebody's house, trying to fix himself. This wasn't supposed to be the direction his life had taken. The Sam that had lived in New York would never have accepted this as an outcome. The Sam that had lived in New York would have been so judgmental of this, of all of this, the crystals and the shaman and the green juices that he couldn't even drink because they had too much salt. He'd gone soft, living in Los Angeles. Soft and gullible, too willing to believe anyone who told him what he wanted to hear.

Yet in some ways he was harder, too, than he had been in New York, angrier and more wounded, less open in ways both big and small. Sam wished that he could go back in time, to be a different him, like the him that had lived in New York before everything had broken.

He tried to go back to the beginning of what happened in New York, but all those beginnings were arbitrary. *Pick one*, he thought.

A young man with dark hair and blue eyes standing by the bar, looking over his shoulder in Sam's direction.

Sam breathed in and out. *Not yet*, he thought.

There. He settled there, right in his mind's eye. The bar on Second Avenue—what was it called? No, not that—the Roseland. Oh, no, there was something before that, even. The roof of the apartment on Eighty-First Street.

Yes, like that.

It was fall in New York City.

It was fall in New York City, which was the best season in the only city, and Sam was moving out.

Out of the spare room of a drag queen's Chelsea apartment he'd found on Craigslist his junior year of college. He'd chatted with her for five minutes, at most, before making the decision to move in, not realizing that he would spend the next two years in an apartment where every surface was covered in rainbow glitter and clumps of hair-weave.

In the drag queen's bedroom, on shelves that encircled its perimeter just below the ceiling, were dozens of colorless mannequin heads cheerfully adorned with wigs: not just a wispy platinum Farrah but jewel tones, too, like a cranberry Reba, slightly askew. Sam's room had a bunk bed with an efficiency desk in place of a lower bunk, where he sat on a tiny stool, hunched over his laptop, finishing his papers as graduation loomed. In a third, more generously proportioned bedroom, from which Sam was certain his room had been carved in some earlier reimagining of the floor plan, a sinuously built Czech go-go dancer surfaced only at night, wearing skintight Diesel jeans and an Andrew Christian tank top. He spoke no English, nor did he need to.

By day, the drag queen worked at the Container Store on Sixth Avenue. The cupboards spilled over with trays and cubbies, closets stuffed with thin suede hangers and translucent tubs for storage. Sam stuffed his winter coats into stackable plastic bins. A cheap window air-conditioning unit whirred all summer long. Ethan Hawke lived in a brownstone across the street. Sam sat on the stoop some nights and smoked cigarettes. It made him feel close to something.

"Can you host?" No. No, Sam could not host.

Moving out, and moving up. For months, he'd been talking about getting a place with Brett, his best friend in New York. They'd met on Twitter while Sam was in undergrad. They both tweeted incessantly about pop culture, the way some people followed sports, and both had a soft spot for pop divas, especially the unlucky ones at the bottom of the pyramid. Twitter was a high school cafeteria made meritocratic, and every retweet was a little dopamine hit. When Brett followed Sam back, it meant something. *You're funny. You matter.*

Do you want to come with me to the taping of a live concert Kelly Rowland is doing for Walmart? Brett asked him over direct message.

I thought you'd never ask, Sam said.

Sam loved Brett instantly. He was short and scruffy. Britney Spears was his patron saint: he called her Godney. When something was really funny, he dissolved into a fit of giggles so convulsive that Sam thought he might choke.

That first night, they investigated each other in the uneasy way that gay men did, trying to figure out if the other was a romantic prospect or competition. Instead they cried from laughter on the subway over a meme. There was no kiss. It was exactly right.

Brett was the first person Sam had ever met who wanted the same things he wanted. To talk endlessly about the way a swell of synths or a propulsive drum beat made a song tear at the heart. To scour Scandinavian music blogs looking for the next big star who would play a tiny show at a Lower East Side dive bar to a crowd of jaded label A&Rs.

To hang an oversize portrait of Christina Aguilera in the living room.

When Sam got a job writing for a music blog out of college, Brett took it as a sign. Brett had been living upstate with his parents and commuting to Westchester for a corporate job he hated. "That's it," he said. "I'm moving to the city to chase my dreams." He mimed getting into a taxi. *"Take me to the center of everything."*

Sam found a listing for a two-bedroom in Yorkville, many avenues from the subway. "Eighty-First and York?" a co-worker at his new job said, frowning. "That's basically upstate." It was all they could afford, and they couldn't even really afford that. It was probably stupid to try to live in Manhattan on their incomes, but it felt important. They met at Grand Central Station and took the 6 uptown.

Sam hadn't been up to the Upper East Side in years. Not since high school, when most of his friends had lived there. As they walked down Eighty-Sixth Street toward the East River, Sam noticed the places that were familiar to him through some foggy lens: the building on that corner where he had snorted Adderall with some girls from school. The sushi place where he relapsed on sake bombs after his second stint in rehab, or maybe it was the third. He couldn't remember.

Being there brought back his past in more vivid color than he particularly wanted to see. The privilege he'd had as a prep school kid in Manhattan, before his father had cut him loose financially, not long after Sam got sober. Sam had even managed to pay for college himself, through some combination of scholarship, loans and working retail. He had been terrible before he got sober. He knew that. What a relief to never be that ugly again.

Things were different now, because Sam was different now. He was twenty-three, over four years sober, financially independent and, miraculously somehow, employed with a real job. And now here they were, about to move into what he was sure would be their dream apartment.

"God," Brett said. "This place is far from the train."

They heaved and grunted, making their way up five flights of stairs, the building manager fumbling with the lock. The pictures on Craigslist had been a little bit deceptive, as was standard in New York. The ceilings were unexpectedly low. The kitchen had been shoddily renovated. The grout between the tiles flaked off in little clumps that stuck in the grooves of Sam's sneakers. But the living room was big, with a wall of exposed red brick, and at least it was clean. Sam looked at Brett as if to say, *Not bad*. Brett shrugged.

The building manager sensed their uncertainty. "You *have* to see the outdoor garden."

Up yet another flight of stairs they trundled, out onto the roof. It wasn't a garden so much as a fenced-in square, perhaps ten feet by ten feet, with a wooden gate and a table with two chairs seated at it. There was no greenery, no photo-worthy staging. But it wasn't hard to imagine that with some string lights and a few planters or some paper lanterns, it could come to life, their own outdoor paradise in the middle of Manhattan.

Sam imagined throwing parties up there, everyone crowding in on a dreamy summer evening, one of their aspiring pop star friends strumming away at a guitar, all of them singing along. He could see in Brett's face that he liked it, too. On their way back to the train, they decided to take it.

They would make it a home, Sam thought, and it would be a place where music would always play. To love something as purely as they both loved the mysterious alchemy of a perfect pop song, all those chords in mathematical symmetry, the explosion of a euphoric chorus, the key change on the middle eight that felt like speedballing to heaven, some young woman (never men) singing about crying at the disco over a sparkly beat, that gorgeous intersection of happy and sad. Even years later, the sound of a synth loop from one of the songs they'd loved could transport Sam back to that era, efficient as boarding a time machine. There, both of their names on the lease, nobody could judge them for the songs they wanted to hear.

The space never ended up looking quite done. They spent all their money on first and last month's rent, barely scraping together enough for the security deposit, and there was little left over for furniture. They had an IKEA sofa and a few bookshelves that Brett had brought from his childhood bedroom, a moon-shaped mirror they found at the thrift store, and Sam did indeed go to Times Square one afternoon to have a sidewalk artist draw a black-and-white pastel portrait of Christina Aguilera from a photo that Sam had printed out for him. She wasn't quite recognizable in the drawing, but they pinned it to the wall with a thumbtack anyway. Sam tried to convince himself that the sparse furnishings of his bedroom gave the appearance of luxurious minimalism instead of betraying the reality that he didn't have the means to buy anything except the bed and a little side table. He bought a mattress with his first paycheck, but couldn't afford sheets until the next one, so he slept on it bare, waking up with the sunlight, happy.

They didn't put up paper lanterns on the roof. But Sam still spent a lot of time up there, at the round card table with the wooden folding chairs, all the high-rises towering above him, casting shadows on the afternoon. He called old friends or sat with his laptop and chipped away at the manuscript for the book he wanted to write. He didn't expect anyone would ever publish it. He knew that he was a nobody, just another aspirant in the city with dreams of big success, churning out hot takes about Top 40 hits for a blog nobody read. His boss was always talking about traffic and uniques, and Sam knew those things were important but also couldn't imagine caring about them.

Yet to write something that would make other people feel the way his favorite songs made him feel—this was the prize, and the act of pushing toward it made Sam feel like he mattered. He could see himself, there, in this memory he had polished to a silvery brightness, in this thing that he loved to remember.

Did you feel broken back then? Sam asked himself. He returned to the present moment.

The room was dark and silent. *Was it bad back then?* He squinted. The answer came to him: *No. You were hopeful.* And the memory of that hope filled him up for a moment—oh, to feel that again. *Am I on ayahuasca yet?* he asked himself. *No, I am not,* he answered, and so he returned to the memory, tapping his feet nervously against the floor of Buck's house, bored by the familiarity of this tape and yet disinterested in changing it. *Is this what I need to see?* he asked. *Sure. Might as well be.*

The Upper East Side. When Sam was a teenager, it had felt fancy, traveling through his friends' park-facing apartments. Now, as an adult, he could see the neighborhood wasn't all day-drunk private school kids and well-heeled Fifth Avenue frauen. There were a lot of young professionals in Yorkville, too. Frat bros who filled the sports bars along First Avenue, and twentysomething public relations girls who had migrated north from Murray Hill to keep the nail salons and blow-dry bars doing brisk business, and families who were more middle-class, if such a thing still existed in Manhattan, than those who lived west of Lexington. The cool kids had all moved to Brooklyn, but the city wasn't quite dead yet. When he walked home from the train at night, he imagined he could feel some magic in the air, the romantic fantasy of being young and hungry and making it in New York, a city that remained alive with possibilities.

It was exactly the right place to be for the book he was trying to write, a memoir about those teenage years getting into trouble with a pack of rich kids, his adventures in rehab and subsequent recovery. So much of his misbehavior had taken place in that same neighborhood that if he wanted to seek inspiration, all he had to do was step outside and there it all was. All those memories.

Sam wondered sometimes, living there, if he would ever be able to reclaim those streets in his adulthood or if they would always feel like they belonged to some lost version of him, some irretrievably young self who knew so little.

Memory was like this, a house of mirrors. Sam remembered, at twenty-three, what it had felt like to be full of possibilities at eighteen, and how he had written those memories down, trying to bleed them onto the page, to create a record of the person he had been and the person he was then, remembering them with five years' distance; and now, at twenty-eight, lying on the floor of Buck's house with another five years' distance, he could not believe how young he had been at twenty-three, when he had felt so precociously weathered by experience that he had been possessed to write a book about all that he remembered; and suddenly, Sam, the present-day Sam, the one lying on the floor of Buck's house, felt a powerful bitterness at how stupid he had been at twenty-three and the self-importance that had led him to write that book in the first place.

Now after cherry-picking the memories that served the narrative he had wanted to tell, the ones he never wrote were lost to time. Now his story, when he remembered it, was as clean and narratively resolute as flipping through the pages of his book. Was it even possible for him to remember what had actually happened, instead of the record of it that he had committed to the page? He remembered himself remembering eighteen from the vantage point of twenty-three, but now, at twenty-eight, he had nothing from eighteen except what he had published in that book.

Suddenly, fiercely, he wished that he could be twenty-three again, to be able to look back on his life as it had actually happened, to exist in all the uncomfortable ambiguity of the person he had been. Maybe this was all he was supposed to do here, on this shamanic journey—to simply remember what had gone wrong and why.

What would it be like, Sam wondered, to remember things as they had actually happened—not to prove a thesis, or eliding the moments that felt inconsequential, or didn't serve the story? Could he actually just recall an experience without wondering where it fit into a narrative, without trying to map the interconnectedness of things or place it within some big and convenient pattern? The very act of telling the story was not like photography; he didn't know how to capture moments as they were. It was more like sculpture, starting from the raw materials of lived experience and chiseling away at it until it had revealed what he wanted to see, or what he thought the world wanted to see.

He turned over on his side, tasting the smoke and the brine. He exhaled the memory, trying to blow it out of his mouth.

Up on the roof, writing alone. He had been lonely in that apartment, living with Brett. Maybe that was why he had done it. Perhaps he had imagined that if he wrote a book, he would finally feel fixed, somehow rendered whole. If people were reading his story, he would never be truly alone.

On the weekends Brett went out to the gay bars in Hell's Kitchen, to dance or to DJ songs by chart-middling pop stars while Sam usually stayed in. Much as Sam loved Brett, he was envious of him, of the freedom that Brett found in going out and getting wasted in packed nightclubs, making out with cute boys and getting pizza at 2:00 a.m. Sam would be at home, cracking self-deprecating jokes on Twitter, chasing that rush of validation as retweets and favorites rolled in while he watched old sitcoms on Netflix or sat on his fire escape, looking up at the moon. But all those notifications—they weren't the same as having a person. *Where is he?* Sam wondered on those nights. *When will I be loved?* And so he went on dates.

First there was Adam, a blogger. Over drinks, Sam learned that, like Sam, Adam was stockily built and baby-faced, and also like Sam, his taste skewed thrillingly lowbrow, Bravo docuseries about wealthy white women throwing wine at one another and singles from mostly forgotten turn-of-the-millennium one-hit wonders. There was so much common ground, Sam thought, it had to be fated, and there was something gentle about Adam, something alluringly soft about the way he put his hand on the small of Sam's back as they were standing at a bar, something wounded and puppyish in his eyes when he talked about the shows he loved. But over the course of subsequent dates, what had telegraphed as sweetness seemed to turn into toothlessness. Where was his *edge*, Sam wondered. Where was the bite?

Quickly what had once been charming grew irksome, Adam's snoring through the night in Sam's bed, which forced Sam to drag a blanket and pillow out to the IKEA sofa in the living room and collapse there, with the junky old window air-conditioning unit blasting on high, even though it was the dead of winter, to generate enough ambient noise to dull Adam's asthmatic breathing in the other room, and in the morning Adam lumbered out to the living room like a bear stumbling through a campsite, wiping sleep from his eyes and apologizing profusely, even though of course it hadn't been his fault—who can control their own snoring?

But more than the irritation of the sleepless night, it was Adam's radiant embarrassment that was a turnoff, as though Adam found himself inherently burdensome and had been trying to hide that from Sam and suddenly he'd been exposed, that the way Adam actually felt about himself was newly transparent.

Something about the interaction haunted Sam, maybe because, although he wasn't conscious of it at the time, it was a reflection of the way Sam himself felt, moving through the world in a body that was too big for him, making too much noise, graceless and self-conscious; to see it in Adam, for Sam, was like staring at his most vulnerable places in the mirror, and Sam knew that he could not forgive that quality in himself enough to forgive it in someone else.

Not long after, Sam called Adam and told him he thought they were better off as friends. He could hear the little break in Adam's voice, the way he paused before he said, "I understand," and Sam knew that he had hurt this young man, but he knew, too, that it hadn't been quite right, in ways that couldn't be bridged. Still, he felt guilty about it.

"I will never find anyone kinder than him," Sam told Brett.

Next there was Eric, a comedian whose sensibility tended toward the macabre, tweeting weird and surrealist jokes about celebrities, particularly Oscar-winning actresses over the age of forty; after a deep dive into his feed, Sam knew that he would never look at Laura Linney the same way again. They met for coffee, taking a long walk through Union Square Park on a frosty winter day, and Sam couldn't believe how good-looking Eric was, tall and brawny with a chiseled jaw and piercing eyes like a Disney prince. What would it feel like, Sam wondered, to be loved by a man like that?

Eric worked as a bartender at the Gansevoort and soon Sam was meeting him in the Meatpacking District to while away the hours at dive bars after he got off work, or Eric would come with Sam to the concerts that Sam had to cover for his job, and Sam felt the building tension the more they spent time together, the realization that if they hadn't hooked up by now, they probably never would, and clearly Eric didn't even want to, or he would have made a move—and what was holding him back? Sam was sure that it was because he was fat, instead of naturally athletic like Eric, and about this he felt such bitterness—that the only thing making it impossible to be together, or so he convinced himself, was his body, which was especially cruel given they were so good together, riffing on extended bits of pop culture detritus and texting each other jokes throughout the night.

Eric drank too much, although that wasn't surprising—they were gay and in their early twenties; it was par for the course—and this tendency he had to get quickly intoxicated kept Sam hoping, in some private and bleakly opportunistic corner of his heart, that the stars would align and Eric would get just drunk enough to want to sleep with Sam, to over-look Sam's physical imperfections enough to desire him, if only for a night.

One evening Sam scored an invite to a fashion week after-party and brought Eric as his date. By the end of the night, Eric was flushed and ebullient after so many vodka tonics in some West Village penthouse, and when Eric muttered, "Let's get out of here," Sam knew it was finally going to happen. But back at Sam's apartment, Eric's drunkenness had turned ag-gressive, ugly, pawing through Sam's refrigerator for the beers Brett had bought for a party they'd never ended up throwing.

"You want one?" he snarled at Sam.

"I don't drink, Eric," Sam said. "You know that."

"Whatever," Eric said, slamming the refrigerator door shut. He passed out on Sam's bed, face-first in a pile of pillows. Even after that, Sam lay down beside him, tucking his arms around Eric and hugging his ribs, smelling his musk and the lingering spice of his cologne, wishing that he could change the ways in which Eric was flawed. Maybe that's how Eric felt about him, too, and this realization felt like the most vi-cious twist of the knife—that you had to see people as they truly were, not for who you wanted them to be.

In the morning, Eric was terse and awkward, talking too loudly as if his hearing had been damaged the night before, packing up his things to go home to Brooklyn. Sam knew it was over, this thing, whatever it had been.

"I will never find anyone funnier than him," Sam told Brett.

Then there was Robert. Oh, how heavy Sam had hung his hopes on Robert, a culture pundit who sat atop the pyramid of the cool kids of media, and who wrote with a strange and dazzling lyricism that made the intellectual snob inside Sam, the version of him who cared about that sort of thing more than looks or personality or any other quality, weak-kneed. Late into the night for weeks on end, they direct-messaged about beloved books from childhood and the curious interpersonal politics of New York media, this world Sam felt adjacent to but never quite a part of, like he always just missed the mark—not arch enough, not clever enough—and in those little missives, those text dispatches from across the city, Robert was affectionate and encouraging, intimate as a dinner-party whisper. They joked about how long it had taken for them to find one another, about a New England wedding, in a way that only a fool would have mistaken for anything serious, but surely, Sam thought, there had to be some modest kernel of truth underneath it—right?

Yet when they finally met at a cigar bar downtown—one of the few places left in Manhattan where you could still smoke inside, thankfully—Robert was chillier and more caustic than Sam had expected, hidden behind a beard and glasses, a cipher who revealed nothing. No affection, none of that desire that had been in all their correspondence. The screen, so cool and impersonal, had communicated warmth, but in person, it was cold. Still Sam bought the whiskey that he knew Robert drank, just to have on hand for the nights that he imagined they would be spending together. But Robert only came over once, declining Sam's offer for a drink, and so it sat unopened on the kitchen counter for as long as Sam lived in that apartment, a reminder.

They spent that night together, awkwardly fumbling in bed in that unfamiliar way, like the encounter was freighted with too many expectations for it to ever carry an erotic charge, like Robert had come over because he felt like he had to in order to be sure that Sam was as much of a disappointment as he suspected. Or maybe Robert was the one who felt like a disappointment, like he could never live up to the lofty bar set by his online persona as a writer, impressive as it was.

Soon after, Robert ghosted—or maybe it wasn't a full ghost, but it was certainly ghostly, in that he took days to respond to Sam's messages and dodged attempts to make follow-up plans. And as he ignored Sam's texts, Robert continued tweeting and blogging cheerfully, which made Sam irate as he sat at home on weekend nights, staring incredulously at the glow of his laptop—at the sheer gall of this man, to have made such clear gestures at romance, to have allowed something that had felt so promising to wither and die so cruelly.

"I will never find anyone smarter than him," Sam told Brett.

The Robert thing crushed him. Sam could see himself now, pulling up his bedroom window and stepping onto the fire escape. It was winter, and the little balcony overlooked a courtyard frosted with snow. He felt the hot rush of tears coming and soon he was sobbing. Surely it was something about him, some way in which he was undeserving.

He resolved to stop pursuing creative types in their twenties, and he announced so to Brett. "They're all such emotionally stunted alcoholics." (In fact, only two of them were even drinkers; Adam was rather temperate, so he did not fit this narrative, but it was easier for Sam to pretend that it had never happened, let alone that he'd had some agency in how it had ended, than to search for some thread that tied all three together.) "There's only room in a relationship for one of those, and it's going to be me."

Brett turned down the volume on the Kylie Minogue record that was blasting from the speakers like a glitter cannon and set down his takeout. "Okay, so no more alcoholics," he said. "What is it that you actually want?"

"Kind, funny, smart," Sam said. "Just someone decent."

"And you think you're going to find that guy in this city?" Brett said. "Among these queens?" He shook his head. "Good fucking luck. I'm lucky if I take home a guy who doesn't try to steal my wallet."

"Maybe it's the universe's way of telling me that I need to focus on other things," Sam said. "Work. The book. Myself."

"I don't think of you as someone who has a problem focusing on yourself," Brett said, spearing a bite of ziti with his fork.

"Drag me," Sam said. "But don't you feel like every self-help book in the history of the world is like, 'Become the kind of person that you would want to date'?"

"That doesn't sound right," Brett said. "Two bottoms don't make a top."

"You know what I mean! Maybe instead of trying to get these guys to love me, I try to become a better version of myself. Unpack some of this baggage."

"Get it down to a carry-on, girl," Brett said. "Stop paying those checked baggage fees."

Baggage. That was always the problem. Sam had too much of that. And now he was conscious of his body, not in memory but in the moment, in Buck's house, and he put his hands on his chest and sighed. The heaviness of it was almost unbearable.

What had he said after that? He couldn't remember. That was where the memory stopped, and in his mind's eye it was as blurry as a watercolor, Brett's funny little smile disappearing into a kaleidoscope of static. Sam pointed his toes and flexed his feet. The room was full of smoke now, and it irritated his throat, making him cough.

Is anything happening yet? he asked. No. Nothing was. He tried to settle back into his mind, to drop back into those months of fruitlessly dating through a New York winter. The snow was packed on the ground and crusted on the barren trees like they were wearing gloves made of ice. By the time it all began to thaw, Sam had changed, too.

He had known on some level, even if he couldn't articulate it clearly at the time, that the problem, the thing that kept him from being loved, was his tendency toward excess, the big hunger inside of him, the same force that had made him drink and drug that had mutated in sobriety to other things—mostly food and validation—and he stuffed the emptiness however he could. His need was bottomless.

Where did that come from, Sam wondered—why was he like that? The only time he had been thin was in high school, when he was living in the city with his father, the same years that he was writing about in the memoir.

Sam's father had wanted him thin, Sam remembered; it had mattered to him. Like Sam, his father had been chubby as a kid, but had leaned out in adulthood as he fixated on fitness. He exercised for multiple hours a day, training for triathlons, biking to work and taking long runs through Central Park.

Sam had dropped the weight as soon as he started abusing amphetamines when he was fifteen; even more than the speedy high, Sam loved the feeling of satiety. His days were no longer ruled by hunger. For the first time during those years, Sam joined his father at the gym, barely grazing when they went out to eat, and by the time Sam was a senior in high school, he was gaunt enough that teachers at school were expressing concern. Sam thought he looked great. Not only was he desirable to the older men he dated, but his father was proud of him. Sam could feel it in the warmth of his demeanor, the way he seemed affectionate with Sam in a way he hadn't been before. When Sam was fat, he had been a manifestation of his father's shortcomings as a parent, a mirror of the heavyset kid his father himself had been and spent so many years running from. When Sam was thin, there could be no other problem. Never mind that Sam rarely ate or slept, consuming only cigarettes and Adderall. His thinness was a blinding light that kept his father from seeing anything else.

Once Sam got clean at nineteen, the weight came back with a swiftness that surprised even him. When he saw his father a few months after he'd sobered up, Sam could feel his discomfort; it radiated out of him. It wasn't disappointment so much as it was an inability to reconcile the fact that Sam was doing well—he was sober now and had gone back to school—with the fact that Sam was also fat, which had to mean that something was wrong. These truths were in such deep conflict with one another that it seemed easier not to deal with Sam at all.

At seventeen or eighteen or nineteen, Sam had been unable to understand with any insight why his relationship with his father felt so fraught, but with a few years' distance, he had come to see the ways in which the dynamic had been, and still was, sick. This implicit rejection of him because of the way that he looked. An anger stemming from his time as a latchkey kid in New York City, which itself could be a tacit condemnation of his father's negligence.

This was why Sam had been a drug addict and a fuckup— because the person who had been supposed to take care of him hadn't been around.

But this, too, was an overly tidy and convenient story that

Sam liked to tell himself, one that reinforced his sense of victimhood and flattened out the complexity of what had actually been, wasn't it? Maybe his father had just wanted Sam to be healthy. Was that so wrong? And this, the many levels of memory and narrative, began to feel dizzying once again, and lying on the floor of Buck's house, Sam touched his hands to his temples and rubbed them anxiously, trying to soothe a headache that wasn't really there.

He anchored himself back in the memory of the apartment on Eighty-First Street. Of himself, standing on the street finishing a phone call in the cold early-spring light, of an enormous bodega coffee. It was in the spring that Sam had committed to losing the weight, motivated more by self-loathing than by self-love; instead of eating, he just drank coffee, and he started walking everywhere instead of taking the train, from his office in the Flatiron on Twenty-Ninth Street all the way home to the Upper East Side, or if he had appointments in the East Village or shows in Chelsea, he walked home from those, too, long evening walks in the city where he called friends from out of town or jotted down notes on his phone or listened to music or just had the luxury of being alone with his thoughts.

Sam was broke, too, broker than he had ever been before, so broke that sometimes the $2.25 of a MetroCard swipe felt like an expense that wasn't worth indulging, so he subsisted on coffee using K-Cups that he took from the office, justifying that he sometimes worked from home so it wasn't really theft, and he walked and smoked (because cigarettes were one expense on which he wouldn't compromise), and occasionally he'd stop and get a greasy slice of dollar pizza, but mostly his stomach was empty and he let the smoke and grime of the city feed him as he chugged through the hazy days that turned into crystalline nights. Sometimes as he walked, Sam imagined he was on a reality show where he would narrate his own life with self-important theatricality. *This city is tough,* he would say over a montage of taxis swerving, clickety-clack girls in stilettos stumbling down Washington Street, the sun setting over a brownstone roof. *But so am I.*

And it didn't take long before he could feel his hip bones jutting into the waistband of his jeans and his belly was flatter than it had been in a long time. He saw it in his face, too, the way the youthful curve of his cheeks went tauter than it had been before; he almost had a jawline now. When Brett wasn't home, Sam stood for what felt like hours in front of the mirror that hung in the living room of that apartment, sucking in his stomach, putting on clothes that had fit snugly only a few months earlier to feel how expansive they now were. He had always been unstoppable when he set his mind to something, and so he had set his mind to no longer being fat, and it had worked. The hunger for love, a love that he was sure he would find if only he was thin enough, had finally grown more urgent than the hunger for food.

Never mind that his body was still a battlefield of trigger points and insecurities. He wasn't in shape, and in photos he could see that he had a look he had come to associate with fat people who had starved themselves thin; a not-quite-healthy sense of proportions, a head that looked a little too big for his body, and when he studied his reflection, he tugged at the flesh of his thighs and the loose skin on his upper arms with dissatisfaction. It was still all wrong. He wasn't even thin, really—he had just undereaten to the point of no longer being too fat to date, to fit within the range of what was considered normal, to look decent in clothes, especially if he kept his jacket on or wore a slightly bulky sweater.

It made Sam want to see his father. Or, rather, it made Sam

want to be seen by his father, if only so he could have a moment to gloat.

Still, things were easier not being fat. The world had a curious way of rewarding him for it—both in the warm, wide-eyed reception he received when he ran into people he hadn't seen in a couple months, and the way that men looked at him on the street when he walked past, and even when he went out to the gay bars with Brett now, he got cruised in a way he never had before. They didn't know that he was an imposter, a fat person hiding in an unfat body, that behind the fitted shirt he was wearing was a mess of stretch marks and baggy flesh. That was how he felt, like a bulbous skin-sack that never contained its contents quite right. He wanted to be a little babe, spoonable, fuckable, but he was too tall and broad and lumpy to ever be that, and so he had to exist like this, though still he dreamed of one day inhabiting a different body, just waking up in the morning to discover that he was someone else.

The men of New York were just like his father: they preferred him thin. Or even more essentially, his value was contingent upon being thin—and this was not some wild eating-disordered distortion, it was true. He now received attention in a way he hadn't since high school, when he was strung out and skinny and pliant. In the years that he had been working hard to finish school and building a foundation of sobriety in adulthood, when he was kind or funny or smart, but fat, he'd been all but invisible. He was the same person he'd been before, with the same assets and flaws, just in a smaller body, but he was treated so differently.

In his relationships, there was something that reminded Sam of his father, this familiar pattern of seeking attention and approval only to be ignored. He had to change the way he thought about men, he decided, to be more independent and less desperate for validation, to telegraph satiety instead of hunger, which he knew would be hard because he was hungry literally all the time, especially now, but he would simply have to put on a brave face and pretend to be someone that he was not. Someone autonomous and confident and self-sufficient. Someone who didn't have a black hole of need inside him.

"Maybe," he said to Brett, like a mathematician who, in a moment of profound epiphany, had just solved a seemingly impossible equation, "the problem isn't that I keep dating my father, but just that the men I'm dating are dating my father's son," to which Brett rolled his eyes and put the Carly Rae Jepsen album back on.

My father's son. Those words rolled around in Sam's head for a minute, reverberating. *My father's son. My father's son. My father's son.*

He returned to the present moment and opened his eyes. The smoke in the room had thinned. Was a window open? How much time had passed since they'd begun the ceremony? Was anything even happening?

Sam looked over at Buck, who was lying supine under a blanket, his eyes closed. He wondered what Buck was thinking about. Weren't some spirits supposed to show up and start healing them?

He looked across the room to Jacob, who was seated cross-legged in a meditative posture, his eyes closed. The shaman didn't look like he was conjuring much of anything.

Sam lay back down.

In his mind's eye, he scanned his memory like he was looking over a reel of film, trying to find exactly the right frame. And there, he landed on it.

It was late spring, and the air in New York had grown balmy with the threat of another sticky summer. Brett and Sam were going to a concert at the Roseland Ballroom. It was

Justin Timberlake, whom neither of them particularly liked—
"I can't believe we're going to see a *man* play a concert," Brett
grumbled—but Sam had gotten the tickets comped through
work and so they had decided to make a night of it.

It was sweltering in the venue, and so crowded they couldn't
get anywhere close to the stage. Sam blotted the sweat from
his forehead. "Do we have to stay for the whole set?" Sam
shouted to Brett.

"I've got twenty minutes of this in me, max!" Brett yelled
over the din.

At the back of the theater, they lingered not far from the
door, as though they might need to flee at any moment. Halfway through one song, the chorus swelling as drunk girls sang
along in one big sloppy choir, Sam tapped Brett's shoulder,
shouting at him, "You need a drink?" and Brett shook his
head no, and so Sam made his way to the bar. A harried bartender was tending to a line of men all queued up like stock-
brokers trying to get his attention.

Down at the end of the bar was a young man with glasses
and dark hair in a cream-colored track jacket, tipping the
bartender. When he turned to look toward Sam, there was
some odd familiarity in his face, like Sam had seen him in
a dream or, more accurately, as if the sight of him triggered
some long-dormant memory. Sam lifted a hand to wave at
him and the young man waved back like he recognized Sam,
too, although Sam was sure that he couldn't place him. But
still Sam walked toward him—it would be weird not to after
this moment of acknowledgment. Sam smiled and cocked his
head quizzically.

"I know you," Sam said.

"What?" the man said.

"I know you!" Sam said, louder this time.

"Yeah," the man said. "I had the same thing." He extended

his hand and Sam shook it, formally. "What's up," he said. "I'm Charles." His eyes were very blue behind his round glasses and his hair was ink black and his lips were a little bit pouty. His face was handsome in a patrician way, like a royal portrait. He was sturdily built, and he looked like he was in his late twenties, maybe, but it was hard to tell exactly.

"I'm Sam," Sam said. "I can't place you."

Charles shook his head. "I know," he said. "Where are you from?"

"Here," Sam said.

"The Roseland?" Charles said.

Sam laughed. "No," he said. "The city."

"We probably went to the same parties."

"Probably," Sam said. He thought back to high school, where there was always some Greek shipping heir with a town house teeming with underage kids blowing lines on a Friday night, and it seemed likely that this was where they had seen one another, years ago, in some earlier iteration of themselves. Maybe Charles had poured him a drink when Sam was sixteen or bummed him a cigarette on a terrace. Sam was always half blacked-out in those years, anyway. No wonder the memory hadn't stuck.

"I should get back to my friend," Charles said. "He spilled a drink on some girl and she's really pissed."

"That sounds important," Sam said.

"It was nice to meet you," Charles said. "Nice to see you again, I guess." And he was gone.

That was it. There were no fireworks, no violins, no big transcendent moment of connection.

But after the show, the crowd pouring out onto Fifty-Second Street in clouds of cigarette smoke, hailing taxis and shouting into the sultry night, Sam saw him again, standing on the corner of Broadway, propping up another man, who was gesticulating wildly in the way very drunk people did. Sam and Brett passed them and Sam made eye contact with Charles again.

"It's you," Charles said.

Sam paused. "Is your friend all right?" he said. The man Charles was standing with collapsed against the wall and slowly slid down it into a sitting position.

"Yeah," Charles said. "He'll be fine. Enzo just had a few too many. Didn't you, Enzo?"

"Charlie," Enzo slurred. "Let's go to—let's go to fuckin' Le Bernardin." He was very tall and very good-looking and very drunk and very French, which was too many things to be at once. "I want a fuckin' cheeseburger from Le Bernardin." He kicked his Ferragamo loafers against the ground impatiently, like a little kid throwing a tantrum.

"I'm sorry," Charles said. "He's a mess. I always end up babysitting him." Charles turned to Brett. "What's up," he said. Brett raised a hand in greeting.

"It sounds like we're going to Le Bernardin," Charles said. "Do you want to come?"

The invitation surprised Sam. He looked at Brett, whose face communicated total disinterest. "I think we're going to pass," Sam said. "But good luck with this."

Charles looked surprised for a moment, and the thought struck Sam that maybe this was someone who was used to people saying yes to him. "I should probably get him home anyway," he said.

"Yeah, it looks like it," Sam said. "Good luck."

And then Brett turned to walk away, and Sam was about to turn, too, but for a second he glimpsed something in Charles's eyes, some desire, and so Sam said, "I'm around if you want to get a drink later, though."

Brett looked at Sam, startled.

"Okay," Charles said. "I'm going to take him back to the Upper East Side. Want to meet at the Penrose at eleven thirty?"

"Sure," Sam said. "I'll see you there."

As they walked away, Brett looked at Sam like he had snapped. "What was that?" Brett said.

"I know that guy from high school," Sam said. "Sort of. He's cute, right?"

Brett shrugged. "He looks like he has a trust fund and does a lot of coke."

"All right, I see the caliber of guys slinking out of your bedroom in the morning," Sam said. "Didn't the boy yesterday have a lip ring?"

Brett laughed. "I came out to have a good time and I'm honestly feeling so attacked right now," he said, hailing a cab.

That was where the memory stopped. Sam couldn't remember the cab ride back, or how it had felt to be at his apartment after the show, or if he had changed his clothes between the concert and meeting Charles at the bar, or the walk down Eighty-First Street to Second Avenue. There was just a big gray nothing, a gap in the reel of film, missing frames. Then the Penrose.

It was a place that felt defiantly unlike everything that this unfashionable stretch of Yorkville stood for. It belonged in Williamsburg; the drinks were served in mason jars, good-looking young people gathered in booths made of tufted brown leather against a backdrop of exposed brick, eating salmon tartare and Gouda macaroni and cheese, the hot rush of conversations lifting over music that grooved and crashed rudely.

Charles was already there when Sam walked in, still wearing that track jacket and now an apologetic half smile, seated at the bar. He had a Cartier watch around his wrist and Sam noticed now that he, like Enzo, was wearing designer loaf-ers. It made him look a little out of place there, like he should have been drinking closer to the park.

"What's up," Charles said. He had said it that same way earlier in the night and it struck Sam now because it wasn't something people really said anymore—not the way Charles said it. It reminded Sam of the straight boys from prep school whose approval he had always wanted, how they were slightly reticent in that boyish way. Not expressive, as Sam was, which always played as feminine.

"Your friend get home safe?" Sam said.

Charles shook his head, beleaguered. "Yeah, he'll be fine," he said. "Just needs to sleep it off. I'm sorry. I realize it's not a great first impression." He cared about making an impres-sion. Sam liked that.

"It's fine," Sam said. "That was me in high school. And it would be me now, if I still drank."

"You're sober?" Charles said.

Sam nodded.

"My best friend, Eleanor, got sober when she was really young, too. I've been to meetings with her. Eleanor Ruben-stein? Do you know her? She went to Chapin. Always in and out of rehab when we were growing up."

"I don't think so," Sam said. "That was me, though. Seven rehabs by the time I was nineteen. And then I finally got sober."

"Sounds like a lot of kids I know from the city," Charles said.

"Yeah, I guess it's par for the course," Sam said. "But I only did my last few years of high school in the city. Did you grow up here?"

Charles nodded. "Between here and Florida," he said. "My dad lives in Miami. But I went to school here. And I still live on the Upper East Side." He motioned north. "Ninety-First and York."

"You came back to the neighborhood?" Sam said.

"Well, it's my mom's apartment, but she's not there much," Charles said. "She stays with her boyfriend on Sutton Place most nights. So I've been living at her place." He sounded slightly self-conscious about this, like he was trying to minimize the admission that he lived at home.

"Listen—Manhattan real estate is a killer," Sam said. "If I still had family in the city, I'd be staying with them, too."

"Your family isn't here anymore?"

Sam shook his head. "My dad moved away a few years ago. I never thought I'd end up back on the Upper East Side. But we—my roommate and I—found a great place nearby."

"We're neighbors," Charles said. "Surprised our paths haven't crossed sooner."

"Yeah," Sam said. "And city kids all seem to know each other, don't they? *They*. We, I guess."

"We do," Charles said. "It's a universe unto itself."

"I don't have many friends from that chapter of my life anymore," Sam said, a little more abruptly than he'd intended.

"Why not?" Charles said.

"Sort of hard to explain," Sam said. "After I got clean, I had to put some distance between them and me, I guess. You know—city kids party. And my life is just—it's different now."

"I know what you mean." Charles leaned a little bit closer to Sam and his eyes were very bright. "I bet your friends from the city miss you, though," he said.

The moment was intimate, more so than Sam knew how to navigate. "Yeah," Sam said. "Maybe I'll call one of them up and see if there's, like, a gala I can tag along to." His palms were sweaty. He wiped them discreetly on the front of his jeans. "So," he said. "What do you do?"

"I'm a risk analyst," Charles said.

"Cool," Sam said, although he had no idea what that meant. "Is that...finance?"

Charles laughed. "Yeah," he said. "What about you?"

"I'm a music journalist," Sam said. It sounded more official, and impressive, than saying that he wrote two-hundred-word posts about pop stars' album tracklists for a blog.

"Wow," Charles said. It had worked—he sounded impressed. "Is that what you studied in school, journalism?"

"No," Sam said. "I studied creative writing. I always wanted to write a memoir. I mean, I am writing a memoir. Or trying to, at least."

"About what?" Charles said.

"That world," Sam said. "Our world. My years running amok all over the city. Kind of a *Less Than Zero* type thing."

"Why do you want to write it?" Charles said. It was a funny question, Sam thought. He bit his lip.

"A lot of reasons, I guess. Probably for the attention. That's a big part of it. I love attention."

Charles laughed. "That's honest," he said.

"That's not the only reason, though," Sam said quickly. "I guess the other reason is because—well, when you're an addict, you blow through peoples' lives like a hurricane, causing all this damage. And then you get sober and you get better but you can never really undo the damage. So what was it all for? For you to grow and learn from? That's nice, but it feels so insubstantial compared to how much fucking chaos you've created. And the idea of making something from it—to actually create something useful out of all that wreckage—is appealing." He looked at Charles. "Does that sound really grandiose?"

"No," Charles said. "It's a nice impulse." He took a sip of his drink. "I'll read it," he said.

"I have to finish it first," Sam said.

And then the tape went blank again. What happened after that? Sam squinted. Charles must have walked him home, because then they were standing outside Sam's apartment building. It smelled like smoke. Was that in Buck's den or in the memory? Oh, it was both. Sam had taken out his cigarettes, a little bit guiltily, and Charles had said, "Oh God, can I bum one—I've been trying to quit," and they had stood outside for a moment in comfortable silence. Suddenly Sam could see himself, his younger self, so clearly, as if he was watching a recording of it. He had been wearing a light gray cardigan and a lemon-yellow shirt. Had there ever been a more perfect spring night than that one? It was late by then and the midevening stickiness had burned off.

And Charles had looked up at Sam's apartment building and back at Sam and then he had kissed Sam. "Normally I would try to come up," he said. "But I think you might be special."

"I hope that's a risk worth taking," Sam said.

That was it. *Risk.* Why did that word feel so charged now?

Sam looked up at the streetlamp illuminating Eighty-First Street and the light was almost blinding, and then the light circled him, taking residence just behind his eyes, and began to pulsate like a strobe. He couldn't even see Charles anymore, couldn't see the shadowed street, the stairs leading up to the apartment, the cherry of his cigarette. There was only this pulsating white light in his periphery.

Sam's hand twitched. He opened his eyes and stared up at the ceiling. He looked around. He could see the books on the shelves, Buck lying next to him and Jacob lying cross-legged on the other side of the room. Now it was bright enough to see clearly. Who had turned on a lamp? Where was the light coming from?

He sat up. Groggily it dawned on him, with some mix of

horror and astonishment, that there was no light. The room was completely dark. And yet he had the full use of his vision. He could see in the dark. Like a cat.

Like a cat, he thought. *What the actual fuck.*

Sam felt a tension in his groin and realized that he had to pee. He wobbled to his feet, stepping over Buck's outstretched body, and stumbling through the living room to the bathroom around the corner. There was a candle burning in the hallway. Sam shielded his eyes from it; it was searingly bright, like gazing directly into the sun.

In the bathroom, urinating was a powerful relief; it felt like he'd had to pee for a hundred years. A candle was burning on the floor of the bathtub, with the shower curtain drawn so the light wouldn't be too bright, but still it illuminated the whole room so well that Sam could see his reflection.

He studied his face. He couldn't tell how altered a state he was in. On one hand, he felt pretty sober. On the other hand, he was basically a cat, so he didn't want to overestimate his clearheadedness.

As he blinked at his reflection, it started again—that pulsing white light that felt like it was coming from right behind his eyeballs. What *was* that?

He made his way back to the living room and lay back down. He closed his eyes again. Still the white light was flickering.

What was that thing that his teacher had said? *It's not about what you remember. It's about why you remember it that way.*

The details that stuck with him now, all these years later—why had he committed those to memory? The boorish people at the concert and Charles's drunk friend and the conversation they'd had about Sam's sobriety—it was because it had been hard, hadn't it? Harder than Sam had wanted to admit at the time, when he was so committed to the performance of having it all together. But it was so terribly lonely and frightening to be sober in an unsober world, and this was something that Sam hadn't wanted to say out loud, at the beginning. He didn't even want to think it, as if allowing the thought to exist would drive him to drink.

Maybe he had been jealous of Charles from the very beginning. Maybe Charles had represented the ease and security that Sam imagined came with money. Like all the kids Sam had known from high school with whom he no longer kept in touch.

And rich gays were the worst of all. It was part of why Sam had left New York, but it was just as bad in Los Angeles. Noah had been rich, too, which was annoying. *Noah*, he thought, and a memory threatened to crack open, but Sam couldn't go there yet, and he opened his eyes and looked up at the ceiling to steady himself in the clear voice of his inner narrator, not in something as immersive as a memory.

Rich gays. Even Buck, who had been so generous to him—on some level Sam resented him, too. These gays who were handsome and effortless and spent money however they liked. That was all Sam had ever wanted to be. It was so shallow and petty. He didn't want that to be the only thing he felt—surely there was something more profound than that, something deeper than simple envy, some grave wound that he could heal. And in an instant Sam wanted, desperately, to know what it was, to touch that deeper pain and to tear it out at its root. But he couldn't remember what it was.

He rolled over onto his side and curled up in a fetal position. What a stupid exercise this was—analyzing his own memories like they were a work of literature. He had already remembered all of this a thousand times and it never told him anything new. He sighed heavily.

And then, as if on command, Sam heard a heavy thud, like

the beat of a drum. Then another. He turned his head to listen. It *was* a drum—he had forgotten Jacob had brought one in. The beat was slow and steady, evoking something ancient.

Jacob began to sing in the high, eerie voice that he'd used in Portland when he was touching Sam's belly. "Hari om namo narayana," he sang. "Hari om namo narayana."

In Jacob's reedy voice, the song was shot through with grief; the sadness was beyond words. Every syllable was an elegy. The sound of it made Sam shake, and something heavy dropped in his chest, like his heart itself was a leaden weight.

He turned over again. When did the healing part start?

Sam didn't want to go back to Eighty-First Street. He didn't want to remember anything more than this. He wanted to curl up inside the pain of the song and stay there, right there, immobilized by everything that still hurt. "Fuck," he said under his breath.

And there Sam was, standing under the streetlamp again in his memory, on another night, maybe a week later, holding an umbrella. It was raining. What had he been wearing? He could see himself in a rain slicker with a little hood over a button-down shirt and the plain black Tod's loafers that he had found at a secondhand store that winter for fifteen dollars; he couldn't believe what a coup it was, to find this sort of preppy essential, the kind he could not normally afford, at such a steal, even if the pebbled soles were already almost worn through.

It had been pouring all day, a torrential spring rain, uncharacteristic for the season, with thunder and lightning to boot. Charles had suggested they have dinner at a new restaurant in the West Village and Sam had agreed, planning to take a long walk downtown, but the weather had preempted that plan. Why don't we just go somewhere in the neighborhood? Sam had texted Charles.

I can drive us if you want, he said.

You have a car?

I'll pick you up, Charles had said.

Sam squinted through the rain as a long black Mercedes pulled up in front of the building, turning on its flashers. Was that him? The passenger-side window rolled down and Sam could see Charles inside, wearing a leather jacket and those goofy round glasses again. Sam made his way through the rain toward the car, shaking out his umbrella before sliding in.

"What's up," Charles said.

"I don't think a guy has ever picked me up for a date in a car before," Sam said. "Nobody in the city has a car."

"It's my mom's," Charles said, pulling out onto York Avenue. "Having a car in the city is like having a superpower."

"You're so fancy," Sam said. Charles shrugged.

"If I'm going to be living at home, I might as well take full advantage of it," he said. He looked down at Sam's shoes—the secondhand Tod's. "I have those shoes," he said.

Sam wiggled his toes in them. "Me, too," he said, needlessly, and he looked over at Charles.

They left the car in a garage on Horatio Street and made their way to the restaurant, jumping over puddles and swerving to avoid the spray from passing taxis. Inside, Charles murmured his name to the hostess and they were shown to a corner booth. Charles looked natural in this context, at an expensive place surrounded by expensive-looking people. Everything about him seemed expensive, but not in a performative way. It looked right on him.

It was then, that night, that Sam learned more about Charles's life—wasn't it? Sam couldn't remember what Charles had said, exactly, but he remembered the stories, how he had listened intently while not eating his burrata; it had been so long since Sam had spent time with anyone like this, not since high school.

Charles explained that his father, an American, had grown up in Texas, while his mother, the French heir to an agricultural fortune, was raised in Algiers. She moved to Paris when she was a teenager to study fashion and worked for Azzedine Alaïa before moving to New York. Charles's parents met at Studio 54 and fell madly in love, then had Charles, followed by a messy divorce when Charles was a teenager. When the economy tanked a few years later, Charles's father went broke and moved to Florida.

"He had to sell all his planes," Charles said, sounding a little melancholy.

"That's a very glamorous sentence," Sam said. "In fact, having to sell *all* your planes might be even more glamorous than having planes in the first place."

"I think true glamour is keeping your planes through the Great Recession," Charles said, pushing his glasses up his nose.

On someone else, it would have been unbearable, but on Charles, it wasn't, somehow; he was funny and self-conscious about his station. He wore his privilege like a loose garment, a part of him but not defining. He told Sam a story from his childhood; he'd grown up with a driver, and so the first time he was ever on board a public bus, he whispered his address in the driver's ear. He thought that was how it worked. Charles laughed helplessly at this, mortified by the memory.

It reminded Sam of the culture shock he'd experienced when he had moved to Manhattan as a teenager and realized that the flashy, name-dropping way that rich people talked in the movies was totally inaccurate—the way fictional characters always pointed out their privilege, as though insecure that it might go unnoticed by those around them. This, he had learned, was a parvenu tell—people born of true privilege never have to acknowledge it, because it just *is*. Sam's friends in high school had scorned the flashy monogrammed purses that the upwardly mobile carried; they wore slinky Marni dresses, tasteful Celine totes. Living well wasn't a point to be proven—it was the stage on which life played out.

Sam wondered if Charles's lifestyle would have alienated someone who hadn't spent a few years traveling in those same circles, who didn't already speak this language, and he was grateful to be familiar enough with it that it didn't rattle him, because he thought he might like the person underneath it.

He couldn't remember leaving the restaurant—couldn't remember doing the delicate dance of reaching for the check, though he was sure that Charles had paid, which was probably a relief to Sam at the time—the bill for a dinner like that could have wiped out the balance of his checking account, spread thin as he was financially. He couldn't remember anything until later that night, when the date was over, sitting up on his roof and talking to Kat on the phone. Charles would have dropped him off at home. How funny that Sam now couldn't remember the kiss as he was getting out of the car, if it was polite or lusty or something else altogether. How tragic it was that those details just got lost to time, disappearing like ghosts in the night.

But he knew this—that he had sat on that roof and called Kat. "What do you do if you meet a cute boy who is into you and you're into him but you worry that you're only into him because he represents the unattainability of your unfulfilled past?" Sam said.

"Get married?" Kat said. "Who is this dude?"

"We met last week at a show," Sam said. "The good news is that he's French so our kids would have dual citizenship and be better than everyone else."

"Chic!" Kat said.

"The bad news is that he works in finance which means he's probably a cokehead and I bet all his friends suck."

"That's less good for you," Kat said.

"But I think I'm mostly attracted to him because he reminds me of the super rich kids I partied with in high school whose approval I craved except even when I got it, it was still never enough for me because I'm a black hole that endlessly sucks in validation and gives nothing back."

"Relatable," Kat said.

"So do you think we should raise our kids in Paris or send them to boarding school?" Sam said. "It's very important to us that Colette is bilingual."

Why had he joked about it that way? Maybe it was some way of externalizing the anxiety he already felt about the fact that he'd met someone, out in the real world, and that someone liked him back. It was so much easier to spin his wheels about the potential problems than to just exist in this thing that felt good and simple. But there was also a real fear there—that Charles represented some sort of resolution to the things that were still sticky in Sam's past, the way he'd grown up, the very story he was trying to tell in this book that he wanted to write but was afraid that he would never finish. There could be no more fitting partner than a true Upper East Side blue blood when Sam was trying to tell the story of how he'd fit in among them; it was a way of coming back to the person he'd been running from for the past half decade. Perhaps it would even help him write the book.

Sam came back into his body, wriggling his fingers as if to remember that he still had them at all. His eyes darted around the room, which was still as brightly lit as if there was a lamp on, even though there was nothing to illuminate it.

Jacob was singing a different song now, in a foreign language, with a slow and dirgelike melody. Was it Sanskrit? Sam didn't know if he had ever even heard Sanskrit before—how would he recognize it if that was indeed what it was? Yet it plucked at the strings of something private and primal, and with a heavy sigh he went deeper into himself, back into this film he couldn't help but play to its final frame.

It must have been only a few days later that he had met Charles for a third time, for dinner at a little bistro on Third Avenue. Sam couldn't recall the name of the restaurant now. But he remembered standing on the corner and seeing Charles's silhouette approaching him in the spring dusk. He had a slightly flat-footed walk and a bottle of water wedged into the pocket of his jacket and he kissed Sam on the cheek. That was all Sam could remember with any clarity.

Maybe it had been one of those arbitrarily punishing New York days where there was no hot water for his shower and when he stepped out into the rain, he realized that the umbrella, which he had grabbed on his way out of the door, had broken tines crumpled up like the legs of a dead insect and he didn't have cash to buy one from a street vendor and he couldn't get a taxi and so he sprinted to the train and then it ran express for no reason, skipping his stop, so he was late to work and then the line at the deli that sold sad desk salads to sleepy-eyed corporate zombies was so long that he had missed his one o'clock meeting, rushing back down lower Fifth Avenue clutching his lunch in a brown paper bag and walking in red-faced and embarrassed to a disdainful glance from his boss.

Or maybe it had been something else entirely. But whatever the reason the city on that particular day had not felt like a place where all things were possible, instead feeling like a place where all things were difficult, and pointlessly so, and so Sam's frustration with the city had leaked out of him over dinner. Somehow the subject of New York and what it would mean to stay there had come up, and Sam had been overly dismissive of the charms of the city, saying something offhanded about how it was very difficult to imagine growing old in New York, although of course he understood implicitly that it was and always would be the center of the world, but that he thought often about moving to Los Angeles, where the sun would always shine and things might be a little bit easier, that maybe when his lease was up he would just go and do something else, get out of the rat race and just *live*.

And somehow this conversation had bloomed like a weed, and Charles had said that he couldn't imagine leaving New York—why would you ever live anywhere else?—and when Sam said he would probably go to Los Angeles eventually, Charles looked crestfallen. It was emotive in a way that was premature, given that they barely knew each other, but Sam could see it now, as clear as a photograph, some faint but distinct wounded shock in Charles's eyes, the way his mouth went tight into a thin horizontal line.

"I don't know," Charles had said. "I love it here. I know it's hard sometimes. But it's worth it to me." And then maybe they had switched subjects, skating through that loaded little moment as gracefully as possible.

But this, now this, Sam remembered clearly. They had finished dinner and were standing on the street and Charles kissed him and his mouth felt exactly right on Sam's; even his breath was sweet. *I want this forever*, Sam thought. It was such a dumb, romantic thought, but he thought it anyway.

And then Charles pulled away from Sam and gripped his hips and looked at Sam with his piercing blue eyes and it was like Sam was seeing him for the first time clearly, all of it—this sweetness, this impossibly lovely tenderness, as Charles shifted so effortlessly from a little boy playing dress-up in his father's business clothes to a man in his own right, self-possessed and confident with a swagger all his own. In an instant, Charles was all of the things—he was kind, and he was funny, and he was smart, and he was the only one who could be all of those things at once. It no longer felt difficult to be loved. It felt easy.

"Don't go to California," Charles said plainly.

And Sam realized that he didn't want to anymore.

"Okay," Sam said. "I won't." And he couldn't believe it but he really meant it.

God, how Sam wished he could go back there, that he could rewrite his own history, that the story could have gone differently. But it wasn't real anymore. It was all just memory.

This is all just memory.

He didn't want to be in this story anymore. He hated this story now. He closed his eyes and tried to conjure up anything else—a memory of something different, a fantasy that he had yet to live, a mantra or a prayer, but his mind was blank. He had to drop back down into it.

Everything sped up after that—it was harder to isolate specific evenings. Back when Sam had used drugs, he had loved the way amphetamines had made things feel so quick and glossy, like time passed in a different way, like life was happening around him but he didn't have to be present for anything but the best moments, which he could step into and feel with such acuity and then return to autopilot, like his body was a machine. Falling in love with Charles was a little bit like that, those big surges of dopamine whenever he saw him, and everything in between was just white noise, as he floated through life in an altered state waiting for the next rush.

But maybe it was the next night, on his fourth date with Charles, that Sam had met his friends; some heiress was having a '70s-themed birthday party downtown. Rich people loved costume parties as they loved any occasion to buy a new outfit; for Sam, who lacked both time and money to think through and purchase a period-specific costume, it was a deeply stressful invitation. Still, he had rallied, running to the Goodwill on First Avenue that afternoon to forage for bell-bottom jeans and a tacky plaid blazer, which he'd hastily thrown on before heading to meet Charles, spritzing himself with cologne to cover the musty aroma of secondhand clothes.

There was a photo booth, and streamers everywhere, and all Charles's friends had names like Isabelle and Chloe and Lucie, gamine young women in suede dresses and patterned jumpsuits, some lo-fi disco number tinkling in the background.

How is it? Are they terrible? Are they your new best friends? Brett had texted him, and Sam had written back, *They are both and it's fine.*

That was the first night Sam had spent with Charles. He could picture the blazer folded on the arm of the overstuffed chair in his bedroom, the way Sam had creased it so Charles wouldn't see the chain-store label and think less of him. There, cocooned in his bedroom, lost in his limbs, Sam told Charles that he had a bad history with men, that he always seemed to scare them away by being too intense, too intimate, too vulnerable and too needy, that from all the men he'd ever really cared about going back to his father, he'd had the same terrible pattern: once men realized that Sam was simply too much, it was only a matter of time before they left.

Charles looked at Sam with something like bewilderment, and he said so quietly, "I think all of those guys were really dumb." It was a line, but a good one, and Sam had the passing thought, almost too implausible to hold tightly, that maybe this might really be something.

Sam let the memory pass through him, allowing himself to feel a twinge of longing and regret, but only shallowly; he couldn't bear to touch the big emptiness underneath it.

Sam hadn't been in an apartment like Charles's since high school, a five-bedroom colossus in an enormous postwar building on York Avenue with panoramic views of the East River; there was a capacious formal dining room, and servants' quarters that were actually inhabited by a real-life live-in maid, an unsmiling Ukrainian woman named Yana, and a guest bedroom that was cluttered with old stuff, designer shoeboxes and racks of clothing and—Sam gasped when he saw it—a portrait, nearly as tall as Sam, of Charles as a young boy, painted by some middling artist and encased in a gilded frame. It wasn't entirely up to date—everything in the apartment was wood-paneled, which must have been a trend in the '90s but made the space feel more like the interior of a yacht than an actual home in the city—but it was still luxurious.

It would be weeks before Sam finally met Charles's mother, who spent most nights with her boyfriend across town, and it was easy to see why even in his late twenties Charles had continued living there: there were always groceries in the pantry and Yana kept the house tidy; when they ran out for coffee in the morning, they returned to find Charles's bed made and the clothes all folded neatly on the overstuffed chair in the corner and the little toothpaste spots wiped off the mirror in the bathroom, which was an emerald-tiled cube, all its fixtures so glossy and pristine. When Sam opened the vanity, there were so many fancy toiletries, bottles of Molton Brown black pepper and coriander body wash and little silver jars of Dr. Brandt moisturizer and La Mer eye cream and endless bottles of Creed cologne. The closet, too, was crowded with nice things, Gucci loafers and fur-trimmed Moncler parkas and effortless Saint Laurent topcoats and cashmere sweaters in every color. It activated something in Sam, some desire to be a part of this world where everything was put in its right place, where there was no dust or lint on anything, where things were expensive and beautiful and fit where they belonged.

Charles's apartment was ten blocks north of Sam's, on

Ninety-First Street, and soon every night Sam was walking those ten blocks up York Avenue to stay over, a duffel
bag stuffed with the next day's work clothes, or just to meet
Charles for a cigarette downstairs to say hi and give him a
squeeze and talk about the day. Quickly he learned every step
of that walk: the pizzeria and the dry cleaner and the pharmacy and the Gristedes where, he was sure, nobody had ever
shopped. A few awnings down Eighty-Sixth Street toward
First Avenue, there was the building where Sam's stepmother
had lived when he was in high school, and he looked often at
that awning and the doorman standing underneath it in his
jaunty cap—how that doorman had hated him, when Sam
was a bratty teenager—and in those moments it felt terribly
poignant, that ten blocks could contain an entire life in so
many respects. This ten blocks that represented, in its totality, the person he was at Eighty-First Street and the person he
had been at Eighty-Sixth Street and now, perhaps, the person
he was becoming at Ninety-First Street.

Sometimes Charles came over to Sam's apartment, too,
though it was always cold and a little bit empty and it was
strange to see him there, this polished man in this unpol-
ished place, but he crawled into bed with Sam and lay with
him until they fell asleep or they would sit out on the fire escape smoking cigarettes. That summer Sam was listening to
the new Taylor Swift album around the clock, and Charles
walked in one night while Sam was playing it full blast in
his bedroom, leaning out the window blowing smoke circles
and singing along.

Charles laughed at the sight of him. "You really like Taylor Swift, huh?" he said.

"Oh, I love her so much," Sam said.

"Why?"

"I mean, she's somebody who writes about her life, like

I do, so I guess I like that," he said. "She's pop music's best memoirist. She's a master of perspective. Have you heard this song, 'Mine'?"

Charles shook his head.

"Oh my God," Sam said. "You have to hear this." He turned it on. "It's a song about falling in love, but it's not just a song about falling in love—it's a song about remembering falling in love. Like a lot of her songs. Have you ever noticed that, like, most of the best modern pop songs are in the present tense? Taylor is so good at writing in the past tense. It's about memory—about lived experience. On 'Mine,' she's singing about something that happened a long time ago. Listen to these lyrics."

They listened to the song together, Sam tapping his feet to that kicky guitar loop. "On the chorus," Sam said, "she goes, 'I remember we were sitting there by the water, you put your arms around me for the first time.' That 'I remember'—that's the shit that really blows me away. We're not with her in the present as she's falling in love, we're with her as she goes back into her memories, with all the grief and longing and distance that comes with the passage of time. But then in the second part of that chorus—'You made a rebel of a careless man's careful daughter, you are the best thing that's ever been mine'—I mean, first of all, my God, have you ever heard a more spectacular turn of phrase than 'a careless man's careful daughter'? It just tells you everything you need to know about her, her backstory, her as a character. But then she does this beautiful little twist. 'You are the best thing that's ever been mine.' Not *were*, but *are*. We've been in her past. Suddenly we're with her in the present."

He looked at Charles—wanting him to understand, wanting him to feel the way that he felt, wishing he could pluck the feeling that was in his chest and transplant it into Charles so he could feel it, too. "Isn't it incredible?"

Charles laughed. He didn't look like he felt it the same way that Sam did. He looked like he felt something else. He touched Sam's shoulder, and suddenly Sam was embarrassed.

"Sorry," Sam said. "I just—you know, I always wanted to write something that makes other people feel the way a song like this makes me feel. It just makes me feel so, like— I don't know!" He lifted his hands and pressed them to his collarbones. "It makes me feel like my heart is doing jumping jacks in the rain."

"You know, I've never met anyone like you," Charles said. He studied Sam for a moment. "You're really intense, huh?"

Sam felt himself blush. He'd been too unedited.

But then Charles's face softened. "I really like it," he said. And then he squeezed Sam's hand.

Then, later, on the northwest corner of Eighty-Sixth Street, there was a little courtyard with some benches outside a bank, and it was there that, a few weeks after they had begun dating, Sam had sat with Charles and it had spilled out of him, some grandiose and sentimental confession: *I know that we just met and it would be easy for this to feel like a lot and I know I'm always a little bit a lot but that's just who I am and I just, I mean, I've never felt like this before, not with anyone, and it feels like this is something big, Charles, something real, the kind of thing that epic stories get told about—they write books about this sort of thing, don't they? Don't they?*

And Sam could see in Charles's eyes that something had begun that neither of them could stop, that there would be no pumping the brakes now, that they were both in too deep.

Sentimental, Sam thought. That was what it had been. *You're so fucking sentimental.* And suddenly he was furious with himself for getting trapped in all these platitudes.

But there was no original way to describe what it had felt like to be in love with Charles, no gimlet-eyed turn of phrase that could make it anything other than ordinary. It had felt so special at that time. Maybe it was. Or maybe it was just as pedestrian as Sam was, as trite as his best bit of imagery.

You are the best thing that's ever been mine. There was something there, in that lyric, but Sam couldn't quite crack it—couldn't remember what it was.

Jacob was whistling now, and the sound of it threatened to pull Sam out of this memory, but he persisted through it, like he was traveling down a long hallway lined with doors, and as he flung open each door there was another new heartbreak inside.

This—this was the last memory from that time before darkness fell. They had been seeing each other for five weeks. Sam remembered because they had joked about it, how it was their five-week anniversary—"We should just celebrate our anniversary every Sunday night," Charles had said—and they had gone out to the Hamptons to stay with one of Charles's friends.

Her name was Eleanor, the one Charles had mentioned at their first dinner, and Sam had liked her instantly, the night he'd met her at the '70s party. She had long curly blond hair and a prominent nose and a big, friendly laugh and they had talked for a moment outside over a cigarette, comparing notes about their coked-out prep school years—Eleanor had gotten sober young, too—and the best twelve-step meetings in the city, in which their paths had never crossed because Eleanor mostly went to meetings downtown but now, surely, they would have to go together—and when Charles had come outside, Eleanor had looked at him and pointed at Sam and said, "I like this one—he's a keeper."

Her parents had a house in Sagaponack where Charles said

he spent many weekends. "We have to go over Memorial Day," Charles had said. "It's the best."

And although it seemed premature, going away with this guy he'd just met and his friends—"You're going away with him *already*?" Brett said incredulously—Sam couldn't say no, and so he'd packed a bag and left the city with Charles on Friday afternoon, speeding down the Long Island Expressway in the Mercedes, Sam playing DJ and singing along to the bad radio pop he loved, the sunlight glinting off Charles's sunglasses, the curl of his muscular arm peeking out of his polo, and it felt like a strange dream, that these were just things that Sam got to do now, a weekend in the Hamptons with a boy he loved.

When they arrived at the house that evening, there were already people there, lithe young women in insouciant sundresses and rumple-haired boys in oversize linen shirts, and Eleanor screamed and threw her arms around Sam as if they were old friends—"You came!" They sat in the kitchen and talked into the night, the conversation drifting seamlessly into French from English and back again, someone ordering duck confit pizza from World Pie in Bridgehampton, and then everyone was sitting outside drinking wine in clouds of cigarette smoke, all these chic new friends talking about somebody's parents' garden party in Amagansett tomorrow that nobody wanted to go to, and Charles had his arm around Sam almost protectively, like he was worried that all this might be a bit too much for Sam, but instead Sam was charming and cracked a few jokes and leaned his head against Charles's shoulder, inhaling the now-familiar smell of him and the salt of the ocean.

Sam wanted to get past this, the smooth veneer of his nostalgic self-regard, the way time had let him sand down the rough edges of the truth until everything was rosy and airbrushed as a movie still. He searched his memory for the flinty edges of anxiety that must have been there—they must have—the newness of these people, the foreignness of the environment. Somebody passing a joint around outside, Charles inhaling, looking over at Sam with concern, Sam smiling to show Charles that he didn't mind, that Sam wasn't that kind of sober, tightly wound and self-protective, but that he was chill. Anything but the truth, which was that he had fought and scraped to continue using through so many stints in rehab and failed attempts at sobriety, that even though he'd gotten clean at nineteen, he felt he'd done so on borrowed time, well past his expiration date, and that the aroma of cannabis, innocuous as it was, cracked open in him some deep sense memory, some longing to be both a part of and apart from in that blissfully benumbed way. It had been years now since he'd felt that, since he'd been able to disappear. Charles reached over him, passing the joint to the girl sitting next to Sam, and Sam inhaled that smell, the earthy perfume of it.

But Sam didn't want to remember that. It didn't fit the narrative he had chosen—the story about how everything had been perfect in the beginning. He wanted everything that came later to come as a surprise; he didn't want to scour the past for the red flags he'd missed, those auguries of pain to come. He could excavate the deep and the dark later. He wasn't ready yet.

Maybe then it was morning and they were sitting on the lawn, drinking coffee, and there was Eleanor, pulling out of the driveway in her baby blue convertible, her long blond hair blowing in the wind, her eyes shielded behind Yoko Ono sunglasses. "You boys wanna come to SoulCycle?" she yelled.

Charles and Sam looked at each other and shook their heads no.

"Your loss!" she shouted and sped away, and then, with

the house to themselves, they crept up to the bedroom to fool around.

Maybe it was that afternoon that they were dancing at Surf Lodge in Montauk, their feet in the sand, and Sam was swaying and feeling the beat in his body, and Charles's hands were on his waist. It wasn't about the specifics—it was about the tenor of it, that rapturous young freedom and desire, this weekend and its honeyed beams of potential, of that luminous thought—*maybe it will just be like this forever*, a tangerine blur of dumbstruck euphoria, that vertiginous buzz as good as any drug.

And then, suddenly, it was Sunday afternoon and the weekend was over. Soon they would be sitting in traffic on the Van Wyck, the great dark skyline of the city approaching on the horizon. Charles was folding his clothes and putting them away in his duffel bag, a big black Louis Vuitton checkered canvas thing that Sam would have thought was tacky on anyone else but on Charles seemed somehow just right, and Sam was lying in bed gazing out the window at the lawn when a terrible thought cut through him like razor wire.

What was it? Sam squinted. He couldn't remember. He had just felt it.

"Are you all right?" Charles said, looking over at him. Sam nodded. Charles came over and sat down on the bed next to him, rubbing Sam's shoulders gently. Something malignant formed in his stomach.

"I'm just stressed about the workweek," Sam said. "Sunday scaries."

Charles looked out the window and in the golden hour, the light caught him just right.

"I know," he said breezily. "I love it out here. I never want to leave."

Stay, Sam thought. *Then stay.*

But it was already too late, and soon Charles and the memory were very far away, like Sam was reaching through time and space so he might grab ahold of Charles by the collar of his shirt, to twist that fabric in his fingers, to feel Charles's skin, the smooth expanse of it—and yet he couldn't. It was all too remote now.

All Sam could hear was Jacob's whistling, that high and eerie note, until it wasn't Jacob whistling anymore. It was the sound of the wind in the desert, an open window, driving fast on the freeway, the dry heat on red rock mountains. Now Sam was sitting in the passenger seat of a car. He looked over expecting to see Charles there, but it wasn't Charles in the driver's seat.

It was Noah, in a hoodie and baseball cap. He looked over at Sam and smiled guiltily, like he knew what they were doing was wrong.

It hadn't been wrong, had it?

This was from a different time. After Charles, and after what happened in New York, and after Sam had come to California. Not long after Sam and Noah had started seeing each other, but before reality had set in, the buzzkill that came to dampen the high of the early days. They had still been magic to each other then, the erotic surprise of feeling unexpectedly connected to someone new, all that heady want. *I don't want to*, Sam thought, but the memory kept playing.

"Let's take a little holiday," Noah had said simply, a quiet command, and Sam had said, "Okay," because he wanted Noah and that made him want to do whatever Noah wanted to do.

"The desert," Noah had said, and Sam had nodded.

What am I doing here? Sam asked. It didn't make sense. This story wasn't about Noah. This was supposed to be about Charles, and what happened in New York. That was the big wound—the big thing he needed to see. Right? *Why am I remembering this?* he asked, but there was no answer.

He tried to conjure Charles again but in his mind's eye he couldn't even make out his face now—it was just Noah. *Fuck it*, he thought, and he settled into the memory, into the desert.

Into Noah, who had a friend with a house in Palm Springs, and so they had fled Los Angeles on a sunny fall morning, taking the 10 east out of West Hollywood, feeling the heat rise as they passed through Riverside County, drinking iced coffees and finding out more about one another than they already knew.

Noah told Sam about the project he was working on, and all about his family back in England, in Manchester, where he'd grown up. "You'll love them," he said easily. It sounded like a promise.

"I'm sure I will," Sam said.

Noah was affectionate, but there was an edge to him, something dangerous, the residual addict that lives inside people in recovery long after they get clean. Sam liked it. He liked the rush of it even as it made him nervous.

And it was good to be there, in the desert. Sam loved the desert, loved the way the ruddy brown-red of the mountains contrasted against the artificial bright green of the grass like a shock, loved the luxurious kitsch of the midcentury modern houses, white-haired men in golf shirts and voluminous khaki pants and their younger, surgeried wives, the eerie calm of it. The bedroom was clean. White walls, salvage wood, a Navajo quilt, crisp white sheets.

As soon as they set down their bags, their hands were all over each other. It was primal. Noah fucked him twice. Sam gripped the blanket in his sweat-slick hands, feeling the scratchy woolen fibers in his fingers, tasting Noah's spit in his mouth, inhaling the metallic smell of his sweat. Even with the blinds drawn, the sun was so bright, slicing through the room in bars. Noah's five o'clock shadow. The hair on his chest. Noah's hands around Sam's neck. As soon as Noah was finished, Sam wanted more. He could be such a glutton. Such a pig.

Then they were hiking up a mountainside. There was nobody else around, nobody for miles. The air was cold and still. Dust and rocks. It was strange the way it could be so hot in the light of the sun and so cold once that same sun dipped behind the clouds. Sam followed Noah up the side of a cliff, kicking up dirt behind their sneakers. He was a man. Sam could see him now, in his black T-shirt and faded black jeans, all the pieces of him that didn't care. Sam was always pretending not to care. What would it be like, he wondered, to actually be at ease in the way that Noah seemed to be—to not obsess over every little thing?

And then the sun went down and they were splashing around in the pool and Noah put his arms under Sam's shoulders, lifting him up by his armpits, and for an instant Sam felt like he was weightless, just this feathery thing that could float away in the tide. It was so different from how Sam felt on land—heavy, dowdy, flat-footed. And when Noah kissed him hard, Sam thought maybe this was something more than just lust—something real. Sam had always thought of himself as a hopeless romantic, but what if instead they got to be hopeful romantics—blue sky people, the saxophone riff on "Run Away With Me," freeways cleared of traffic and bonedry desert nights?

But lying in bed that night, after Noah had dozed off, Sam couldn't sleep. His thoughts raced. Noah looked so contented in his slumber. Sam wondered what it would be like to be Noah instead of himself, to have that loose, fluid comfort. Sam wished that he could make a home in Noah's body, to live in him like a parasite, to see through his eyes.

The great curse of being a person in the world—you only ever get to be yourself.

Sam went outside to smoke a cigarette. The desert was freezing. All the heat had gone away. He shivered.

In the morning, the house felt different to Sam, like he no longer belonged in it: conspicuously stylish, with a rich gay aesthetic, modern and colorful, dotted with stacks of Taschen books and Jonathan Adler sculptures, an oversize Marilyn in the living room, everything as crisp as could be.

"I'm going to swim again," Noah said, and he walked out to the surface of the pool, dipping his toe in the water. He stripped down to his underwear, then pulled those off, too. Naked, he plunged under the surface, flicking back his hair. Sam sat in the shade, watching him, wanting him, wanting to be him. There was a piece of Sam that wished he could join, but he didn't know how. He was too self-conscious about his body to ever let go, now, in the clear light of day. This body that Noah worshiped. This body that Noah wanted to fuck all the time. Not even his desire was enough to make Sam feel at home in it.

What is it? Sam knew, but he still wasn't deep enough. There were places he could not face yet. Words he was not ready to say. Things he refused to investigate for fear of what he might find there, the way a child might turn over a rock in a garden to see what was underneath and discover so many bugs crawling in the earth, squirming and wriggling, some revulsion at all the things that lived but were so rarely seen.

Sam had done that, once, when he was young, but there were a lot of things he had done when he was young that felt far away now.

"Are you still experiencing effects?"

It was Jacob. His voice snapped Sam out of darkness. Sam

pointed his toes and made circles with his wrists, returning back into his body fully. He opened his eyes. The blinking light had stopped. The room was dark again.

"No," he said.

"Neither am I," Buck said. He was only two feet away from Sam, but somehow Sam had completely forgotten he was even there. Sam reached for Buck's hand and he squeezed it. "Hey, buddy," he said quietly, like it was a secret.

"Shall we close for the evening?" Jacob said. Sam pulled himself up into a seated position, reorienting himself to the space, and rested his hands on his knees, palms upturned toward the sky. He took a deep breath.

"What did you experience?" Jacob asked.

"I didn't feel much," Sam said. "Memories. Thinking about the past. But that's not new for me. The light got sort of weird, I guess."

"I didn't feel anything," Buck said, sounding a little indignant.

"That's not surprising," Jacob said, a smile in his voice. "I gave you so little, it's not likely that you would have had a powerful experience."

"Right," Sam said. "Gotta ease us into it." He still didn't fully understand the logic of the whole journey, but he wanted to seem compliant, trusting.

"But, man, there was a lot of debris out there," Jacob said. Sam could feel Buck tense slightly.

"Yeah?" Buck said.

"Where?" Sam said.

"In the other dimension," Jacob said. "Yeah, it was really—there was a lot of energy to clear. You might not have been able to feel it, but I definitely did."

"Huh," Buck said. "What kind of energy?"

"Just clutter," Jacob said. "I have to make sure there's a clear path for her to enter."

"The spirit," Sam said.

"Yes," Jacob said, as though this should be obvious by now.

Suddenly it all seemed colossally silly again, the spell of the ceremony broken now, these three grown men sitting on the floor of a house in the Hills with all their mystical knick-knacks, praying for—what? Salvation? Sam wasn't quite sure anymore.

"You'll probably have much more of an experience tomorrow," Jacob said, as though he could feel Sam's uncertainty. "The second night is usually the night where things really happen."

"I'm looking forward to it," Sam said.

"Should we have something to eat?" Jacob said. Slowly and deliberately, they made their way to their feet and padded out to the kitchen. Buck switched on an overhead light, and Sam winced. It seemed too bright, more so than his eyes could handle.

He steadied himself against a wall, feeling a wave of faint dizziness. He scanned the kitchen. The appliances, which had looked ordinary a few hours earlier, suddenly seemed foreign, like they had been sent from the future, and the light reflecting off the window was eerie. It was curious. Sam wasn't altered but he felt weird, in a nonspecific way, like things were subtly different, like the objects in his line of sight had been rearranged while he was midblink.

Buck reheated some of the grilled chicken and quinoa on the stove and they sat quietly in the dining room, eating it. It didn't taste like much. Maybe it wasn't supposed to.

Sam was just about to crawl into bed in the guest bedroom when he heard a knock on the door and Buck entered. He sat down next to Sam on the bed.

"How was your journey, really?" Sam said. "What happened?"

"Nothing," Buck said. "Nothing! Even calling it a journey feels, well, pretty generous. I mean, I was so bored! Nobody told me shamanic work was boring!"

Sam laughed. He felt a rush of affection toward Buck. "I'm just down to have this experience with you," Sam said. "No expectations." This was a lie, of course—his expectations were incredibly lofty—but it felt like the right thing to say.

"Did anything happen for you?" Buck said.

"Not really," Sam said. And it was true. All Sam had really done was go for a ride through his memories, and that was something he could do anywhere—sitting in traffic or on a conference call or just zoning out in the middle of whatever he was doing. Had he felt anything mystical, or even just psychedelic?

He hesitated. "But I do feel—I don't know. Weird, I guess. Don't you feel weird?"

"I mean, the situation is weird," Buck said. "Anyway, I'm going to bed. Get some sleep, kiddo."

And then he was gone and the house was silent. Sam looked around the bedroom. He turned his phone back on and flipped numbly through Instagram.

Muscular gays in trimly tailored suits smiling blandly on the step-and-repeat outside the Chateau for some brand's party. Had Sam been invited? Probably not. Memes. Flat tummy tea. *Don't look at this screen.* But he couldn't put it down. Sam inhaled; the sweater he'd worn during the ceremony smelled like campfire now, all those foreign smoky smells lingering in the fibers. His phone looked alien, possessed—all the things he hadn't done, all the people whose lives he wanted—and something dark bloomed inside him, like a pen bleeding ink.

As he scrolled, letting the darkness envelop him, he thought about Kat, about the end of the world she was so sure was coming. He imagined a tsunami roaring from the sea and decimating New York as in a disaster movie, its surging gray-black waves weaving through skyscrapers like snakes, carrying taxicabs and mailboxes and bicycles and bodies. He imagined Los Angeles burning to the ground, canyons and beaches ablaze, cinder and ash. *Take me with you*, he thought. *Take me with you.*

8

The Ocean

There was a note from Jacob in the kitchen when Sam awakened the next morning, wiping sleep-grit from his eyes, craving coffee he wasn't supposed to be drinking, blinking at the blare of morning sunlight, and he stopped at the half-folded piece of yellow legal paper on the counter and read the chicken scratch scrawled on the front:

GONE TO TENNIS AND YOGA. BACK LATER. J.
PS: REMEMBER THE FOUR COMMITMENTS.

Sam snorted. The shaman was out at tennis and yoga while they were on house arrest? Please. This whole thing was such a grift.

The door to Buck's bedroom was closed; Sam figured he

was still asleep. So he paced around the house. He studied the books lined neatly on the shelves, the little objets d'art laid out on countertops. He refreshed his Twitter feed, scrolling and scrolling and scrolling, for moments, then miles. He took selfies from various angles, trying to find the best lighting.

He had imagined that everything about this weekend would feel serious, imbued with divine and mystical energy, but instead it was just more of the same. In his head, he called out to the great spirit of the medicine.

Hello? he said. He listened for an answer but got nothing back.

He stepped outside to call Kat, sitting in the shade of an oak tree in the yard on a bench.

"How are you?" he asked.

"Oh my God," she said. "I had the worst nightmares last night."

Sam rubbed his eyes. The morning was cool and damp. Maybe he'd make a cup of herbal tea. "What were the nightmares about?"

"I was swimming," she said, "and suddenly there were jellyfish everywhere. And I wanted to touch them, because they were beautiful, but I couldn't, because I knew they would sting me, and I couldn't swim past them, because they were surrounding me. When I looked overhead to swim up to the surface, they were above me, too. I could feel my lungs filling up with water but I couldn't move past them. So I drowned. I actually felt myself die. And death wasn't peaceful. It was terrifying."

"Jesus, Kat." He wanted to tell her about his own thoughts from the night before, but he didn't want to make matters even worse. "What do you think it meant?"

"I'm not sure. Should I call your mom and ask?"

"Honestly, she would love that." A long pause. "You there?" Sam asked.

"Yeah," she said. "I just looked it up. Apparently dreaming of jellyfish is about painful memories rising up from your subconscious."

"Maybe they were mine," Sam said. As soon as he'd said it, he knew that it sounded crazy, but it also felt true. "The painful memories. Is that weird?"

"No," Kat said. "I mean, I'm an empath. Duh." She paused, like she was waiting for Sam to volunteer some more information. "Is that what was coming up for you? In your ceremony?"

"Sort of," he said. "But like, nothing really happened. I didn't feel anything." He felt suddenly defensive. "The shaman said that the first night is more about, um, clearing energetic debris."

"Debris," Kat repeated. "What kind of debris?"

"You know, like…" Sam was unable to explain what kind of debris it might be. It had sounded much more plausible when Jacob had said it the night before, at the end of ceremony, than it did now, in the harsh light of day. "Just like, cosmic debris or whatever."

"Oh, *cosmic* debris." He could hear her rolling her eyes.

"Maybe my expectations were too high for this whole thing."

"Your expectations are too high for everything, though," Kat said. "It's, like, part of who you are."

After he finished his call, Sam walked the perimeter of the property, the fence that enclosed the backyard and path through the garden, along the side of the house, that led to the driveway. Distantly, he could hear the whistling of traffic.

It was Friday morning, all those commuters forcing their way down Laurel Canyon from the Valley, braking and honking.

Sam's head throbbed. For a moment he considered getting in the car and leaving, just to be a part of the world again, to escape the chilling quietude of this house and this ceremony. His car, parked on the street right outside the gate. Jacob was gone. Nobody was awake. He could go, quickly, and get an iced green tea. Traffic was moving in the other direction— he'd be back in fifteen minutes. It wouldn't be coffee—it was barely cheating.

Sam walked down the driveway that led to the gate. As he approached, his movements slowed slightly, as if his limbs were growing sluggish, something leaden settling into his body, which was suddenly leviathan. His breath quickened, even as the rest of him lagged.

That's weird, Sam thought. Maybe he needed that shot of caffeine more urgently than he'd even realized.

But as he approached the gate the feeling, at once sedate and anxious, seemed to rise in his throat like he might vomit. The sunlight was too bright, and everything was wrong. He stopped at the gate and rested his hands on his knees, panting. He leaned forward, the crown of his head grazing the wooden slats of the gate, and the feeling made little shocks of electricity descend down his neck and through the tissues of his back, and he was sure he would throw up. He couldn't go any farther. It wasn't that he didn't want to anymore—it was that he *couldn't*.

Slowly he backed away from the gate and straightened his spine. He turned away, facing the house again. Sensation returned to his face. He pressed the back of his hand against his forehead and it was hot to the touch. His breath slowed. He felt normal again.

Shaken, he returned to the house.

★ ★ ★

The day passed restlessly, Sam flipping through coffee table books from Buck's library, or flopped on the couch scrolling endlessly through his Instagram. Finally, begrudgingly, Sam unpacked his laptop. "I'm going to go sit on the lawn and do some writing," he said to Buck, who had returned to bed, where he was lying atop the covers, corpse-like, with his hands folded across his chest and his eyes closed.

Buck nodded wordlessly and Sam went to sit outside in the shade in the backyard, until he noticed that the yurt was still erected on the edge of the grass, and so he crawled through the open flap and sprawled out on the ground, awkwardly resting his back against a cushion, breathing in that damp canvas smell.

He did need to do some writing, although of course when he said he was going to do some writing, that almost never meant actually writing; rather, he just read and reread the pages he'd already written, the same pages that Elijah had found so disappointing. It rarely felt productive. It was more like a tic, something useless and ritualized, something he did because he had always done it and because he could no longer stop. He began to cry, feeling frustrated, although he wasn't sure exactly why.

It was at that moment—of course it was—that the flap to the yurt opened and Buck poked his head inside. "There you are," he said. "At least someone's getting some use out of this gorgeous yurt."

Sam wiped away a few tears. Buck sat down next to him. "Jacob's back," he said. Then, a little snidely: "Our fearless leader."

"Okay," Sam said. "I just need a minute."

"You all right?" he asked. Sam shrugged. "What is it?" Buck said.

There it was—that question, again. *What is it?*

"I don't know," Sam said helplessly. He looked at Buck. "Do you know what yours is?"

"Fear, probably," Buck said.

"Of what?"

"Oh, everything," Buck said. He ran his hands through his silvery hair, making the muscles in his arms tighten and bulge. "Being alone. Getting older. Losing what I have. All of those things at once, really. I don't want to be this age without someone to build a life with. I don't want to keep picking the wrong people. I'm scared, you know? That I'll never get it right." He sighed. "I don't believe that life was meant to be lived alone, but I've spent so much of mine that way. And I can't understand why. I mean, is this how I grow old and die? Chasing after younger men, this Peter Pan syndrome, trying to touch a youth I spent closeted and scared—to make up for lost time I can't ever really get back?" He shook his head. "You know, my generation—the ones who lived through the plague—sometimes it feels like we're all so terrified of our own mortality that we're doomed to spend our lives fighting it. Just trying to be young forever. Running against time."

Sam looked at Buck, and his chiseled form seemed suddenly to sag, making what Sam had always seen as strength look like something else—puffed up, like an inflatable thing that could be punctured at any moment.

"Is that really how you feel?" Sam asked.

"Sometimes," Buck said. "Not all the time. But, you know, those of us who survived—we saw things you can't unsee. That changes you. It makes you want to be invincible."

"If you're strong, you can't be sick," Sam said.

"Yes."

"Is that why gay men are all so obsessed with youth and

beauty and our bodies?" Sam said. "Or is that a terrible generalization? Or is the whole world like that?"

Buck shrugged. He pointed at Sam's open laptop. "What are you writing?"

"I don't know anymore," Sam said. He thought about Kat's dream, about the jellyfish, about the ocean. "You know how they say, like, the majority of the ocean is still undiscovered, because you can't get deep enough to study it? That's what it feels like. I want to go deep enough to see what lives there, but I can't."

"She's good for that." They looked up and Jacob was sitting cross-legged at the opening to the yurt, hands on his knees. How long had he been there? "I know last night may have been underwhelming," he continued. "That's very common. But for many people, the second night is the night where a lot of healing happens. You're open. Ask for her to come to you." And now Jacob was tender in a way Sam hadn't seen him be before, that firmness falling away to reveal something unexpectedly soft. "She wants that for you," he said. "Can you put your faith in her?"

Sam nodded. "I'll try," he said.

"Good," Jacob said. "You *are* ready. You found me for a reason. So often we mistake fear for unwillingness. But your courage is a measure of how you push through fear to discover what's on the other side of it. Self-knowledge. Healing. Change."

Some chattering part of Sam's mind thought, *That sounds like a basic inspirational quote I'd see on Instagram.* And then another part of him thought, *I hope that's true.* He wondered if this weekend would make him basic. He wondered if he already was.

"Are you ready for ceremony?" Jacob said.

Sam looked at Buck, who nodded. "Yeah," Sam said.

"All right," Jacob said. He smiled at Sam. "Hey," he said. "I'm glad you didn't leave."

Sam froze. Some part of him wanted to feign obliviousness, to pretend like he didn't know what Jacob meant, even though he did. But he knew this probably wouldn't work. It wasn't even worth the attempt. So he decided, once again, to accept the weird surreality of this, the impossible possibility that the shaman knew what had happened earlier at the gate, that in his seeing-beyond power, he had actually seen something that he could not possibly have seen.

Sam let that feeling crash over him like a wave.

9

Little Things Feel Like Big Things

Back in the main house, the three men gathered in the den again, rearranging the cushions and pillows, folding up the blankets that had been left strewn messily across the floor. Sam felt serene as he lay back against the side of the sofa, arranging his legs out before him with his ankles turned outward, feeling the gentle stretch through his hamstrings and calves. If he had been listless during the day, sundown had brought with it a relaxation. All he had to do was get through the night.

Jacob poured the medicine again, waving a feather around him and whooshing through his teeth. He drank, then called Buck up to the mat. Again, more murmuring. Then he called Sam up.

Sam took it again like a shot, one smooth gulp. It tasted more bitter than it had the night before.

He settled back against the cushions and closed his eyes. He breathed slowly and deliberately.

This is boring, he thought. *Boring*.

There was silence in the room. The smell of smoke. The rustling of feathers. And then Jacob began beating on the drum, softly, then harder.

I really need this to work, Sam thought. *Can something please just happen tonight?*

The sound of the drum was hypnotic. Its slow, steady clap was like Sam's heartbeat, pounding loudly in his ears, and then it sounded less like a drum and more like the sharp slap of waves crashing against rocks, and as the sound ceased to be Jacob's drum and became the rushing of water, Sam felt himself sinking, like he was being submerged in an elevator through the ocean and dropping down a few stories into a memory that was a little deeper than the previous night's tape—deep but filled with light, like the glint of the sun on the bay, and Sam squinted, but he couldn't remember where it was, this place; and then he felt his face smile because it was such a good place, a sun-warmed place where he had felt so loved and hopeful.

He was with Charles at their favorite restaurant, overlooking the water on Three Mile Harbor in East Hampton. They were celebrating, but then, they were always celebrating something; Charles was so good at that, not just real special occasions but the most minor of things—a promising meeting at work, or a friend's good fortune—merited a nice dinner out. For the first few months they were together, they had celebrated their anniversary every Sunday night, at one of the restaurants Charles liked, Le Bilboquet or JoJo, or picking up fried seaweed and chicken satay from Philippe and eating it in bed on ornate silver trays, which always made Sam feel a bit like a Victorian dowager in a novel he would have read as a kid; but really, why would they go outside and face the city when a whole world existed in this bedroom, the wood-paneled womb, watching romantic comedies on Netflix and smoking out the window?

"Happy anniversary," they'd say to each other, grinning at the pleasure of having found one another, at the stupid and endlessly affirming joy of being in love.

What were they celebrating that night? Sam could see the shape of Charles's pink mouth, his flute fizzing with rosé, could taste the sweet and bitter tones of his iced tea. "To Woodhollow Drive," Charles said, and Sam had laughed, delighted.

"To Woodhollow Drive!" he said. Had he ever been happier?

Sam had found it, the house on Woodhollow Drive, on a lark. It was in the woods of East Hampton, where homes were more modestly priced than the shingled megamansions and oversize farmhouses that dotted the land south of the highway. "Look at this house," he said to Charles, pointing excitedly at his laptop, where he had pulled up pictures on the listing. *The house on Woodhollow Drive*, they repeated to one another, marveling at how cinematic it sounded.

Sam patted a necklace of imaginary pearls. "Darling, I simply can't tolerate the city in the summer," he said in an affected voice. "Have the driver bring the car around. I *must* go to the house on Woodhollow Drive." He mimed wrapping a scarf around his neck.

"Why are you putting a scarf on in the summer?" Charles laughed.

"Because rich people are always cold," Sam said. "Duh.

Haven't you ever noticed that? Rich people are always, like, reaching for a pashmina or a shawl. Also, they never sweat. Have you ever seen a very rich person sweat? They don't. Being cold is the ultimate luxury." He hugged his arms around himself. "I can't wait to be rich so I can be freezing cold all the time."

"You're so dumb," Charles said, messing up Sam's hair.

On a sunny Saturday morning, they drove to see it, up a winding country road lined with trees. The forest in the Hamptons was greener than anywhere else Sam had ever been—almost mint green, bright green, luminescent. They parked at the base of the driveway and hiked up through the overgrown bush to the house, which was perched at the top of a hill. The gate was open, so they quietly walked around the side, shushing each other and giggling.

"Is this considered breaking and entering?" Charles said.

"It's, like, B-and-E adjacent," Sam said.

Through the dusty windows, they could see the interior of the house, spread across three levels. The decor was outmoded; much of the house had seen better days. But the grounds were spectacular. Long beams of gray wood decking framed an enormous swimming pool, perhaps forty feet long, with tiered levels that would create a waterfall cascading down; the pool had long been emptied, and Sam caught a whiff of rotting stink from an animal that must have died nearby, but it was easy to imagine how breathtaking it would be when the house was up and running. It looked like a resort, a little enclave surrounded by dense, verdant woods, and it was so quiet all Sam could hear were their footsteps. Stairs led up to levels of decking that circled the main house, and they climbed up to the highest story to peer into the kitchen, then to look down onto the pool. From there, you could see the bay in the distance beyond the tree line.

Sam held Charles's hand and they gazed out over this, what might be their kingdom. Sam looked at Charles and he could see some gleam of madness in his eyes.

"We have to have it," Charles said.

Sam blinked.

Jacob was still beating on the drum. Sam opened and closed his eyes to the beat for a few seconds. He wanted to be in this memory, because it was happy, but he didn't, because it was so embarrassing now—that he had been so entitled, so greedy, to think this was something they could do. He sighed and gave in to it.

It was when Sam was twenty-five; it had been a year since he had met Charles. Now it was summer, and he had stockpiled vacation days to take a month away from work to finish writing his book, and Charles had rented a house in East Hampton for the month of June. He would drive out from the city on weekends and during the week Sam would be alone to write.

Sam loved it out there—not so much on the weekends, when the highway would grow clotted with cars from the city trying to get to Surf Lodge, or when Charles would bring a carful of friends to the spare bedrooms of the house, getting high by the pool and sloshing drinks in plastic cups and putting on pastel dress shirts to mill around parties at somebody's share in Montauk, but he loved it during the week, when the little town of East Hampton was conspicuously quiet, the gorgeous silence of those empty streets. Sam would awaken early before the day got too hot and sit in the shade by the pool, drinking iced coffee and chain-smoking and pounding away at his computer, then drive into town to get a sandwich with Brie and turkey at the Golden Pear, then go back to the house to write more as the day grew steamier, until some indeterminate point in the midafternoon when he'd strip down and go for a swim. It was an amber-hued summer dream and even when the work was difficult, he loved the solitude, the quiet, the serenity.

"This is my favorite place in the world," Sam said to Charles.

He rolled his eyes. "You and every rich person in Manhattan," he said. Then he softened. "I know," he said. "I love it out here, too."

Charles had inherited some money earlier that year; initially he had intended to buy an apartment in the city but slowly, first half jokingly and then over time more seriously, they had been talking about buying a house in the Hamptons instead. "Property values are going up like crazy out here," Sam said with the authority of someone who knew what he was talking about, although of course he did not. "We could keep renting in the city and have a house out east for weekends and the summer. We could rent it out for just one month of the summer and pay the taxes and maintenance for it all year long."

Sam said *we* although this was Charles's money, but it didn't feel like he was overstepping. They were building a future together. But it wasn't until they found the house on Woodhollow Drive that this bit began to feel like a reality.

"It's a steal at that price, but it needs a lot of work," Charles said, pursing his lips.

"I know," Sam said. "But listen. I could quit my job and move out here for the fall and supervise the renovation." He got higher off the fantasy, like he was taking sips of a powerful inhalant. "Maybe I'll drive a white Range Rover and go to the farmers market and get organic produce and make a light summer salad and sit out on the veranda or tend to my herb garden, and Gwyneth Paltrow will stop by on her way back from Barry's and I'll say, 'Oh, Gwyneth, it's so lovely to see you—I just whipped up some watermelon gazpacho, would you like some?' and she'll say, 'No, thank you, too much sodium,' and I'll say, 'Of course, I understand—please help yourself to some cucumber water from that carafe on the table.' And I'll have pastel trousers in every color and the slightly leathered look that older leisure gays have but I won't even bother driving to Sag Harbor to get a vampire facial because I'll be aging naturally, you know?"

"Wow," Charles said. "You are really going to make a fantastic Hamptons housewife."

"I think it's my calling," Sam said manically. His career and his life in the city felt so far away.

"We should buy an apartment in the city," Charles said. "It's where we live."

"I mean, sure," Sam said. "But at the same price point, which would you rather own—some five-hundred-square-foot shitbox in the sky on Garbage Island, or your literal dream mansion in Fancy White Lady Paradise?" He shot Charles a pointed look. "*You* do the math."

"I'm doing the math!" Charles protested. And indeed he was. After he crunched some numbers—a process which, to Sam, seemed a little bit opaque, but it hardly mattered if they were going to get the house—Charles decided to put in an offer. "It's a smart investment," he said, a little bit uncertainly. "In our future."

It had been so crazy, Sam thought. But at the time it had felt entirely sensible. They were young and in love and successful and Charles had the money—why shouldn't they buy their dream house in the Hamptons? Why shouldn't they have everything that they wanted? Never mind that Sam made a modest salary and was still paying off his student loans; never mind that they'd only been together for a little more than a year; never mind that they were both still in their twenties. It seemed like the only truly foolish thing would be to temper their expectations—to ask for anything less than that. And Sam opened his eyes again, staring around at the darkness of the room, and he almost couldn't believe it, that this had been his life for a little while.

All of it would have been unthinkable only a year earlier, at the beginning. But life had changed for Sam, and quicker than he'd imagined it could.

The first thing, and perhaps the biggest thing, was the book. A friend of a friend had connected Sam with Elijah, who had read his pages and agreed to take him on as a client. The summer that Sam met Charles, he was working on the proposal, going back and forth on rounds of edits and notes, discreetly printing out drafts at his office after everyone else had gone home and going over them with a red pen on the roof of his building until he knew every sentence of it, every punctuation mark; he could have recited the entire manuscript by heart—that was how many times he had read it. And Elijah's attitude about the material was, if not altogether bullish, at least encouraging; surely, Sam reasoned, Elijah wouldn't bother taking the time to work with him on it unless he thought it would sell.

The problem with the material, Sam now knew, with a rush of shame, was that he had focused too much on the style and not enough on the substance; he had been so concerned with the beauty of his sentences he hadn't thought through what he was saying, which seemed to him now exactly the kind of mistake that you would make when you were young and eager to prove yourself in the world. He didn't know that the book he was writing had critical flaws, and it made him sad all over again to know that he could never tell this story again, the indelibility of this thing he had created, and as he started to think about that again he reminded himself,

No, that story belongs to last night, and he felt it drift away from him and he rooted himself back in the summer once again.

While he was writing, that summer, he had felt only excitement—that this was the beginning of something, the career he'd fantasized about for so many years, the first step toward great success and good fortune. In the fall Elijah had declared that the material was ready and so off it went to a handful of editors, and Sam waited, with a heady mix of anticipation and dread that he hadn't felt since he'd applied to college, to learn his fate. And when the book sold—to a real publisher, one of the big ones—Sam almost couldn't believe it; it was so sublime and surreal that for the first few weeks after it happened, he woke up each morning convinced that he had dreamed it, and it took a moment to remember that it had actually happened.

Now, of course, he had to finish writing the book. But there was plenty of time for that, as contracts were negotiated and the first half of the advance appeared in his bank account like magic and Charles picked him up by his arms and twirled him around his apartment and Sam thought something good was beginning. It felt like liftoff, like the series of memories he would spend the rest of his life looking back at to trace the origins of how it had happened, all the happiness that he'd been chasing, and at times he could almost see himself as some august older self, maybe basking in the sun on the balcony of his house in the Hamptons years down the line as Charles busied himself in the kitchen, remembering how it had begun.

And with the little bit of money he had from the book advance, Sam could now afford to pick up the check at a nice dinner from time to time, which was a thrill, and for Christmas that year he bought Charles a beautiful leather backpack that wasn't even on sale, something that he knew Charles would like, and over New Year's they went to Paris, where

Charles's family kept an apartment, in a historic old building in the Marais with a cobblestone courtyard, that sat vacant most of the year. When they arrived there, they found that a window had been left open by the last person who had stayed there—Charles's brother, a year earlier, which they knew by the empty Lanvin and Saint Laurent shoeboxes strewn about on the living room floor, the wreckage of some misbegotten shopping spree—and everything in the apartment was covered in a thin layer of dust.

"Should we just get a room at Maison Souquet?" Charles said, his brow furrowed.

"No," Sam said. "Let's clean it up!"

And so they did, mopping the floors and running the upholstered cushion covers from the sofa down to the laundromat on the corner to be dry-cleaned, and replacing light bulbs and wrestling a new vacuum cleaner from the hardware store into the narrow elevator that rattled sinisterly underfoot, and while it wasn't how Sam had anticipated he would spend his vacation in Paris, it was almost better to be experiencing it this way, with Charles, as some little test of their commitment to one another—that they could make a shared project out of anything, that they worked well together in domestic spaces, that there was goodwill and camaraderie that superseded romance even in the most trying times.

And after the apartment had been put back together, there were dinners at Hôtel Costes and Le Cinq, long walks through shadowed alleyways, a day spent wandering around the Pompidou, where the most sophisticated take either of them could muster was to point at paintings or statues and say, "Me," or "You," or "Same," this dumb joke that somehow never got old. Late one night on a run to the corner store for some macarons, it began to rain, and so they were running through the cobblestone streets of Paris past midnight, holding hands, laughing at the absurdity of it, and Sam thought, *Oh God, this is it, this is the best moment, the moment all other moments will be measured against forever.*

The next thing to change was the job. Sam had gone in for a few interviews before the holidays but it had felt absurd and unlikely—the position, an editor covering culture at a national magazine, was well beyond his skill set, since he had no print experience beyond a few freelance magazine clips. To go from working at a little-read music blog to editor at a real magazine, one that he'd grown up with, was far too much a leap. He was incredulous they made him an offer.

"Now who's fancy," Charles marveled, and for a time, Sam felt like he was.

Everyone at the magazine was so grown-up, so serious and well-informed. In the morning meeting, each section editor addressed the latest news in their domain, and the quickness and density of it was numbing, the names of world leaders and experimental drugs for cancer and buzzy congresspeople, and every few moments one of the top editors would make an arch joke in reference to an earlier comment that would make everyone in the room laugh, and Sam laughed, too, even though he never got the jokes, and when it came around to him he would stammer and stutter about Beyoncé or the Oscar race, always feeling like he was doing it wrong, never quite sticking the landing.

His area of expertise was arts and entertainment, and nobody expected him to also possess granular knowledge of any subject beyond that one, and yet, surrounded by so many people covering politics and international affairs, science and the economy, he felt so frivolous in those first months. And soon he came to realize that the workload was extraordinary—the sheer volume of emails that landed in his inbox by the time he woke up, missives from the Hong Kong bureau and time-sensitive requests and breaking news that required him to be quick on his feet with a plan for how it should be covered, and magazine pages that had to be closed every week (every week!), and meetings and conference calls and lunches with entertainment industry executives and soon he was at the office late every night.

Still, it gave him a thrill to walk into that skyscraper on Sixth Avenue in his blazer and loafers, like so many generations of magazine editors had done before him, responding to quickfire rounds of emails on his phone. He felt important in new and different ways, purposeful somehow. He tried it out when people asked him what he did for a living—"I'm a magazine editor," he said confidently—and the sheer adultness of it was thrilling beyond words.

And it was worth it then—the sacrifice of having this job at the same time that he was under contract to deliver the book, as overwhelming a prospect as that was. He had known that it would be difficult, that it would mean many sleepless nights spent writing while Charles dozed in the other room, or more frequently, the mornings—that he would rise at 4:00 or 5:00 a.m. to sit in Charles's cavernous dining room, the dull thud of his keyboard as he hammered away at some scene, trying to see how long he could go without looking at the work emails that were already coming in from overseas, or stealing an hour in the middle of the day, pretending to be on a conference call while revising his pages.

What he hadn't considered was the sense of mounting pressure that would make it easier than he'd anticipated to wake up in the darkness before dawn, that he would spring forth out of bed, his brain noisy trying to remember if a story running in the magazine had been fact-checked or whether he'd sent off a round of edits to a freelancer, or from nightmares in which the book was savaged by critics or bombed commercially. So he would rise, padding silently out of the bedroom, to begin working again.

And when he wasn't working, Sam felt guilty, that needling feeling of having forgotten something critical at home as you're heading out on a long trip, knowing that he needed, desperately, to prove himself in both of these spaces of his life—both at the magazine and in the writing of this book, the latter of which was so permanent. He would only get one shot to do this right, and every moment spent doing something besides writing felt like squandered promise. But in the mornings in those fits of anxiety, his body felt tired and he kept thinking, *Maybe I should go to the doctor*, but then he would put that thought away.

The final thing to change that felt really significant was the apartment. That was in February, the month after Sam started the new job, three months after he'd gotten the book deal, eight months after he'd met Charles, and the lease was coming up on the apartment on Eighty-First Street, the home he had built with Brett, and the truth was that Sam felt bad about it, the place where he lived, which was no longer a place where he wanted to be.

Sam went to Charles's place almost every night—and with each passing day, his own apartment looked worse than it had the day before: the cheap kitchen appliances and the half-furnished living room and his bed frame that creaked ominously every time he flopped onto it and the floors that were always a little grimy no matter how frequently they were cleaned up, and God, reaching the bottom of his stairs and realizing that he had forgotten his keys or his wallet and having to hike five flights of stairs back up. When the lease was up, Sam knew he had to take the out.

Charles had been wanting to get his own place for a while. As comfortable as his family home was, with a live-in housekeeper and his mother hardly ever there, he said, he felt infantilized living there as an adult man, and it was probably time for him to grow up a little bit. Sam nodded because he knew this was true and more critically, he knew that he couldn't in good conscience move into Charles's mother's apartment and so the best thing for the both of them would be for Charles to move out. And yes, sure, it was soon for them to be moving in together—it had only been eight months, after all—but this was New York, where people surely did crazier things for real estate. And when Sam thought about where he'd lived in college, in that drag queen's apartment in Chelsea, it seemed silly to overthink the decision to move in with Charles, who loved Sam and who Sam loved, and who he knew so intimately now, even if it had been only a few months. Sam broached the topic with Brett gingerly.

"I'm thinking about getting a place with Charles," he said as they were eating takeout on the couch one night.

"Really?" Brett said. He forked some noodles into his mouth. "It's a little soon, no?"

"Yeah—I mean, the lease is up after next month, and it just seems like...I don't know. We're ready. You know?"

"If you say so," Brett said, and for a split second Sam felt guilty for doing this to his friend, but he wanted to be with Charles more than he wanted to do right by Brett.

"I'm sure you can find another roommate who wants to take my room," Sam said. "I'll help."

"Maybe I'll just get a studio," Brett said. "I dunno." He sighed. "You gonna move in somewhere super bougie?"

Sam shrugged. "We haven't really started looking yet," he said. "But I'd be happy to live somewhere, you know...nice."

Brett looked around the living room, and something fell across his face. "I love our apartment," he said softly.

"I do, too," Sam said, too quickly. "I didn't mean—"

"I get it," Brett said. There was no bitterness in his voice—just resignation.

"I'm sorry."

"It's fine!" Brett said. "Nothing lasts forever."

The memory was too much for Sam. He curled up on his side, fetal, and the pain of it pierced him in his chest. He could almost cry out from the sadness. Brett, his friend, who he had loved so much. Sam had been selfish. If only he had known then that those would be some of the happiest nights, sprawled out on the couch in that apartment watching reality TV.

The white light was blinking again in the background and Sam scrunched his eyes up, trying to blot it out.

But it hadn't been enough to deter him. And so he and Charles had gone to see the listing for an apartment on Sixty-Third Street and Third Avenue, in a modern high-rise. Charles had wanted to live somewhere new, and the photos on the realtor's website looked appealing enough—the elegant mirrored lobby, a doorman in a hat with a brim, the long gray awning that Sam saw himself waiting underneath for a taxi on a rainy day, wearing a trench coat and holding an umbrella, looking toward Second Avenue for a cab with its numbers lit up.

In the lobby they met the realtor. "Let me show you the unit," she said. *The unit*—Sam hated that, the clinical sound of it. It wasn't a unit. It was the place that would be their home.

As soon as they walked in, Sam knew that Charles would love it—loftlike dimensions, dark hardwood floors, a kitchen that gleamed, closets for days. There were other things that Sam noticed. The bathroom, modern but cramped. There was no overhead lighting, which made the place feel a little sad and dim. The windows faced the block, with a view of a nearly identical building across the street—double-paned windows like expressionless faces, all those other people paying too much just to live their lives. And there were odder things, too—in the living room there were holes in the walls, presumably from where there had once been shelving or paintings hung, but there was one round depression where the wall itself looked caved-in, and Sam had the clear, disturbing thought that it looked as if someone's head had been smashed into it. Surely that hadn't happened, though. It was just a thought.

"Oh, it's chic," Charles said.

"Are they going to fix that?" Sam said, pointing to the wall.

The realtor rolled her eyes as if it was a stupid question. "Of course," she said. "It'll be spick-and-span by the time you move in. And the rent is subsidized, because they're breaking their lease and they want to get out of here. So it's less expensive than other units in the building."

"Why are they breaking their lease?" Sam asked.

She shrugged. "I don't know," she said. "I put them in here. Nice young couple. Courtney and Brian."

"Did they break up?" Sam asked.

She shrugged again.

"So they broke up," Sam said.

Charles had a lot of reasons they should move in: the convenient location; the price that was reasonable, again by Manhattan standards, for a one-bedroom in a doorman building on the Upper East Side. And he was right that it was nice— the nicest place Sam had ever lived in New York by a mile.

But Sam didn't want to live there. It was superstitious, he knew, but he was skittish about building a home in the dissolution of someone else's relationship. Still, they reluctantly signed the lease.

That night, Sam took a cab down to Enchantments, a hole-in-the-wall storefront in the East Village that sold witchy knickknacks. There he bought a smudge stick and carried it through the apartment as ash sprinkled down onto a white porcelain plate, letting plumes of fragrant white smoke snake through the living room. He didn't really believe it would work, nor did he really believe that it wouldn't, but it was the kind of thing that his mother would have done. So he said a little prayer, asking that whatever darkness left behind would evaporate.

It would never really be their apartment. It was Courtney and Brian's apartment. Even after it had been painted, there were little things that Sam kept noticing in the days after they moved in, things that gave him pause. Like the chip in the granite on the kitchen sink. Sam made up stories about it. He imagined Brian cracking a beer open there, too drunk to find the bottle opener—did Courtney hate his drinking?— her sniping at him, resenting him a little bit more every time she washed a dish and saw that aberration in the smooth line of the granite.

For months they got Courtney's mail. Sam should have forwarded it to her, but usually he just threw it away, which was shitty of him, he knew, but he flinched every time he saw Courtney's name attached to their address. He wanted to erase any indication that an unhappy couple had lived there before they did.

The apartment. It had been the apartment's fault. Lying on the floor now, Sam was sure of it, and he twisted over onto one side again, remembering the apartment, hating the apartment.

What had been good? They had eked some joy out of moving in, out of the project of building a home together, taking weekend runs upstate to tool through vintage stores in sleepy Connecticut towns, and driving to outlet malls, a Restoration Hardware deep in Queens where they had the only French wall tower clock, five feet in diameter, left in the tristate area, and they rented a U-Haul and drove it there, loading the clock in the back, and Charles drove home, the clock rattling in the trailer, and Sam gripped his arm, laughing and yelling, "Please don't crash!" That was a nice memory. Maybe he could stay there.

But then he was standing in the apartment, right by the clock, which had been hung on the wall above the dining room table, looming approvingly over the space, and it was dusk; or maybe it wasn't dusk, because the apartment never got any natural light, so you never really knew; and Charles was in the kitchen, filling up a big silver bowl with ice and beer. Sam squinted. When was this? Then it flooded him, like diving into a pool: the housewarming party. He didn't want to go back there, but he couldn't resist it, the memory tugging at him.

It was a couple months after they had moved in, the bulk of the apartment furnished, and Charles had wanted for everyone to see how good it looked. He was insistent that they throw a housewarming party. The thought made Sam's stomach turn, and he kept pushing it off, but Charles continued to bring it up. "Just a few people," he said.

"Oh God," Sam said. "Do we have to? As a sober alcoholic who sweats a lot, hosting a house party in a one-bedroom apartment in the dead of summer is my worst nightmare."

"Can't you just do this for me?" Charles said, and there was something hard in his voice and in his eyes that made Sam certain he had to let Charles win this one. This was how it was: relationships were about compromise.

They argued about this from time to time—how they socialized, and with whom, and when, and how much Charles's friends partied, even if Charles himself was pretty moderate.

Sam had been sober for long enough now to develop an intuitive understanding of how to survive social situations that revolved around drinking—for him, it was all about knowing where to find the nearest available exits. There was always an escape route planned. He had learned early on, after getting sober, that environments that seemed innocuous could quickly shift into ones that were, if not altogether dangerous, uncomfortable enough that he'd need to leave. A long, boozy dinner where everyone else was drinking but Sam wasn't—that was tolerable, since at least there was something there for him to consume. He rarely had a great time out at bars but he didn't mind weathering them, usually just to stop by and say hello—and he took comfort in the knowledge that he could leave whenever he wanted to, that he never had to be in a space that made him uncomfortable.

But people were always on their worst behavior at house parties. A cramped apartment that always ended up getting humid with too many bodies packed into it. Depending on the vibe, people using drugs out in the open. And leaving always felt more conspicuous in someone's home.

As the evening approached, the feeling had built inside him, the feeling of not being able to do this, no matter how simple a thing it was, some overactive fight-or-flight mechanism gone haywire.

It was a sweltering summer night, and Sam was sitting in front of the air-conditioning in the living room, trying to cool himself down, waiting for guests to arrive, as Charles flitted around in the kitchen, setting out finger food and drinks. He was cheerful, excited to see what fun the night would bring. But Sam felt a profound dread rising from his gut and up through his throat. He was wearing a fancy button-down shirt that Charles had bought him and he could feel the fabric sticking to the perspiration on his chest. His heart pounded. Why did he have to get so worked up about stupid things like this? Why couldn't he just be normal? Why did everything have to be so difficult? He had been so angry with himself, so angry with Charles, so angry with the world for making him this way, and Sam wanted to reach through time, to grab the person he had been who didn't have the words to explain that this, this night, would be the one that broke him—not the book or the job or anything else but a housewarming party, that it was too much for him to bear.

Sitting in the chair by the window, Sam rocked back and forth, making a soothing noise to himself, some tuneless song. But the heat was building in him, the fear, the hellishness of this mundane thing that he simply could not do. *Why is it so hard for you to do things? What is the matter with you?* He took long, deliberate breaths but his heart was pounding like a drum.

"What are you doing?" he heard Charles say.

Sam shook his head.

"Are you okay?" Charles said.

Sam shook his head no.

"What's wrong?"

"I don't know," Sam said. "I don't know."

Charles walked over to him and put a hand on Sam's shoulder but Sam shrugged it away. He didn't want to be touched.

"It's just a party, babe," Charles said. Sam shook his head again. "It's just a little thing."

"I don't know why all the little things feel like big things," Sam said. "I don't know." He wanted Charles to call it off, to say he'd turn everyone away at the door, to say that it wasn't that important. But Charles's face tightened instead.

"Let's just get through the night," Charles said. "It'll be over in a few hours."

Sam looked around the apartment, at the place they had built, and he just wanted to be alone in it, to be cocooned in the safety and security of the world they had built there. But when he heard the first knock on the door, it vibrated through him and he knew he had to perform. He stood up and spread his face into a smile.

Guests began to filter in, saying all the right things about the expensive furniture, and Sam felt himself shift into the role of the gracious host, being welcoming and charming, moving from friend to friend, smiling warmly each time the door opened and someone new arrived. It was as if his body was operating without his mind. But that was almost worse. He felt like a liar, like a fraud, like he was pretending to be someone he wasn't, and this, too, was sickening; sometimes it felt as if this was all Charles wanted of him—to be on his arm at a fancy party or dinner with friends, looking at him with visible adoration and gratitude. Even though Charles was gay, he was still somehow conventional in his expectations, some old-world model of how a couple should be.

It wasn't an hour into the party that Sam saw one of Charles's friends, a gay who worked as a promoter for a Meatpacking District nightclub, exiting the bathroom, leading a pretty girl in a camouflage miniskirt out by the hand. She licked her lips, working her jaw; he swiped at his nose with his other hand and sniffled. Sam felt his stomach twist like he was going to vomit and the whole performance fractured. *No.*

And so Sam did what he always did in these situations: he left. He slipped through the crowds of people swilling rosé in the kitchen, convening around the dining room table, past the window where someone was passing around a joint, through the foyer and into the elevator down to the lobby, where some friends were checking in with the doorman—"Oh, hi! I'm just stepping out for some air," Sam said to them breezily—and outside into the muggy summer night. Suddenly he felt his breath rise in his throat and his eyes spilled over with tears and he sobbed. There was a piece of it that was darkly satisfying: the grim pleasure he took in being right, in having ammunition to use against Charles for the next time they argued about whether they would go out. *Oh, so I can get trapped in another house party with your garbage cokehead friends?* Sam would snarl, and he would win by default.

He sent Charles a text. Can you just get everybody out? it read.

What? Charles replied. Then: Where are you?

Outside, Sam said. There's people doing coke in the bathroom.

Soon the guests were straggling out, hailing taxis and wandering uptown. Some of them in small groups of new friends, headed up Third Avenue to J.G. Melon for late-night burgers, maybe, or downtown to Rose Bar, sloshing their drinks and taking bumps from a little saran bag, sips of euphoria to keep the good vibes of the night going. Sam watched them from the shadows across the street until he was sure that everyone was gone. He couldn't bear to see any of them, let alone speak to them.

Back up in the apartment, Charles was rounding up the empty beer bottles. They looked at each other for a long moment. Sam could read every little modulation on Charles's face, the tiniest crinkles in his forehead, the curve of his mouth, the version of him that hung behind his eyes. Right now he was sorry but also defensive, flexed, ready to apologize but only so much, because—in his mind—Sam bore half the responsibility for being so sensitive, so prudish, so judgmental. This was where they always broke down. Charles couldn't understand why Sam couldn't just be a little more chill.

Privately, neither did Sam. But not knowing how to change it, he always just doubled down instead, insisting that it was Charles's fault.

"I'm sorry," Charles said.

"I know," Sam said. He looked around their nice home,

full of all the nice things they had bought, and for a moment he didn't want to live there at all, and then he felt ungrateful. He sat down at the dining room table. "I really didn't want to have this party," he said.

"I know."

"Why did you make me?"

"I thought it would be fun," Charles said. He sounded like a little boy.

"Fun?" Sam said. He could hear the iciness in his voice, the rage. "What about this would be fun for me?"

"You invited all your friends, too."

"Because I was trying to counterbalance the stress of having to deal with yours."

"I am sorry that it went down like this," Charles said. "But I can't control what my friends do, or police their behavior—"

"Police their behavior?" Sam said. "All your friends know what my deal is. All your friends know I don't drink or use. What kind of person does coke in a recovering addict's home?"

"I don't think they knew, babe," Charles said. "You can't expect everyone to be that sensitive to you."

"It's not being sensitive—it's being fucking decent. Here's a general rule of thumb—don't do coke in random people's houses."

"Why are you so mad at me? I'm not the one who did anything."

"Because I want you to care more about protecting me than about whether your friends are impressed by our nice shit," Sam said. "Do you have any idea how hard it's been to stay clean and sober these last six years? How hard, and lonely?"

"Oh God, not this again," Charles said, and he turned back into the kitchen. Sam stood up and followed him.

"You don't, do you?" Sam said. "You don't have any idea, and you don't care."

"Right, Sam," Charles said. "You're such a fucking martyr because you occasionally participate in social activities and don't get fucked up during them. Welcome to the real world. Some people do drugs. Why does it bother you so much?"

"Why does it *bother* me so much?" Sam said, agape. "There were other sober people here tonight. Did you even consider how that looks to them?"

"That's what this is about, then. You always make me out to be so image obsessed, like I care so much about what other people think. But you're just worried about fucking up your brand."

"I don't care about my brand. I care about having a partner who gives a shit about my safety. Which you don't, clearly."

"Your safety is not in jeopardy because some kid did a little coke in the bathroom," Charles said. "Grow up, Sam."

"I knew something bad was going to happen tonight," Sam said. "I fucking knew it. I felt it."

"Oh, congratulations," Charles said. "You manifested another shitty night."

I don't want to do this, Sam thought, and he no longer knew whether he was thinking that in the memory or in the present, whether that feeling belonged to the version of him that had been there in that apartment, or the version of him that was lying on the floor of Buck's house. *Take me out of this, please.* He rolled over on his side and opened his eyes, coming back into his body.

He sat up. He was completely lucid. He looked around the darkened room. There wasn't even a trace of the spooky glow-in-the-dark effects of the previous night. He looked over at Buck's nest, but it was empty. He could see the outline of Jacob, sitting cross-legged a few feet away. He closed his eyes again. He lay back down.

He couldn't go back into the fights, to look at how ugly they had turned, the mysterious way that love could spoil, how the depth of their love was commensurate with the depth of their rage. Not here. Not yet. Not when there was no single fight but rather something more like a supercut of fights; there had been so many that the individual fights had lost their shape—there were only moments, frames that he could freeze on.

The way Charles had looked, so crestfallen and so surprised by Sam's capacity for cruelty, when Sam had said something unforgivable in the fever pitch of anger—he couldn't remember what it was now. Another night, sitting up in bed at the apartment on Sixty-Third Street, and Charles was yelling, spittle flying out of his mouth, and Sam was saying, "Just hit me then, if you hate me so much, just fucking hit me, you faggot, you coward, you fucking pussy," and he could see Charles straighten—he wanted to do it, Sam knew, and Sam wanted him to, because that was his inviolable boundary—if Charles hit him, then Sam would leave.

How did they get there? Sam rolled over again. It must have been something Sam had done, or something that he kept doing, some way that he was inciting Charles's anger— something Sam had done because he was rotten to the core.

No. He didn't want to do this. He didn't want to go there. He wasn't ready. He wanted to stay in the electric gold of that night in the Hamptons, the whisper of an acoustic guitar, the sun over the bay, the way Charles's car hugged the country roads, mosquitoes buzzing by lamplight, the fantasy of the house on Woodhollow Drive.

Sam had liked that version of himself, the him that lived in the house on Woodhollow Drive. It looked right, to be someone who summered in the Hamptons—to be someone who summered, period—someone who wore white pants and ivy green Tod's to a dinner out at a little restaurant over-looking a dock with his good-looking, moneyed boyfriend. There he was. Exactly as he should be. He could see himself there, how right it all was.

That was one of the good nights, one of the ones that Sam had committed to memory as if to remind himself of how it should be. But he felt himself pulled, insistently, deeper into the memory, into what happened next, and he shook his head, not wanting to remember it, how just as the server was set-ting down the ceviche, Charles's phone rang. He looked at it.

"It's the broker," he said.

"Oh my God," Sam said, grabbing Charles's arm. "This is it."

Charles picked up the call and put it on speakerphone.

"How are you?" the broker said, his voice crackling from a lousy connection.

"Give us good news!" Charles said.

"Listen, guys," the broker said, "unfortunately the seller has rejected your offer."

Sam furrowed his brow. "What?" he said. "I don't under-stand. We came in almost at the asking price. He doesn't want to counter?" This sounded like something people would say, though he didn't understand exactly how it all worked, be-cause he was twenty-five and could barely manage the logis-tics of paying his cell phone bill; buying a house was entirely beyond his ken.

"I'll be honest with you," the broker said. "I don't think he really wants to sell this house. It's been on the market for nearly two years. If he wanted to sell it by now, he would have."

"So what do we do?" Charles said helplessly.

"At your budget?" the broker said. Sam heard him clicking his tongue. "Maybe you should consider getting a condo. There's a really nice new development in Sag."

Suddenly the whole thing felt absurd. Some elitist, entitled joke that they had pulled on themselves. Being with Charles, it was so easy to expect that the world would open up its riches to them. But life didn't always work out that way. Sometimes it all just felt average and staid and anticlimactic. There would be no watermelon gazpacho, no drop-ins from Gwyneth, no house on Woodhollow Drive.

They drove back to the rental house in silence. The dream was ending. Sam looked over at Charles as he navigated the country roads. He was so handsome—dark hair and a strong, wide build; an expressive face that modulated so quickly from boyish to manly. He was the one that Sam had been imagining for years, that Sam had hoped the universe would deliver to him.

Most of the time.

"We'll find another house," he said.

"I know," Sam said, but he was disappointed. They both were.

Would things have gone differently if they had bought the house on Woodhollow Drive? Sam often thought that they would have. That in some quantum permutation of the universe, there was a version of him who was sun-kissed and happy there, tending to his herb garden, while his good-looking finance boyfriend drove in from the city on a Friday night. Sam would kiss his face when he arrived and ask him about his day and point to the dining room table, a slab of salvaged wood dotted with tea candles, where Sam would have thoughtfully curated an array of hors d'oeuvres for him. He would sit and Sam would rub his shoulders and smile and be relaxed and at ease and later suck his dick just because. He would be the man Charles had wanted him to be.

And though it would have been just as easy to populate this fictional universe with a different man, or put them in a different house, in Sam's mind it was always Charles, and the house on Woodhollow Drive.

Sam opened his eyes again. He stood and silently loped out of the room into the hallway. One candle was burning at the far end of the hall, below a mirror, and Sam looked at his silhouette, as if he wasn't quite sure that it was really him. He raised a hand at his reflection and waved it at himself.

He turned the corner into the bathroom and sat down on the edge of the tub for a moment.

What was all this, even? It was halfway through the second night and he had yet to experience anything that felt remotely like healing. This, the slideshow of memories that he'd been replaying in his mind for years already, wasn't anything new or revelatory.

The intolerability of it came on quickly like a head rush. He didn't want to go back in there, didn't want to lie there listening to a drumbeat, remembering all of the dumb things he'd done and mistakes he'd made. It wasn't cathartic, or spiritual. It was pointless.

And yet, he also knew that he'd made a commitment to Jacob that he would see the whole thing through, and as unimportant as that felt, he was also afraid of what might happen if he broke it. He thought back to that morning at the gate. Chills ran through him. He still believed enough to keep going, or at least, he believed that something bad might happen if he didn't, although he didn't believe enough to feel confident that the whole experience would offer any ultimate benefit. It was just that if he didn't stay there, in this sustained suffering, there might be an even worse outcome.

So he stood and trudged back into the den, where everything was still and silent, stepping over Buck's motionless body and crawling back into his nest. Sam closed his eyes and tried to recenter. After a moment, Jacob began to sing again.

"*Usa mi cuerpo, hazme brillar, con brillo de estrellas, con calor de sol.*"

Sam put his hands over his chest cavity and took a deep breath. *Do we have to do this?* he asked, and somehow, he knew that he did; he felt it intuitively, the way you just know some things, and for a moment it made him wonder if she was there with him, the spirit, but he stayed very still for a moment and tried to feel something mystical, and there was nothing—just the sound of his breath in his lungs. His lungs. *His lungs.*

Jacob had said there was something in his lungs, Sam remembered. He wondered what it was. It wasn't as though he was constantly ill. He'd get a head cold maybe twice a year, which lasted for less than a week, and occasionally he had a flare-up of seasonal allergies, and sometimes it was difficult to tell which of those was which, but both felt like little more than unpleasant inconveniences to be weathered, an infrequent tax on an otherwise healthy life, not a sign of spiritual unrest.

But there were a handful of times that Sam had gotten sick with a mysterious twenty-four-hour virus that passed as quickly as it came. It happened twice in New York, both when he was living with Charles. The first time it was late winter and it started as a heat, and then soon Sam's entire body ached as though he was meat that had been tenderized; it hurt to stand and it hurt to lie down. Sam's teeth chattered and he dripped with sweat.

When Charles got home from work, he took one look at Sam and fled uptown to his mother's apartment; he was a hypochondriac who washed his hands compulsively and took a dizzying regimen of vitamins to keep his immunity up, and they had been entrenched in a low-level fight about something for the past few days anyway, so if his affection for Sam had barely been strong enough to override his paranoia about getting sick at the very best of times, it certainly wasn't enough now.

But Sam was grateful that he was gone. He drew the blinds, turned on the air conditioner and sprawled wide across their big bed with its grand hammered steel headboard, punching the pillows soft, feeling the thick crinkled linen of the duvet turn from chilly to hot as his body warmed it. His fever climbed to 101, then 102. He felt wild-eyed and delirious, like a movie character, driven mad by some mysterious illness and consigned to life as an invalid.

After several hours of this decadent misery, he walked the six blocks uptown to an urgent care clinic, where a doctor inspected him, declared it a random virus that would probably pass quickly and advised him to rest and drink lots of fluid. But Sam did not want to get better, to go back to phone calls that needed to be returned and dry cleaning that needed to be picked up and bills that needed to be paid. He wanted to stay in the center of the fever, which was too encompassing to fight through. He wanted to be too sick to do anything forever, because he was sick enough that being sick felt like its own activity, one to which he was forced to surrender. He embraced his powerlessness, let the sickness envelop him like an unwelcome hug.

The next morning he woke up and felt fine—better than fine, even, with the clarity that only comes after a fog has lifted.

Sam was more surprised the one time it had happened in Los Angeles; for whatever reason he assumed that New York, such a cesspool of scuzzy germs and filth and inclement weather, was a place where people got sick with strange illnesses, ones that were probably carried by rats and roaches, then infected you when you touched the credit card console at Duane Reade and didn't immediately wash your hands. But Los Angeles, with its sunshiny, slightly vacant good vibes, did not seem like a place for sickness. Nonetheless it passed in a day, and Sam woke up in the morning with the previous night's suffering feeling far away.

And then there was one other time that he had been sick like that, he remembered—he was in Morocco, on a holiday with Charles, and he had fallen ill their last night in Marrakesh and Sam became hysterical, convinced that he had come down with some rare North African flu and Charles hated the riad where they were renting a room—"I don't like it here," he said, "I don't want to stay"—and so they decided to leave Marrakesh early to drive to Casablanca, and Charles hired a driver to take them out of town. They drove through the night, along long, badly lit desert roads, past gas stations with prices in Arabic, as Sam moaned and keened with his head leaned against the window, letting his breath steam up the glass, and the next thing he remembered he was sitting on the floor of the shower at the Sofitel in Casablanca, shaking from fever, and then in the morning he was all right, again. As sick as he had been, he was not sick anymore.

Was all that normal? Remembering it, it felt stranger than it had when Sam had lived through it, those little sicknesses that came and went so fast. But that was the strange thing about being sick, at least in that way—the sickness that came with fever chills, body aches; those fluish maladies—the transience of it almost felt like magic. How curious a thing that the body could be so susceptible to something that was utterly incapacitating, then would pass in a single day, leaving you restored to your original condition. And then it was always forgotten once your health returned. Sam did not think about what it was like to be sick unless he was already sick, and then what it was like to be sick was all that he could think about.

That was why it was so significant the last time Sam had gotten sick, a few months earlier, when he came down with a fever and began to feel a little bit dizzy. Sam had thought to himself then, "Oh, it's another twenty-four-hour bug." It had always followed a predictable pattern from which he had never known it to deviate. He knew the lay of the land, knew how sick he would get and how bad it would feel, knew that the end of it, a return to health, was already on the horizon— that it would pass, because the condition of being sick, as Sam had always known it, was a fundamentally brief one, and so he assumed that it always would be.

But it wasn't. That time was different.

Do we have to do this? Sam asked again, and again, the answer was yes.

It had started the week between Christmas and New Year's the previous year, during that overlong holiday interregnum where the world seems to stand still in its normal rhythms of work and events and errands. Sam had been coming to the tail end of several weeks of travel that had left him feeling depleted—not ill just yet, but more susceptible than normal, maybe. It was in the late afternoon after a morning flight from Las Vegas, where Sam had spent the weekend with Noah, when he realized he was warm in that feverish way, and a little dizzy.

Why had they gone to Las Vegas in the first place? Noah liked it—that was why. "It's peak America, isn't it?" he said. "All that tacky splendor." They had both been traveling for the holidays, Sam with his mother and Noah back in England with his family. They had only been seeing each other for a few months, which made that Christmas trip feel like an eternity; time meant such different things at different moments. Sam was nervous landing at McCarran, nervous as he tugged himself out of the taxi downstairs at the side entrance to the casino, where Noah was waiting, beaming, like he was so proud of himself. Sam dropped his bag onto the concrete and fell into his arms. His smell, leather and smoke.

"Come on," Noah said, pulling Sam by the hand into the casino. It felt like a maze, being led through endless hallways of gold-plated everything, the musty, malodorous hallucination of it. They barely made it into the room before Noah's hands were all over him, in the waistband of Sam's jeans, pulling down his fly with one hand, kissing him hard, their teeth clinking, and then Noah pulled away and Sam saw something hungry and primal in his eyes—that look, that *I need to have you right now* that always made Sam go numb and bright.

This was how it always happened: then Noah's hands were down the back of Sam's pants, cupping his ass; and then he pushed Sam down on the bed; and then he pulled off his own shirt, revealing his strong, lean chest and the pale pink of his nipples, the fur that led from his navel down; and it was here, in this moment, that the feeling inside Sam burst from desire into something more like need.

Then Noah's underwear was off and he spit on his hand and rubbed it on his cock and pushed himself inside Sam and for an instant Sam was complete. Noah leaned forward to kiss him, Sam's ankles on his shoulders, the metallic taste of his spit, tugging Sam's lower lip with his teeth; and then as he got closer, his weight shifting in and out, he looked at Sam and his eyes fluttered and groaned, spasming and quaking, and Sam wanted all of Noah, wanted to belong to him—and once, only once, did Noah say the thing that made Sam's face flush so hot he could hardly bear it, but now was not the time to remember that, not here, not in this sacred ceremony on the floor of Buck's house. But the memory of it made Sam stiffen in his briefs and he turned over on his side and worked his jaw, trying to back away from the waves of desire that rolled over him and into him, the shame of wanting it that badly.

Not that part. Anything but that.

Fast forward to what came later, as they sprawled out on the bed, and Sam pacing around in his underwear, smoking and telling Noah about the week he'd spent with his family; the black coffee they drank looking out over the Strip. Noah fucked him again before they went to dinner. Raw and savage, standing up this time, Sam's face pressed against the wall.

Sam hadn't known then what it was—he knew it wasn't love, but it was a lust more palpable than anything he'd experienced before, so potent it almost felt like it was enough to build a relationship on.

Out in the hallway, the stench of smoke and medicinal cleaners. It had been so sickening. No wonder he'd gotten sick.

"*Namah shivaya. Namah shivaya. Namah shivaya. Namah shivaya namah om.*" Jacob was singing this now, at a faster pace, and the sound of it made Sam bounce inside his body, the muscles in his thighs and legs shaking, and the memories seemed to move more quickly, too, cycling through his mind's eye in double time. *Can we not?* he asked, but there was no answer—only memory.

These memories. Rapid-fire. Crispy rice and spicy tuna at Nobu. They wasted money at the slot machines. They fucked for hours. They went to Cirque du Soleil and let the erotic charge build, Noah's leg sturdy, pressing up against Sam's. Sam wanted him all the time.

And then they were walking along the Strip, neon lights flashing, jets of water in fountains erupting from a pool opposite one another like an elaborate pas de deux, and Sam was walking ahead—*why was this moment important?* Sam couldn't remember, but he dropped back into it anyway—as they approached a set of revolving doors that led into the next casino. One compartment was closing as the door turned and Sam was waiting for the next to open, but suddenly he felt a force on his shoulders as Noah shoved him into the door. Sam stumbled into the container, narrowly missing the glass barrier. Noah followed him into the next one, smiling naughtily. Sam's heart was pounding. He turned to face Noah as he came through the door.

"What the fuck was that?" Sam said. He saw Noah's expression turn. Noah had been trying to be playful, but it had caught Sam off guard. "Don't do that."

"I was just kidding around," Noah said, abashed.

This little interaction—it was so telling. Noah, a little more fun and impulsive, and Sam, forever with his guard up, never able to just let something slide, never able to just relax.

And then it was the next morning and they had to leave, but they stayed in bed too late, Noah's arms and legs wrapped around Sam like interlocking pieces. Sam was tall enough that it was hard to find someone who made him feel small but Noah—long, lean Noah, with his whiskey eyes—he always could. Sam didn't want to put on clothes, didn't want to go to the airport, didn't want to return to the world. Even as they were checking out of the hotel, Sam could feel the way things were starting to unravel, somehow—some tension, some misalignment that he couldn't yet name.

Traffic was bad on the way to the airport, the wide streets of the Strip giving way to a desert highway, horns blaring, plumes of dust everywhere. They were going to miss their flight. Noah was a bad traveler, Sam realized; he looked as if he might cry, and Sam couldn't believe that this tree of a man could be reduced to rubble so quickly, and he wanted to comfort him but he didn't know how. At security, Noah's line moved more quickly, and suddenly he was passing through the metal detector and walking into the terminal while Sam was still untying his shoes to stuff in a bin, and Sam called, "Wait!" but Noah didn't turn back.

When he finally caught up with Noah at the gate, Sam was furious and humiliated.

"What?" Noah said.

"You left me," Sam said.

"What are you on about?" Noah said, and there was something confused and unsympathetic in his voice. "I'm right here."

They didn't speak on the flight. The tension grew almost unbearable. About halfway through, Sam reached across the aisle for Noah's hand and gripped it, and Noah looked at him, confused. He didn't know what he had done wrong, and Sam didn't know how to explain.

What Sam wanted to say was, *Please don't leave me.* He wanted to say, *Yes, I'm angry right now, for reasons that are too deep to explain, but just promise me that you won't leave me, that you won't let anything come between us, that you won't let me go.* But he didn't say that. He didn't say anything.

Sam turned over on his side again. He heard a rustling, like the flapping of wings. The room was full of smoke. *Controlling, demanding, irritable,* he thought. *That's how you always become, the closer someone gets to you. That's who you really are.*

Back home, Sam didn't hear from Noah for the rest of the day. That evening they spoke on the phone. Something in his voice was different.

"I just don't know if I'm in the right place to be in a relationship right now," Noah said tightly. "I have too much going on to be responsible for someone else's needs. I'm not up for that again."

"You're not responsible for my needs," Sam said, sputtering. He was downstairs by the entrance to his garage, smoking. He inhaled deeply. "Where is this coming from?"

"I just think we might need to slow down," Noah said. "It's too much too soon."

"Noah."

"I do think you're really great—I just need to take care of myself," Noah said. "I'm sorry."

It was so pat. So boilerplate. And it was right then that Sam began to feel not quite right. His face was flushed and his vision blurred slightly.

"Okay," Sam said. "Let's just—let's sit on this for a minute, okay? I'm not feeling super great." He took a long drag of his cigarette, suddenly not wanting it anymore.

"That's all right," Noah said. "We can talk later."

It came on so fast. That was what Sam would remember later, with some incredulity. It was not a daylong decline, creeping fatigue, constriction in the back of his throat, tenderness in his sinuses. It was more like a collision. He was fine and then he was not. And in the new and frightening not-fineness of himself, he walked back up the stairs to his apartment, feeling the heaviness in his limbs, wondering if this was psychosomatic—it probably was, he thought—and he collapsed onto the couch, pulling a blanket up around his shoulders and resting his head on a shapeless throw pillow.

It was hot in his apartment, or maybe his body was hot—he held a hand to his forehead and wasn't sure if it was his hand or his face that was hot—and he stood and turned on the air conditioner, although it was late December, and then he threw open the windows, letting the cold air rush in. Feeling the cold on his face, he laughed slightly, remembering when he had moved to Los Angeles just over a year earlier and he had packed like he was going to the Caribbean, lots of shorts and tropical colors. It had startled him to feel the chill of the winter.

Soon it was cold in his living room but still Sam felt the heat burning inside him, and the fever took him like a kidnapping. Like he was being cooked alive in his body. He took sharp breaths like he had been holding his breath underwater and had just come up to the surface for air. It was so cold and so hot and he bit the inside of his mouth so hard he could taste blood.

He awakened at some point and looked around the apartment. It was the middle of the night but the lights were still on and he felt dried out but his face was damp with sweat. He rocked back and forth. It did not feel like a sickness—it felt like a possession. *This will pass soon*, he thought. *It must.*

Maybe it was morning when the fever broke and Sam drove the three blocks to the pharmacy to buy cold medicine. He made tea and stumbled senselessly around his apartment, looking at himself from different angles in different mirrors, trying to find something deserving of love in his reflection. He ordered green juices and algae shots and turmeric and ginger and sucked it all down, one after another, until he could feel it burning his throat and churning in his stomach, all those sharp strange acids comingling. He vomited and felt better for a few minutes, and then the fever rose again like a curtain— "Showtime!" he sang out to his empty living room, collapsing again onto the couch, burying his sweat-slick face in the cushions.

Noah called to apologize.

"It's fine," Sam said, feeling the way speech made his vocal cords vibrate, feeling the delirious numbness in his head, having everything and nothing to say.

"I overreacted," Noah said.

"I'm really sick," Sam said. It was all there was.

Why this story? What does this have to do with anything? Sam flashed back into his body, returning to ceremony, and he was furious about having to watch this tape again—this thing he had no interest in remembering. Having to live through it once was enough. *Please don't make me do this,* he pleaded with the spirit, but of course there was no one there—it was just him and his memories, and he had no choice but to contend with all this once more, and so he settled back in and let the tape keep playing, surrendering to it and the logic of what he was being shown, as maddening as it was.

Noah had come over, to bring him medicine—on New Year's Eve, Sam remembered. He could feel himself, lying on the couch, looking up at Noah, whose face was so concerned, and Sam was arguing with him, feebly and unconvincingly—about what? There was a party at the home of some film executive and Sam had said some weeks earlier that he would go, and it felt critically important that he follow through on that invitation, even though he was, of course, much too sick to do anything, and Noah was saying, "You can't go," and Sam was saying, "But I have to, even if it's just for a few minutes," and Noah was saying, "Tell them you're sick," and Sam was saying, "What if then he thinks I'm a colossal flake," and Noah was taking Sam's temperature and it was 101 degrees, then 102, and Sam was stumbling to his feet, pulling on real clothes for the first time in so many days, and for some reason the act of tying the laces of his shoes made him cry out in pain, and he panted and heaved, and Noah said, "This is so fucking crazy," and Sam said between gritted teeth, "I have to, Noah—I have to," and then they were in the car, Noah driving, and they wound up into Beverly Hills and approached the motorized gate to a private community and Sam lurched out of the car, pressing the name of the producer on the keypad, and there was a long dull ringing—nobody was answering—and so he called the executive on the phone and it rang and rang and then the answering machine picked up, and he stood there in the cold winter night, feeling so wobbly, like his body was all cartilage, like the whole machine was breaking, and he realized that nobody was coming. And it felt like a sign, and so he stumbled back into the car and put his head on Noah's shoulder and they just turned around and drove home.

Happy New Year, he murmured to himself, or to Noah, or maybe to both of them. *Happy New Year, baby,* and he was singing it alone in his apartment, laughing to himself. *God, you're sick,* and he really was.

He took cold baths. He took hot baths. He prayed to God that it would be over.

The day after New Year's, Sam made an appointment with his primary care doctor. The doctor took Sam's temperature, looked down his throat and felt his glands. "It's the flu," he said.

"Are you sure?" Sam said. He was dumbfounded. It couldn't be the flu. He had never felt anything like this before.

"Yup," the doctor said. "Bad flu going around. Really bad."

The flu. It sounded so innocuous, so no-big-deal. The doctor prescribed something that he said would shorten the duration of it.

Zinc lozenges. Orange juice. Sam couldn't eat. He drifted in and out of reality. After another three days, Sam went back to the doctor. "Still flu," the doctor said.

"It can't be," Sam said. "I can't keep going like this. I feel like I'm dying."

"You're not dying," he said. "It's the flu."

And so Sam went home. And he lay on the couch, waiting for whatever this was to be over. Waiting for what felt like it had to be death. He drifted in and out of consciousness. And then he woke up with a gasp. He felt like his lungs were filling up. He croaked.

There wasn't enough air in the room. He blinked into consciousness, then back into darkness.

He gasped again. He rose to his feet. He became aware that it was raining. He put on a coat.

Down the street he staggered, flicking rainwater from his hair. There was an urgent care clinic a few blocks away. He would go there. They would tell him what to do.

He stumbled through the door. The receptionist looked at him oddly. He collapsed into a seat.

"Flu!" he announced. She nodded. "Flu," he said again.

"We'll get you seen shortly," she said. Sam wheezed in reply, moving his mouth, but no sound came out.

"Samuel?" a nurse called, and Sam rose to his feet, but he wasn't sure if that was his name or not.

Past reception, in an exam room, a doctor took X-rays of his chest. "This isn't the flu," she said briskly. "This is pneumonia. Your lungs are full of fluid. You need to be in the hospital."

Sam gasped and nodded.

"You should go to the emergency room."

Sam worked his mouth but he couldn't speak.

"Is there someone who can take you?"

Sam nodded. And then shook his head no. And then he began to cry.

Stop, Sam thought. *Please stop.* He couldn't be in this memory for one more second. *Stop stop stop you have to stop.* But the memory kept going, kept pushing forward—the doctor's hand on his arm, the stabbing of a needle, the flush in his face, the weakness rippling through him. He didn't want it.

Why are you showing me this? he shouted at her. But there was nothing there—obviously. There was nothing there because God was not real, and spirits were not real, and magic was not real, and he knew that now. He was sure now. *Show me something I don't already know. Show me something, anything, but this.*

"Are you still experiencing effects?" Jacob asked.

Sam opened his eyes, jolting back into consciousness. He looked around the room. "No," he said.

"No," Buck said.

"Let's close the ceremony then," Jacob said. He bowed his head for a long moment of silence.

Sam was the one to break it. "Jacob," he said.

"Yes, Sam," Jacob said.

"Can I ask a question?"

"Sure," he said.

"I know I asked you this already but is this, like, one of those things where it only works if we believe in it?" Sam could hear his voice, trembling with rage. He hadn't realized how angry he was until he had started to speak. "Like, are we going to get to the end of the weekend and nothing happens and it's, like, 'Well, you didn't have an experience because you didn't trust the process enough' or whatever?"

"I take it you did not experience strong effects tonight," Jacob said.

"Nope," Sam said. "I didn't experience anything. And I didn't really experience anything last night, either. Which has me wondering—what the fuck are we doing here?"

"To answer your question, no, your experience is not contingent upon your belief in the effectiveness of the work," Jacob said crisply. "But to be honest with you, I think with this attitude, you're really selling yourself short here."

"Jacob, I have been nothing but open," Sam said, trying to keep his voice steady. "I prepped religiously. I showed up willing to accept whatever this was going to be. But I've spent two nights lying here bored crawling through the catacombs of my mind in the same mundane, torturous way I do every fucking day, and I gotta tell you, it isn't bringing me one iota of relief. Nothing cosmic is happening here. This is not a spiritual experience. I don't even know what this is."

Buck rested his hand on Sam's arm as if to say, *Calm down*. "Actually, I do know what this is," Sam said. "It's a colossal fucking waste of time."

"Jacob," Buck said politely. "Is it possible that there's something...wrong with this medicine? Like, it's not strong enough?"

Jacob laughed. "No," he said. "This is extremely powerful medicine."

"Then why isn't anything happening?" Sam said.

"Well, it can take many ceremonies to experience the full effects of the spirit," Jacob said. "Ten or fifteen, even."

"Ten or fifteen?" Buck said incredulously, sitting up.

"Or more," Jacob said. "Listen, you have no idea what's happening out there in the other dimension, man. It may not feel like there's a lot going on but you just have to trust me on this."

"What difference does it make what's happening in that dimension if I can't feel it in this one?" Sam said.

"You don't get to have this experience on your terms," Jacob said.

"Fine," Sam said. "But I'm tired. I'm hungry. I'm extremely sexually frustrated. I'm, like, weirdly congested? And I am experiencing nothing in the way of healing. So I kind of just want to, like, go home, jerk off, get Shake Shack, take a Benadryl and sleep in my own bed." Sam stood up. "I'm gonna get some air."

Outside in the yard, Sam lit a cigarette, which immediately

sent him into a coughing fit. He hacked and sputtered, feeling sorry for himself. Momentarily, he heard the door slide open and Buck joined him. Buck reached for the cigarette and took a drag.

"You all right?" he asked.

"We are getting scammed, Buck," Sam said. "We are getting straight up taken for a ride. By some white guy who did some spiritual tourism and came back hawking other cultures' traditions for profit! And we bought it! It would be funny if it wasn't so embarrassing."

"Is that really what you think?"

Sam turned to look him square in the eyes. "Ten years of therapy in a single weekend? Like, what the fuck are we doing summoning spirits? I'm a sane, educated person. With a job. And a life. I don't need to be lying on the floor for six hours while some grifter tells me he's cleansing my energy. How dumb are we?"

Buck shook his head. "There's one more night," he said. "Let's not give up on this just yet."

Sam felt tears welling up in his eyes, as his anger gave way to hurt. "I just don't want to feel this way anymore," he said. "I thought things were going to be different. I thought he was going to fix it."

"Fix what?" Buck said. He rubbed his eyes. "Look at you. You're fine."

Sam stared at Buck. He didn't know how to put it into words, to explain what it felt like, what the thing was inside him that felt so bad. Or maybe it wasn't a thing at all but rather an absence where the thing should be—a gnarled, ugly deficiency.

Jacob was seated on the sofa in the living room. "Sam," he called. But Sam walked past him, pushing his way into the bedroom and collapsing into bed.

He lay facedown in the pillows for a few minutes until there was a knock on the door. "Come in," he said. He looked up and it was Buck. At least it wasn't Jacob.

Buck sat down on the bed next to Sam and rested a hand on his shoulder. "This whole thing really meant a lot to you, didn't it?" he said softly.

Sam nodded. "It's almost like—the more I started to believe in being fixed, the more I saw parts of myself that needed fixing."

"There's nothing about you that needs fixing," Buck said, and the tenderness in his voice melted Sam's frustration for just long enough that he could really see Buck, and there, in the dim light of the bedroom, looking directly into Buck's kind eyes, so close to him he could smell his skin, Sam let himself wonder if this was the whole point of this weekend: to bring him closer to Buck, to finally cut the tension between them, to turn their affection for one another into something more than just that, and so Sam reached out and put his hand on Buck's thigh and leaned forward to kiss him.

Buck pulled away. "What are you doing?"

Sam jerked his hand away. He could feel himself turning red. "I'm sorry, I shouldn't have—"

"This isn't— I mean, I'm not—" Buck stammered.

"It's fine," Sam said quickly. "My mistake." He turned over on his side. "I'm gonna go to bed, okay?" Shame rocketed through him. He felt Buck linger for a moment.

"Good night," he finally said, and Sam heard him close the door behind him as he left.

In his dreams that night, the feeling kept going—his anger and embarrassment, the unresolvedness of it. His sleep was restless; he woke up every hour or so to find that he was reaching out for someone, or something, in the night. He didn't know what it was, but he knew that it was what he needed, and yet, when he tried to put his arms around it, there was nothing there.

And then he was deep in a dream, or a vision, or a memory— or maybe all three. He was back in the Hamptons, the night he and Charles had lost the house. As they were packing up to drive back to the city, they had begun to argue—first over something trivial, and then, as it did so often, it escalated into something explosive. Charles had a temper—it was his most frightening quality—and Sam knew at the moment that his eyes went dark and empty that it would be a long night. There could be no walking back the anger once he got that way.

They fought in the car as they drove west, back toward the Long Island Expressway. It was late at night but the freeway was still crowded with cars, all of them heading back to the city, which Sam had come to see as his captor. He hated New York, hated their sterile apartment, hated the muggy summers and frostbitten winters, hated how the city seemed to support and reinforce his workaholic schedule, hated the life he had built there, and most of all, he hated that he didn't appreciate any of it. And the man who had earlier that day felt like the only partner he could imagine a life with was suddenly an enemy. Whatever they were fighting about didn't matter, of course; they were angry about the dissolution of a fantasy.

Sam didn't have the distance to see his part in it; wasn't yet willing to look at how he manipulated Charles by fanning the flames of his anger, then breaking down in tears and begging him to stop yelling. The love that he had been chasing for so many years, that he had finally found with Charles, was something that he knew urgently that he had to destroy, because on some level he was convinced that he didn't deserve it. He didn't deserve the house on Woodhollow Drive any more than he deserved to be loved by a man like Charles.

"You're such a fucking monster when you don't get your way," Charles was saying. "You always do this."

"I can't take one more day like this," Sam said. "I'm at my breaking point."

"Then go, Sam," Charles yelled. "Leave me, then."

That white light was blinking again, faster, then faster still.

At that moment, they drove past a car on fire. It was pulled over on the side of the freeway, and flames were licking at its sides, red-orange and violent. People stood around it in concern, watching it burn. Sam could hear sirens approaching. They fell silent and stared in bewilderment as they passed it.

"Should we stop?" Charles said, his face suddenly a mask of little-boy worry.

"No," Sam said grimly. "Keep going."

Keep going. Keep going. Keep going. The white light stopped flashing. Charles accelerated and the car roared forward into the dark night.

10

The Knowing Place

Something's wrong.

    The morning was brutal, slices of sunlight cutting through the bedroom in zebralike stripes—the most psychedelic thing Sam had experienced all weekend. He rolled over and moaned, pulling the covers up around his neck. He buried his face in the pillow, trying to summon sleep again, wishing feebly that he could fast-forward through the next few hours, at least, until sunset and the final ceremony.

He didn't want to do another day of this, cut off from everyone and everything, mired in this ascetic discomfort, waiting around for epiphanies that weren't coming. He just wanted to be done, to return to his normal life from this preposterous fantasy of healing, to be back in his everyday misery instead of getting teased by the hope of relief.

He pulled on a pair of sweatpants and checked his phone, which he hadn't even looked at the night before.

A text from Kat: You doing okay, babe?

A shudder of embarrassment moved through him, at the realization that he would have to tell her that this whole thing hadn't even worked—that it had left him even more despairing than he'd been before. At least she'd probably be able to commiserate with him over his humiliation at making a pass at Buck.

He opened the door and padded silently out to the kitchen. It was early, still—Buck probably wouldn't rise for hours. *Fuck it*, he thought, and he poured himself a little shot of cold brew from the bottle in the fridge, plopping a few ice cubes into it. He took a sip and its gorgeous bitterness was like rocket fuel, sharp and fast, lights turning on inside his brain.

Ice clinking in the glass, he walked out into the living room—and there was Jacob, seated cross-legged on a cushion on the floor, facing Sam with his eyes closed. He was meditating. Sam turned quickly, hoping to destroy the evidence before Jacob saw, but then he heard Jacob's voice: "Sam."

Shit. Sam turned back around to face him.

"Good morning," Sam said.

Jacob rose to his feet and stood tall. He wore flowing white pants and a loose white T-shirt that made him look like a real guru. "Morning," he said. "How did you sleep?"

"All right," Sam said. He saw Jacob's eyes glance over to the coffee in his cup, but he said nothing, and Sam was grateful for the pass. "You?"

"Good," Jacob said. "Off to yoga."

"Cool," Sam said. "Have fun." In his head, it had been polite, but he heard the way it sounded—nasty, sarcastic. Sam shook his head. "Sorry. That came out wrong," he said. "I'm just going through some shit, I think."

"I know," Jacob said. He sat down at the dining room table and looked at Sam dolefully. "I know you're disappointed. But it's not about me—it's about her, and the type of experience she wants you to have. You need to trust that it's going exactly the way it's supposed to."

"I just feel…" Sam trailed off. What *did* he feel? He tried to scratch at the surface of the feeling but there was only powerless anger. "Do you think this is my fault?" he asked. "Is it something I'm doing wrong?"

Jacob shrugged. "I don't think you really trust the process," he said. "I think you want this to happen on your terms, and it's only ever going to happen on hers. Maybe you aren't ready. Maybe there are things you aren't ready to see."

"I thought she was going to make me ready," Sam said. "I thought that was the whole point. To show me what I need to see. So I can see what I can't see on my own."

"She can," Jacob said. "She has that power. But you have to be willing to open your eyes."

Sam felt a lump in his throat. This was useless, chicken-or-egg nonsense—maddening and counterproductive. "I don't know how," he said. He sat down at the table across from Jacob.

Jacob raised his hands. "Then you might not be humble enough."

"Is that really what you think?" Sam said.

Jacob looked at Sam as though he was boring through him, cutting him open, and Sam inhaled sharply at the effect, at how exposed he suddenly felt. "She is very powerful," Jacob said. "But so are you. In a different way. There is so much darkness inside you. But you resist it. You don't want to embrace it. You don't want to hold it as a piece of you. And yet, the light cannot exist without the dark. These are the things that you want to erase, to ignore, to stomp out. But they are a part of you, too." He smiled. "You're afraid of your shadow. But as you move, so does it. You and it are inextricable. And still you run from it."

"But you felt something in me," Sam said. "That first night, in Portland."

"Yes," Jacob said. "It's what you're afraid of."

"It's still in me," Sam said. "I can't get it out."

"You think it is very deep," Jacob said, "and it is, but it is not irretrievable." Then he leaned forward, across the table, and the voice that came out of him was deep and gravelly, his eyelashes fluttering, his face drained of color.

"Don't you want to know?" he growled. "Wouldn't it be easier to know who you really are, instead of running from the truth? Wouldn't you rather just go to your knowing place?"

Sam was frozen. "Yes," he said quietly.

Jacob rested his back against the chair and became himself again. "Then carry that intention with you into ceremony tonight," he said. He looked at his watch. "I should go," he said. "But meditate on this today. Maybe you'll find some more clarity. Willingness. Something."

"Okay."

Jacob stood and slung a yoga mat over his shoulder. "Good-bye," he said. Sam slumped over at the table, resting his head in his hands. A moment later, he heard the front door click shut.

By the time Buck rose, it was almost midday. He wandered out into the garden in loose terry shorts and a T-shirt, stretching his arms in an exaggerated yawn.

Sam, seated at a picnic table, stared at the ground. "I'm sorry about last night," he said finally.

"Oh, please," Buck said. "We were on ayahuasca!"

Sam looked at him sideways. "Were we?" he said.

"You know what I mean," Buck said. "You were vulnerable. I get it."

"I'm really embarrassed, Buck."

"Don't be." Buck sat down across from him and Sam could tell from the look on his face that Buck didn't want to talk about it anymore. "Did you see Jacob this morning?"

"Yeah," Sam said. "I did."

"Did you kiss and make up?"

"Not exactly," Sam said. "Why, do you think I owe him an apology?"

"I dunno."

"Buck, what if we get to the end of this, and nothing happens and we stay exactly the same way we always were?"

"Are you the same as you always were?"

"Aren't you?"

"Of course not!" Buck said cheerfully. "Every experience changes you, right? So even if there's no actual magic, in the traditional sense of the word, that doesn't mean I'm the same, or that it was all a waste of time. Maybe there's a lesson that hasn't been revealed yet."

Sam frowned at Buck. "How are you so zen about all of this?"

Buck looked reflective. "Age, probably," he said. "It's gotten easier to detach from outcomes as I've gotten older. To just be in an experience. So we don't leave here tomorrow fixed? So what! Look around." He gestured to the garden, illuminated by the sun in ghostly beams. A butterfly flitted from the outstretched fingers of a flower bush, like it was dancing in midair. "It's a beautiful day. Life is good."

"I don't know why I have such a hard time with that," Sam said. "It feels like it shouldn't be this hard." He folded his arms on the table and rested his head on them. "Maybe it shouldn't have been a shaman. Maybe I just need to find a new therapist. Maybe I need to go see a psychopharmacologist again because this is just, like, neurotransmitters firing the wrong way." He sat back up. "Or maybe I just need a boyfriend."

"You know what someone very wise once told me," Buck said, and he leaned in toward Sam.

"What?"

"If dick fixed it," Buck said with a grin, his voice going drag-queen liquid, "then dick would have fixed it by now."

By late afternoon, Sam had begun to feel nauseated. He went into the powder room and knelt before the toilet, the water running in the sink, the cold white porcelain. *What is it?* he wondered. That question again. *What is inside you?* He thought about the medicine, that bloodred brew, stagnating in his gut. He could taste it in his mouth. He didn't want to drink it again tonight.

There was no part of him that could throw up without sticking something down his throat to induce vomiting, but he wanted it out of his body. He gagged. He couldn't do it. Then he sat down on the cool tile and let his eyes flutter closed. After a few moments, he felt a warmth on his face, something radiant. Maybe it was her, he thought idly—the spirit. Maybe she had finally arrived, to do her work. To make him whole.

But when he opened his eyes, he saw that the sun had moved from behind a cloud and light was now streaming through the window. So he rested his head against the wall and closed his eyes again. There was nothing to see.

11

Sick

They gathered again at dusk, settling into their nests of blankets and pillows, trying to get comfortable. By now it was all routine—Jacob's solemn face as he poured the medicine, that heady rush of anticipation tempered by the disbelief that rushed through Sam like a force he couldn't control. *Just please let this end*, Sam thought, and in the same moment he felt a flash of sadness that the weekend was coming to a close already, and so anticlimactically.

He leaned against the front of the sofa. Jacob called Buck up to drink first again, while Sam sat still. Then Jacob motioned to Sam and he made his way up to the mat. Jacob handed him the glass, a grave expression on his face. His eyes revealed nothing.

Sam looked at the medicine. *What are you, anyway?* he

asked it. *Nothing*, it answered back. *I'm nothing.* And then he looked at it again, and the contents of the glass were suddenly so multitudinous it was dazzling—its crimson ink containing all of the stories Sam couldn't tell, all of the blood coursing through his body—and then, in a blink, it was nothing again. Sam shook his head. *This is pointless.*

He took it in one shot and wiped his mouth, handing the glass back to Jacob. He crawled back to his nest and lay back down.

What was there left to do? He closed his eyes and waited for memories to start drifting through him. He had already combed through all of the memories that were easy, accessible—the ones he wasn't afraid to exhume. Now nothing came. His mind was blank. He studied the pinpricks of light under his eyes, scrunching up his eyelids until they grew brighter, like a million little stars.

All he could feel was his body.

Actually, where *was* his body?

He floated off into the little lights. He was no longer gazing at them—he was among them, alone in space. It felt as if he was in the console of a spaceship. He had a distinct feeling of motion, like he was pushing forward. Things moved from the center of his field of vision into the periphery and he watched them go. Some of them were simply colored shapes, interlocking sequences of visual data, patterns that connected together—cosmic geometry. They passed by him like masses of replicating cells, squiggling off into infinity, beautiful threads of colored DNA.

Oh, he thought. *Is this all ayahuasca does?* He felt tranquil, traveling through space, watching little bits of color stream past him. He tried to remember if this was what acid felt like, or mushrooms. It had been so long since he'd done anything like that. Maybe that was all this would be, like a night at the planetarium. At least he'd gotten to go somewhere else, if only for a minute. At least he wasn't in his memories anywhere.

Memory—all those moments he kept spit shining in his mind's eye, finding no new truth anywhere in the same old recitations. He didn't know how to go into the shadows.

You're never going to be able to tell this story, a voice whispered.

I know, Sam said in his head.

You wanna do it anyway? she said softly, but it wasn't quite a question. It felt more like an invitation.

Sure, Sam said. *Let me try.*

Deeper. That was where he wanted to go, and so that was where he went, and the very texture of it was deeper, like descending into a dreamless night's sleep, cushioned by velvety darkness, into an elevator and down a long, dimly lit hallway in shades of gray, faintly patterned slate gray carpeting and light gray walls, fumbling with the key at his front door, and then into the foyer of the apartment on Sixty-Third Street. Sam looked around the apartment. It was his but also not his; all his things were there but the apartment did not belong to him.

It was beautiful, though, the apartment—or at least it was full of beautiful stuff. Stuff that had cost a lot of money. Stuff that had meant something, for a moment. Stuff that had represented the promise of a better life.

Stuff for the apartment, like a candle that reeked luxuriously of musky sandalwood, or an enormous cylindrical dish made of hammered steel to set on the dining room table, stuff he would buy wandering listlessly through a department store after work. These things were typically stark and expensive, which was their style, mostly metallic and grayscale, crisp lines and sharp edges. There was no color there—not even the accent wall Sam had imagined painting when they had first moved in, some cheerful pop of color—except the deep chestnut of the salvaged wood coffee table and the green stem of the white orchid that sat on the console in the foyer. Every few weeks it would die and they would have to buy a new one. "Aren't these supposed to live for, like, a long time?" Sam asked Charles, but he just shrugged. "Lack of light," he said.

Occasionally Sam would buy something sweet, like when he was walking past a little boutique on Lex and saw that they had blown-glass cups for tea candles in a lovely marbled silver, each with a different letter of the alphabet on its front, so he bought one with an S and another with a C and set them on each of their nightstands. When Charles got home that night, dropping his briefcase on the floor with a heavy thud and peeling off his jacket—a black leather Valentino bomber with a matelassé texture, like diamonds—he pointed at them. "Did you buy those?" he asked.

Sam nodded.

"Those are really cute," Charles said, and his eyes crinkled at the corner and his face turned tender, and for a few moments all was right within Sam.

But Sam only had so much space to adorn with expensive things, and so more often than not, he would buy something for himself. There were just so many beautiful things a person could buy. Many, many pairs of loafers, always worn sockless, and breezy tailored dress shirts and cashmere sweaters in every conceivable color and style and coats, so many coats— God, the coats! A brisk cream tailored Bottega Veneta trench coat, and a black Saint Laurent motorcycle jacket with woolen cable-knit front panels and sleek leather sleeves, and a slate-gray checkered Gucci bomber with sporty ribbed cuffs, and a wool herringbone Brunello Cucinelli topcoat that Charles bought Sam for Christmas; Sam had tried it on at Bergdorf's and then looked at the price tag, side-eyeing Charles—*"Trop cher,"* Sam said, and Charles had nodded—but he had remembered and gone back and bought it for Sam.

It wasn't like Sam worked in fashion, or even had particularly good taste. He joked to Brett that he should start a fashion blog called Expensive Shit That Doesn't Look That Dope On Me. "Do you think I'm becoming vain and materialistic?" Sam asked Brett once.

"No," Brett said cheerfully. "You've always been this way. You can just finally afford it."

Somehow buying things always felt like the next right thing to do. It was such an uncomplicated solution.

His coup de grâce was a Fendi shearling coat with panels of flaky black leather, tan felt and tufts of black sherpa at the collar. *I will be my best self in this Fendi shearling coat,* Sam said to his reflection, looking at his shape from every angle, considering how its stiff construction gave his squishy body—he had been gaining weight again—the illusion of structure. *If I buy this Fendi shearling coat, I will be the kind of person who deserves this Fendi shearling coat.* And so he bought the coat, and wore it exactly twice before spring came.

After all, you couldn't wear a coat like that—not in New York. It was not a coat for trudging avenue after avenue to the subway through mountainous piles of gray snow strewn with garbage, when another flurry of sleet could blow through at any moment. That was the winter that went on forever, months of rain and snow and hail. It wasn't just the dark cold of years past; Sam had been through enough New York winters to know that the sun would come out eventually. This one was different. The him that had existed before that winter felt irretrievable.

On the holiday they'd taken in Morocco a few months before spring came, it was unseasonably cold—the coldest winter they'd had in a decade, the concierge said. As they roamed the narrow alleyways of Marrakesh by night, Sam liked the way their silhouettes looked as they walked in unison, their feet slapping on the ground at just the same moment—two tall broad men in the same shoes and pants and shirts and coats, where in the shadows they appeared only in duplicate.

The trill of a cash register and the jagged sound of receipt tape printing. An empty bowl on the table. This was what he remembered. The way things looked—and not just the way things looked, but what the way things looked said about him. He had never loved things that much until they were the best available substitute for love. How did that happen?

Sam returned to his body. He put his hand on his heart. He breathed in and out. He went deeper.

Deeper, into a more distant memory. He was sitting in the bay window of Eleanor's house in the Hamptons again, and it was a few weeks after he and Charles had met, and they were packing up to go back up to the city, and something had struck him. He knew this place, knew it well. He had been here before—not just in his memory, but recently, in ceremony—but he had closed it down before he had reached the memory's critical juncture. He had been so bitter that the moment was gone, so afraid of what was lurking just under the surface. But he wasn't afraid anymore, and instead of nostalgic regret, he felt an affectionate curiosity for his younger self.

He was right there on the verge of something. It was so close. He could taste it, metallic, like blood in his mouth.

He sighed and gave into it.

But what if you have HIV? There was the thought, the first thing, clear and sharp as a diamond. They had been packing up their things in the bedroom to drive back to the city when the thought had cut through Sam, so abruptly that he had to sit down on the bed, as shocking as if it was a new question that he had never considered, instead of something that he had asked himself so many times before. But this time he had a more compelling reason to be anxious: two weeks before Sam had met Charles, he'd slept with a guy in the neighborhood he'd met online; Sam didn't realize until after he had finished that the condom had broken. Sam didn't say anything to the man, didn't ask him if he had been recently tested or if he knew his status; just hurried home, eager to wash the experience from his body.

A few days after that, Sam had gotten a sore throat. He had meant to go get tested, had thought it was something he should do, and then he'd met Charles and in the whirlwind of those first few weeks, he hadn't given it another thought; it hadn't come up. Until now, in this moment, when the whole thing rattled through him like thunder.

"Are you all right?" Charles said, looking over at him. Sam nodded. Charles came over and sat down on the bed next to him, rubbing Sam's shoulders gently. The ugliness of this knowledge spread through him.

"I'm just stressed about the workweek," Sam said. "Sunday scaries."

Charles looked out the window and in the golden hour, the light caught him just right. He was too perfect to keep. And now Sam, with a growing sense of panic, was sure he would lose him.

"I know," Charles said breezily. "I love it out here. I never want to leave."

But they had to leave. And in the car on the ride back to the city, Sam was silent in the front seat while Charles played the music loud, singing along to songs they loved, looking over at Sam, frowning a little when he saw that Sam wasn't singing along, too.

But Sam couldn't. Suddenly it was all he could think about. He knew that he needed to go get tested, but the more he thought about it, the more certain he became that he was positive. He could feel it in his body; feel it in his bloodstream; he was sick, he knew it. He knew that he would test positive and when he did, he was sure that Charles would leave him. Sam had never met anyone so paranoid about getting sick; in fact, that they hadn't had a sexual health conversation at all was shocking considering how conscientious Charles was, but he had just assumed that Sam was healthy, and to be fair, Sam had made the same assumption, at least up until now. They had only been seeing each other for a few weeks, and even though Sam was already in love with him, he also feared that there wasn't enough foundation there for them to weather such a major upheaval.

But he couldn't bring himself to do it, and so he let this, the knowledge that he was positive and that it was a secret he was keeping from Charles, torture him endlessly. Most of the time he buried it somewhere deep, hours passing by without the thought popping back into his consciousness, but certain repetitive moments came to be connected with the thought. When he reached for the shampoo in the shower each morning, it would spring back into his head, and he would think to himself, *Not yet. You'll get tested when you're ready.* When he walked the six blocks uptown to Charles's apartment, he would stand on the corner beneath his building, finishing his cigarette, and he would think about it, the fact that he was sick and that it was only a matter of time before he had to face this, living as an HIV-positive man, the fact that Charles would probably leave him—Sam was sure that he would— and then he would be alone once again, having to disclose his status to every new partner he met, forever feeling the twinge of loss over Charles, the man he had let slip away.

Sam thought perhaps he would write about it someday, years from now, a book or an essay about how he'd lost this great love. Charles was a risk analyst; Sam would call it *Risk*. Sometimes he wondered whether there was an alternate ending to this story, one in which he got on medication and got his viral load down to undetectable and they continued being together, but Sam figured this was probably unlikely, given Charles's hypochondriacal tendencies. There was never any part of Sam that doubted that he was positive, just how long until he had to face it. He would extinguish his cigarette, nod to the doorman and take the elevator upstairs, where he would try to bury the thought for a little while longer.

And of course when they were hooking up, the thought rose to its highest intensity, an almost audible buzzing in the back of Sam's head that contaminated those moments of pleasure. Sam knew enough to know that it was difficult to transmit the virus through oral sex, which was all Charles really seemed interested in anyway, and Sam was fastidious about keeping any of his bodily fluids away from him, but still, the paranoia nagged at him—oh God, what if he gave it to Charles? How would Sam live with himself?

The first time Charles came down with a cold, Sam had wept on the street outside in sheer terror. At home, Sam read and reread the findings of studies about HIV transmission, which provided some temporary relief, the idea that transmission through oral sex was exceedingly rare, but still he couldn't be sure; the only way to relieve this anxiety, he knew, would be to get tested, but he was so certain that he would test positive, and then Charles would leave him. So he tried, desperately, to force it even deeper into himself, to quiet the noise, to promise himself he would do it soon, when he was ready. Just not yet.

He talked himself down, convinced himself that if he had managed to avoid contracting HIV when he was a teenager, before he'd gotten sober, when he was shooting up and having unprotected sex with strangers and waking up with no memory of what he'd done the night before, the odds of getting it now were low. What kind of God would spare him then, when he was at the highest risk, only to let him get infected now after just one mistake?

But he could feel it in his body. He knew he had it.

The fear devoured him from the inside out. He lost a few pounds. Was he getting sicker? Was the disease already ravaging his body? A show they were watching together featured a storyline where a character had tested positive for HIV. He told Charles he didn't like it anymore. "The writing's gotten bad," he said. At dinners and parties and events with his friends, he would forget about it for a few hours, and then all the thoughts would rush back again in a hot wave, like a fever.

He could not tell Charles. He could not tell anyone. This was his and his alone.

It was sick, Sam knew, all of it—the fact that he was so clearly ill but refused to seek treatment; and worse still, the fact that he was putting the person he loved most at risk. The shame bloomed inside him like a vine. What kind of person would do such terrible things? What kind of person could be so selfish?

And yet somehow he managed to keep compartmentalizing it, to enjoy the majority of the best experiences they had together, to lock it away for periods of time. As many moments as it contaminated, it also made Sam all the more grateful for the best times, those instances of pure lovestruck joy; when Charles looked at him with such tenderness he thought his heart might rupture; when he awoke before Charles and nestled his head in the hollow of Charles's chest, feeling his heart beat—feeling as close to him as Sam had ever felt to anyone. Even if he was a liar, he still loved him—that love was never a lie.

Finally, after months of this, he told Kat over dinner while he was home for the holidays. He knew that she wouldn't judge him, but more than that, he knew that she wouldn't immediately dismiss it, like so many other people might; the easiest way to defuse a conversation as charged as this one was to say, "Of course you don't have HIV," which is exactly what Sam would say to any friend who told him they were afraid of that. The odds always felt implausible unless it was happening to him, in which case the worst-case scenario was always the likeliest one.

Kat listened patiently as Sam recounted his tale of punishing anxiety. "Why do you think you have it?" she asked softly. He told her. She considered it. "You might," she said, and Sam blushed. "But hopefully not. And if you do, you'll get through it."

"Do you think I've already given it to Charles?" he said.

She shook her head. "I don't know."

"Would you still be my friend?" he asked.

"God, Sam, it's not a death sentence anymore," she said.

"If I have it and Charles leaves me and I give up my entire life and move out of New York and change my name and decide to live in some small town where nobody knows me and all the terrible selfish things I've done, will you still be my friend then?" Sam asked.

"Always," she said.

But saying it out loud didn't take the power out of it, as he had hoped it might. Instead it made it stronger, like a thing that lived inside him that had its own heartbeat, like a parasite he was carrying. And a few weeks later, he cracked.

He had woken up early from a dream, or a premonition, where he was alone in a hospital bed, sick with some mysterious illness. It was winter and his bedroom was cold, the stark morning light illuminating the dust in the air. Sam ran a bath and stepped into it, letting the water turn almost cold. He knew that he was ready.

There was an urgent care clinic on Eighty-Sixth Street. He walked there and told the nurse that he needed an HIV test.

"Do you have reason to believe you were recently exposed to the virus?" she asked.

"Not recently," he said weakly. "A while ago."

"We'll do a rapid HIV test now, and then we'll take some blood and send it out to the lab for a full sexual health screening," she said.

She returned, pricked his finger and pressed it to the test, leaving an ominously bloody fingerprint on the white adhesive. Sam knew this was it. It was all over. He had to face the consequences for what he'd done. He could not wait any longer. He just prayed that he hadn't already infected Charles. Charles, this man whom he loved so much—his anchor, his missing piece, his person. He knew he had the disease, and that much he could tolerate. He had made peace with it.

But if he had gotten Charles sick, he would kill himself. The thought was not hysterical—it was calm and rational. He could not go on knowing that he had done that to him. For a few seconds, he allowed himself to consider when and how he would do it. A drug overdose, probably. He would make sure Charles knew how sorry he was. A tragic conclusion to this great love story, but he had never really believed he'd have a happy ending, anyway.

The nurse looked at the test. "It's negative," she said. And so it was.

Sam walked home in stunned silence. He wasn't relieved. He was incredulous at his mind's ability to convince him of something that hadn't been true. Was he crazy? He had to be.

He didn't tell Charles about any of it—he wouldn't have known what to say, or how to explain it. But in the days that followed, he thought deeply about how he had let this spiral so madly out of control, to the point where his conviction that he'd had it was almost incapacitating. He talked to Brett, but found that his certainty, which had been such a genuine source of torment at the time, was almost comical in the re-telling. It took on a morosely funny bent, this tale of great anguish over what turned out to be nothing; there was no way to convey how truly harrowing the experience had been when the punchline was so obvious.

"Please!" Brett said. "I spiral like that every time I have sex. Are you even gay if you don't obsess constantly about your sexual health?"

"I'm serious, Brett," he said. "I was so sure. I felt sick."

"I know this girl," Brett said, "who would get tested all the time, even if she wasn't sleeping with anyone. She would go to different doctors asking them to run her blood because she was so convinced that she had it and the tests just weren't picking it up somehow." He considered it. "A true ally."

"But what if I had given it to Charles?"

"You couldn't have," Brett said. "Because you don't have it."

"But what if I did?"

"But you don't!"

Sam rubbed his eyes. "Doesn't it feel like as millennial gays who came into our sexual agency at the tail end of the AIDS epidemic but before treatment was as effective as it is now, we are forever cursed on some level to always see HIV as the biggest of the big bads even though it's actually be-come highly treatable, yet we'll never truly be able to enjoy sex without anxiety because we got it so beaten into us that pleasure invariably leads to sickness and there's an inextricable link between sex and death?"

"That last part could be a Lana Del Rey lyric," Brett said.

"Brett."

"Look, we can all freak out as much as we want but it's pointless and serophobic," Brett said. "Besides, I started taking PrEP."

"What is that?" Sam asked.

"It just hit the market—it's this new drug that's like birth control for HIV!" Brett said brightly. "You can take it and go have as much empty, high-risk, promiscuous, deeply unfulfilling sex as you want while minimizing the risk of catching the big one." He paused. "I guess the sex doesn't have to be unfulfilling, but it probably will be."

"A dream come true," Sam said.

All of this should have assuaged his anxiety, but it didn't feel like enough somehow; the noise was still too loud. He wished that there was a pill he could take every day that would give him a less anxious mind; nothing any psychiatrist had ever prescribed had given him much relief, except the years he was able to spend drifting in and out of a benzodiazepine stupor before he'd gotten sober. He wished that his sickness could live in the body instead of in his head—this sickness that saw fear hiding in every shadow. It was disturbing that his conscious mind was able to convince himself so powerfully that something was true when it patently wasn't; that fear could be so potent and so poisonous that it could actually distort his reality, turning every day into a funhouse mirror. It wasn't even the anxiety that frightened him—it was his certitude.

Sam came back to his body, feeling the cushions against him and the smell of tobacco. *Is that it?* A voice inside his head asked him—petulantly, expectantly—and Sam shook his head no, and he understood, in some deep and instinctual place, that this was an important part of what he had to remember, but it was not where the story ended, as shameful and embarrassing as it felt. There was more here—something else about Charles.

Charles. Sam tried to conjure his memory, but he couldn't—couldn't even picture Charles's face, the face that he had once known so well, every freckle and every hair—all he could see was the apartment again, and in his heart, that little voice said, *Deeper*, and he dropped down another level into a lightless place, into the lightless apartment.

You were so dumb, Sam whispered to himself, feeling his body quiver. *So dumb*.

Being diagnosed negative with Charles should have resolved his anxiety, but it didn't. Instead the energy he'd spent obsessing about his health dispersed, finding new targets. He wanted to locate the turning point where it started to unravel, but there was no defining moment—only a series of moments, equally weighted, like abstract thumbnails that he could click open to see what each one held, and so he did, curious to see what lay behind them, as if he hadn't already lived it.

The first thumbnail led to an ex-boyfriend of Charles's who resurfaced a few months after they started dating, sending late-night text messages to Charles that he would read in bed, his back turned to Sam; Sam knew who it was and Charles insisted it was just a friendship and Sam tried, desperately, to be chill, that most unattainable standard—of course gay men could remain friends after dating without that being cause for concern, especially since Charles and his ex had grown up together in the city and shared many friends in common. And why did it matter if the ex was a little bit more demanding of Charles's attention than seemed appropriate, even a little bit flirty, at least from what Sam could glean from glancing in as chill a way as possible over Charles's shoulder. But over time, his anxiety about it mounted untenably, until Sam was going through Charles's phone early in the morning before Charles had awakened, searching desperately for proof that something illicit was going on, although he never found anything incriminating, just the ex coming on too strong and Charles blankly responding lol, until finally Charles said crisply, "Please stop going through my phone," and Sam knew he had been found out.

It hung over him, this conviction that Charles was going to cheat on him, would leave him to return to this young man. And yet, as Sam descended into this series of memories, he knew this wasn't leading him anywhere fruitful. *This isn't it*, he thought, and he pulled back, and the glow of Charles's phone screen faded away into nothingness.

The next thumbnail was the issue of going out, which caused Sam chronic stress: Charles's social calendar was fairly busy, long and boozy dinners with his friends where he expected Sam to join him, and birthday parties thrown by former New York prep school kids. Sam had been game enough for this in the beginning but as he had grown more and more uncomfortable with his body, he didn't want to be out—he just wanted the comfort and security of being at home, where nobody had to see him. Charles couldn't understand why Sam seemed to struggle so much with it.

"You need to be more supportive of my recovery," Sam snapped, which might have been true, but it must have been confusing for Charles—Sam had been so freewheeling in the beginning. He didn't know how to tell him that it was because he felt bad about himself, as if by saying, "It's because I've gotten fat," Charles would suddenly see him as fat—as if it was something he'd been hiding so far and to vocalize it would make it real in a new and terrible way.

Maybe they had both gained weight, though it was difficult to say exactly how much. Sam's body image was so distorted that he had no way of knowing, and he was petrified to weigh himself, while Charles oscillated in Sam's experience of him from the most exquisitely good-looking man he'd ever seen, no matter his size, to something else, something monstrous, something that snarled and snapped its jaws at him, a jackal whose eyes went coal black with rage.

"You made me this way," Sam would say when they fought. "You made me like this."

That wasn't fair to Charles, but it was true that Sam had changed in ways that startled even him, in terms of the way he lived his life, the way he spent his money and the way he sorted his priorities. Sometimes he looked back so wistfully at the time just a few years earlier when he was poor and hungry. He wasn't sure why he longed for that time now.

But buying things felt like freedom, at least for a while. He had spent so many years broke and unhappy, feeling like everyone in New York was having more fun than he was, doing all the glamorous things he could not afford to do.

And it was funny, too, that they were the same size in everything—or at least they had been when they first met. It was so weird—the boyfriend twin thing, the apex of gay vanity. Sometimes people asked them if they were brothers, but they didn't look alike, exactly—more like they *went* together. They were the same waist size and the same inseam and the same jacket size and the same shoe size and the same height and about the same weight, though perhaps they wore it a bit differently; Charles was almost imperceptibly broader in the shoulders but squarer overall in his dimensions and his calves were leaner than Sam's (Sam was terribly jealous of this), but when Charles put on weight, it went straight to his belly and only to his belly, whereas Sam's fat was distributed equally everywhere.

And yet, as Sam got fatter, he could buy more stuff. Fat stuff. Because it was fat stuff, it meant both more and less to him—more because he needed it more urgently inasmuch as he hated himself so much more, and less because he mattered so much less as a fat person than he did as a thin person, in terms of the way the world experienced him and how he experienced himself.

He could feel the excess, could feel it in his waistline and his hips, could see it in his bank account as the balance dwindled, could see how fatigued Charles had become. But he couldn't stop. He didn't know how to.

The weight had represented so much more than the actual size or shape of his body; it was his happiness, his ability to move through the world as someone who deserved all of the things he had. And underneath the weight was this private conviction that all the things he had assembled while not-fat—his job, his partner, his fancy apartment—were a byproduct of his not being fat, and if he gained back the weight, those things would disappear from his life.

It was all connected, these anxieties, and as Sam continued on to the next thumbnail, he knew that it was one that he didn't want to open; he knew what was inside it, and it wasn't something he was ready to see. *Haven't I had enough?* he thought, but he knew that he had not, that there was more here. And he opened it and it was the book, the memoir.

God, that book had meant so much to him; it had meant more to him than anything, even Charles. It had been the only thing he had ever wanted to do after he got sober—to tell the story of what had happened to him and the things that he had done in his addiction, and it was surreal, the fact that he was actually going to get to do it, after all those years of calling himself a writer—he was proving it. And yet the bigness of the platform and the indelibility of what he was writing also made it daunting in ways he hadn't totally anticipated, in ways that he couldn't manage.

That pressure had started to push him to the edge. He had fallen seriously behind; aside from the month he had taken off work in the Hamptons to write, he had no time to write it. He blew through his first and second checkpoints for his editor to see pages. The publisher pushed back the release date by six months. It was unlike him: he had no problem turning around stories quickly at the magazine, but this book was another animal entirely. All the confidence that had gone into the pages that got him the book deal, which he'd written during the early months of falling in love with Charles when everything felt starry and effortless, had disappeared. Sam had convinced himself that the book would be bad, an embarrassment, but he also knew that he had to finish it. On the weekends he'd try to carve out enough solitude to make some headway on the manuscript, but usually he just ended up staring at his phone for hours on end or taking long walks through the city, chain-smoking anxiously. The more he convinced himself that the book would be bad, the more difficult it became to write; to write was to interface directly with the badness of it, and the more he wrote, the worse it became. It consumed him and terrified him.

He could see himself, sprawled out on the sofa in that dimly lit apartment, his laptop on the floor next to him, open to a blank screen, the same scene he'd been supposed to be writing for weeks now. And then he heard the click of the door as Charles arrived home, setting his briefcase down in the dining room with a heavy thud. Sam had lit the big Diptyque candle on the coffee table to mask the aroma of the burger and fries he'd binged on, depositing the remnants of them in the garbage chute down the hall.

"How was your day?" Charles said.

"Long," Sam said. "I think I'm going to go to a hotel and write this weekend."

Without even looking at Charles's face, Sam knew the expression it bore: disappointment, frustration, fatigue.

"Again?" Charles said. "You did that last weekend."

"I have so much more to do," Sam said. He could feel the fight building already. He wondered how long it would take to rupture. "I can't miss another deadline."

"Do what you need to do," Charles said. "But we have Eleanor's birthday party Saturday night. I hope you'll be up for that."

Sam groaned. "Do I have to go?"

"I thought you liked Eleanor," Charles said. "She's sober."

"I just don't want to be around a bunch of people," Sam said. "I don't feel good." He imagined himself walking into the party and instantly breaking a sweat, the way his clothes would pull on his body, which had expanded so much in size. He couldn't be seen by Charles's friends. They couldn't know how bad things had gotten.

"Fine," Charles said. "I'll go without you."

"I should really focus on the book," Sam said.

Charles snapped. It happened so quick—Sam thought they had at least another few minutes of passive-aggressive sniping at each other, but no.

"Then write it, Sam," he said. "Fucking write it, then. Stop talking about it and fucking write it."

"I'm trying," Sam said. "It's hard. I have one chance to do this right, you know? I get one shot at this. If I fuck it up and it tanks, I don't have family money to fall back on. You have no fucking idea what it's like to actually have your financial future in your hands. I need this to be good. I need it to do well. It's going to follow me around forever. There is so much riding on this. And you're so fucking unsupportive."

"Oh, I'm unsupportive?" Charles said. "I rented you a fucking house in the Hamptons to write in. But that wasn't enough for you. It's never enough for you."

"This book has taken everything from me," Sam said. "You can't imagine what it's like."

"You know it's not going to love you back, right?" Charles said. "You know I'm an actual living, breathing person who is right here, in your life, trying to show up for you."

"Maybe that's true," Sam said. "But this book won't leave me, and I know you will."

Charles shook his head. "You're so fucking crazy," he said.

There was no way to explain it to him—the weight that Sam was carrying, the heaviness of this conviction, how unsolvable it all was.

Deeper. Sam had tried so hard to pin everything that felt wrong on external factors: the stress of his job; the pressure Charles put on him to be more social; his fears about the book; the long and punishing winter; even the apartment, which he had convinced himself was haunted by the ghosts of lovers past.

Charles wanted to buy a place in the city, the dreams of their fantasy house on Woodhollow Drive long since abandoned. On weekends, Sam tore himself away from his manuscript to go visit open houses, although they couldn't agree on what they wanted. Finally, they found a place that they both loved, a renovated duplex in the East Village with an open kitchen, enormous skylights and a little terrace off the back that overlooked an ivy-grown courtyard.

"We could be happy here, right?" Sam said to Charles, searching his face for agreement. "I think I could be happy here."

Charles nodded. "Me, too," he said. He bought it in cash.

It had felt like sleepwalking, the lightless days all blurring together. *Once we move, it'll be better. Once I turn in the book, it'll be better. Once spring comes, it'll be better.* These were Sam's mantras through that last few months, the February doldrums when the snow was hard and black on the ground. He finished a draft of the book, knowing it was terrible, and sent it to his editor and a few trusted readers, awaiting their feedback, and he printed out a hard copy which he kept in a box under the bed, taking it out whenever he was restless to flip through and make red line edits.

And he had gone to Eleanor's birthday party after all, he remembered. It was crowded, marijuana smoke in the air, all of Charles's friends gathered by a window, making small talk and laughing. Sam went to the bathroom and took deep, calming breaths but it didn't work.

Eleanor was working the room in a printed party dress, laughing, in conversation with Charles. "Are you having fun?" Sam asked.

"Oh, sure," Eleanor said. "It's a very me party. I'm drinking soda water while my friends get high and the adults are all in the bedroom doing blow."

Sam grimaced. His collar tightened. A moment later, he grabbed Charles by the sleeve. "I'm gonna go," he said softly.

Charles's face dropped. Sam had expected him to put up a fight, but he didn't. "Okay," he said. "I'll see you back at home." He turned away from Sam.

Sam hung his head. He was so ashamed of his discomfort, of his anxiety, of his inability to just be normal for a night.

On his way to the door, Eleanor stopped him. "Are you leaving?" she said.

"Yeah—I'm sorry, I'm just not feeling well," Sam said. He tried to smile warmly. "I hope you have the best birthday."

"Is it because of the thing I said?" Eleanor asked. Her voice was sharp.

"No—what thing?" Sam lied. "I've just been under the weather."

"Don't leave," she said.

"What?"

"Don't leave!" she said, sounding suddenly bratty. "It's my birthday."

"I know it is," he said. "And this is a great party. I just—I really have to go. I'm sorry."

When Charles got home that night, Sam was waiting for him on the couch. Neither of them spoke. Sam was angry at Charles for staying, irrationally, but he still believed he had the moral high ground.

"Eleanor was upset that you left," Charles said finally. "She wants me to be with someone who knows how to have a good time. That used to be you."

"I'm under a lot of pressure," Sam said weakly.

"She said…" Charles trailed off and looked down. When he looked back up, his eyes were big. "She said if it's that hard for you to do things when you're sober, you should either go to a meeting or relapse already."

Sam laughed coldly. "She's such a fucking bitch."

"She's not."

"Do you agree with her?"

Charles shrugged his shoulders. "I don't know anymore."

The betrayal stung. Sam had imagined that because Eleanor was sober, too, that there was some implicit trust between them, that she would have his back in a situation like this. But she didn't care about him—not really.

And then what? Sam squeezed his eyes shut.

He had awakened one winter morning to find that Charles was already awake, which was unusual—anxiety almost always woke Sam up early, where he would rise and make coffee while Charles continued dozing until the blare of the alarm clock. Sam pulled on sweatpants and made his way out to the kitchen, where he found Charles seated at the dining room table. A stack of papers was next to him—Sam's book.

"Did you read it?" Sam asked.

Charles nodded. He looked stricken.

"I wish you had asked me first," Sam said.

"You've given it to everyone else in your life," Charles said. "I figured it was time I read it, too."

"What did you think?"

"You can't be serious about putting this out."

"What do you mean?"

"The things you write about…" Charles shook his head. He pushed his chair back from the table. An expression Sam hadn't seen often was on his face—disgust. "All the guys you fucked. For drugs, or for money. All the fucked-up shit you did. You want people to know this?"

Tears sprang into Sam's eyes. "It's my story," he said. "And it happened. I need to own that."

"Oh," Charles said. "This you need to own? Your own life. Your mental and physical health. Your ability to participate in this relationship. Those things you can't take an ounce of responsibility for. But this? This you need to own?"

Sam shook his head. "I have to tell this story."

"Why?" Charles yelled. "Why do you have to tell this story?"

"Because I do!" Sam shouted back. "I have a contract, Charles!"

"A contract?" Charles laughed. "You wanted to do this in the first place. You wanted to expose yourself to the world this way. Why?"

"I don't know, okay?" Sam said. "Because I need people to see me. This, right here. This book. These stories. This is who I am, Charles."

"No," he said. "It's not." He gestured around the room. "This is who you are." He pointed at the manuscript. "Not this." He looked at Sam. "This. Us. You and me. Your life here. Not the stories you're always telling about yourself and who you think you are, or who you want to be."

"Those stories are true," Sam said. "And they're important."

"That's not what this is about," Charles said. "You think telling stories is a way of facing yourself. But it's actually how you run from yourself. From who you really are."

"And who am I?" Sam said.

"You're selfish," he said. "You don't care about anything but yourself."

"You have no idea what you're talking about," Sam said.

"You put this first," he said. "Ahead of me. You always talk some bullshit about writing to make sense of your past. But what actually happened is you wrote people right out of your life." Now there were tears in his eyes, too. "I have been here all along," he said. "Trying."

"I've been trying, too," Sam said.

"You haven't, though. Not really. You've been putting all your energy into this. This." He pointed to the stack of pages again. "I can't support you with this. I don't know how I'm supposed to sit back and watch you do this. It's—it's humiliating."

"For who? For me or for you?"

"For both of us," Charles said. "You want me to pretend like I don't care what people think of me—of us? Yes, I care that all of my friends will know about all the things you've done. It's embarrassing to me. I don't have a problem admitting that. But you—you care more about what other people think of you than anyone I've ever met. Which is why I can't understand why you want to do this. To yourself. To us."

"So is that it?" Sam said. "You're done with me, because you think my book is embarrassing?"

"Oh, you'd love that, wouldn't you? If it was that linear—if that could be a part of your story, too." Charles stood. "I'm not going to be that for you." He raised his hands. "You're always telling a story, Sam," he said. "A story about how much pain you're in. How misunderstood you are. How hard things are for you. Once you're done with this one, there will be another one. But I'm not going to wait around for that."

And that was it. Sam should have known that it was ending, but he didn't, somehow—he still thought some part of it was fixable. Maybe he would take a few objectionable parts out of the book for Charles, to sanitize it a bit. Maybe once they moved, things would be better. It had been a funny sort of cognitive dissonance, this inability to see his world crumbling around him, to truly register what was happening.

They never resolved it. It hung over the apartment like a storm cloud for a week or so, until they left for a long-planned vacation that now neither of them seemed particularly interested in taking. Charles's mother had rented a villa in St. Barts for a week, which was the kind of holiday that would have felt unimaginably opulent to Sam a few years earlier, but now, spoiled as he was, the beauty of the place barely registered.

"Let's just try to have a good time, okay?" Charles said softly, and Sam nodded and rested his head on his shoulder.

They splashed around in the water on the beach, but Sam wouldn't swim; a black T-shirt was as naked as he was willing to get. He mostly wished he could be home in the privacy of the apartment, eating Indian takeout, instead of here, with all this tanned, toned flesh on display, reminding him of his own inadequacy. The one thing that still excited him was the prospect of the new apartment. They tooled around design shops for inspiration, studying chaise lounges and high-back barstools, where Sam bought a bottle of room spray for a hundred euro. *Whatever.* "For the new apartment," he said to Charles. They were picking up the keys the next week, once they returned to the city.

But Charles seemed distant the whole trip. Sam overheard him arguing with his mother in French.

"What's wrong?" Sam asked.

"She's driving me nuts," Charles said. Sam knew there had to be more to it, but he didn't want to press the issue.

In bed that night, Sam felt Charles's hands on his body. He swatted them away, as was customary. The idea that Charles would find him desirable now was almost unthinkable. But he was so persistent that Sam relented.

The next night was their last on the island. Sam had dressed for dinner, wearing a tropical blue shirt and white jeans. Charles was buttoning up his shirt in the dressing room of the suite. The door was open to the terrace, making the long sheer white curtain billow in the wind. The night air was salty; Sam could taste it on his lips.

Charles looked up at Sam from across the room and Sam saw it in his eyes, and in an instant, he knew. "Charles," he said.

Charles looked at him.

"What's going on with the apartment?"

He didn't say anything. There was a long moment.

"Am I coming with you?" Sam asked.

He didn't even know where the question came from, or how he knew to ask it. Charles shook his head no.

"Oh God," Sam said.

Slowly, as if he was afraid of what Sam might do, Charles sat down on the bed next to him. "You're not happy," he said. "I don't think I can make you happy anymore. I keep trying and trying. But nothing's working. We're too broken."

"Please don't do this," Sam said. "Please. Take me with you."

"I didn't want to do this here," he said. "I was going to tell you when we got back to the city. But I don't want to lie to you. We've been trying so hard to make this work for so long. And it's just not. You know that, don't you?"

In the morning, they packed their bags in silence. They boarded the ferry to Saint Martin separately. Sam sat on the deck, away from Charles and his family, feeling the spray of the sea as they sped away from the island.

When they landed back in New York, Sam raced through customs. It was snowing and he was still wearing shorts and flip-flops. Stepping out of the terminal onto the street, the cold hit him in a frosty blast. He fished a hoodie out of his bag and trudged across the street to the taxi queue, dirty ice water splashing on his exposed feet, and took his place in the long line that snaked around the median. Horns blared. A bus rolled past, shuddering gray exhaust.

Sam turned to see Charles and his mother leaving the terminal. She was wearing a fur stole, and he had his parka on. They looked cozy, prepared, competent somehow, like people who just knew intuitively how to navigate the world. He watched as a sleek black Mercedes, dusted with snow, pulled up at the curb. They climbed into it and disappeared.

Back home, Sam hauled his bags through the lobby past the doorman, slipping and sliding on the polished floors. Charles was staying at his mother's and Sam had the apartment to himself. He tossed his things onto the floor, tracking slush onto the white area rug in the living room, and collapsed onto the couch and sobbed.

Of course he had thought that Charles would take it back after a few days, that he would change his mind. But Charles was firm. It was over. And so Sam stayed alone in the apartment full of all of the things while he considered what to do.

That was what Sam remembered most about the end—how much stuff there was, and how by that point it all felt dirty and ugly. They ate and fucked and fought and spent and lied and said nasty things, hateful things they could not take back. Sam had grown spoiled and precious and greedy. And the more he consumed, the emptier he had become. He hadn't been able to see it at the time. He hadn't been able to see it until just now.

Charles left piece by piece, over the course of the next several weeks. Sam would arrive home from work to find something new was missing. First it was the kettle that Charles used to brew his tea in the morning. Then the saucepan disappeared from the stove. Next it was the silver-plated tissue box from the nightstand, then the heavy glass Versace ashtray on the coffee table, and finally it was the toiletries—the bottles of Molton Brown body wash, the little silver jars of moisturizer and La Mer eye cream and the bottles of Creed cologne. Rich people always had the best toiletries, the stuff you can only find at some little apothecary in Paris or get imported from Korea.

Sam washed his face with a bar of hotel hand soap he found in his toiletry bag.

One night he came home to find that Charles had taken the lamps—the French cathedral wire-mesh floor lamp from Restoration Hardware and its tabletop counterpart. There was no overhead lighting; everything was dark. Sam laughed at the heavy-handedness of the symbolism. He went down to the corner bodega and bought a flashlight, then used it to illuminate the room, now barren.

Charles's half of the walk-in closet was empty; all of Sam's shirts still crowded onto one rack. All the sweaters that were carefully folded and fluffed on Charles's side were gone now. There were little scuff marks on the shoe racks, specks of lint on the shelf. The hallway closet, which was just for Charles's suits—that was one area where he outpaced Sam; he had dozens, since he actually wore them to work—Sam pulled the door open, afraid of what he would find, his breath catching in his throat—and there it was, just *empty*, everything gone, not only the trim Dior suit jackets and the cropped Thom Browne slacks but the big black Louis Vuitton canvas duffel that always sat on the floor was gone, too, and for some reason the sight of the empty floor rattled Sam.

They had fought over that closet, Sam remembered, when they moved in—"You're going to take the whole thing?" Sam whined, and Charles had snapped, "I have more stuff than you!"—but Sam had relented because Charles let him keep a bookshelf in the living room, a steel-and-glass space-age monstrosity they'd found at the Lillian August in Greenwich with glass doors just opaque enough to obscure its contents, so you couldn't really *see* the books. Still, it was important to Sam that there were books on display, somewhere in that apartment, because Sam was a writer and what kind of writer didn't have a single bookshelf? Sometimes when Charles wasn't home, Sam used to open his closet and look at all those beautiful things lined up on their hangers, all pressed and sorted by color, from lightest to darkest in a perfect gradient. In those moments he wished that he could be as beautiful as any of those things.

The decision to leave New York didn't feel like a major life event; it felt like an inevitability. Sam decided that he would go to Los Angeles. There was nothing left for him in the city anymore. Most of his friendships had disintegrated as he had submerged himself into his life with Charles, his work and his projects.

And so, he thought, he would leave the city. Start over. Try to do things differently this time.

It took about two months to negotiate the transfer with the magazine—two months to fully extricate himself from the life in New York he'd spent so many years building. About six weeks after Charles left, Sam finally allowed himself to have sex with someone else, a burly stranger with a thick Slavic accent he met at Townhouse on First Avenue.

"You have nice apartment," the man said. Sam looked around—it was almost empty now. He waited until the man had gone home to cry.

He cried again the next day when Brett came over to help him pack, and Brett rested a hand on his shoulder sympathetically. "I'm sorry," he said.

"I just don't think I'm ever going to get over this."

"You will."

"Everyone grows tired of me," Sam said.

"Oh, everyone grows tired of everyone." Brett stood up and wandered around the half-packed apartment. Sam sat down on the floor.

"I didn't think it was going to hurt this much," he said.

"Of course it hurts," Brett said. "Breakups always hurt."

"This doesn't feel like a breakup. It feels like I'm dying."

Brett shot him a look. "Okay," he said. "I've listened to you do this for two months. You gotta get your head back in the game. You're going to be knee-deep in quality dick once you get to LA."

"But I'm ruined now."

Brett sighed. "You know, you think your pain is so monumental, but it's actually pretty mundane. This is just normal stuff, not some great human theater. It's what people go through. They fall in love and they get their hearts broken. It's just a part of life."

"Okay." Sam reached for a tissue and blew his nose. "I know I've been really self-absorbed for the past few months. Slash year. Slash forever."

Brett folded his arms. "You haven't even asked me about the monsters I've been dating."

"How are the monsters you've been dating?"

"Terrible."

"I have so much to look forward to," Sam said bitterly.

Brett looked out the window. "It's so crazy that you're leaving New York."

"Should I write a personal essay about it?" Sam said, and then he laughed until he was crying again.

The last time Sam saw Charles there, at the apartment, was a few nights before he left the city for good. They had to sign some documents in order to break the lease. Sam had sold most of the furniture. He had consigned most of the expensive designer clothes—particularly all of those coats, which he knew he wouldn't need in Los Angeles, and God forbid he make it back to New York often enough to need more than one. As for the books that he'd fought to keep—except for a few that had sentimental value, he'd put them all in boxes and dropped them off at the Strand. Only a few things were coming with him to California, like a rectangular foxed-glass mirror from ABC Carpet & Home, inlaid with specks of gold, that he'd thought was the most beautiful thing he'd ever seen. They had hung it in the front hallway because Sam thought it would make him grateful every time he came home and it was the first thing he saw. He couldn't remember when he had stopped seeing it; like everything else, it had just receded into the background. He had been so vain and so stupid. He was just like every other class-conscious white-collar gay with internalized homophobia and something to prove. He had bought into the lie that the way things looked was important. He had bought into the lie that filling his life with beautiful things would fix what was broken within him— that it would make him feel beautiful, too.

The stuff had never meant that much to Charles, maybe because he never needed it as badly as Sam did. But it had mattered to Sam.

Charles stood in the empty hallway like he was a stranger. His eyes were bluer than they had ever been before, blue as glaciers.

"All the stuff is gone," Charles said. He was wearing that Valentino bomber again, the one that Sam had loved, the one that looked like diamonds. It was so effortless on him. Sam looked around and saw the apartment anew. How many things they had picked out together that were no longer there. All those conspicuous vacancies.

"I got rid of it," Sam said. "I got rid of everything." It was astonishing that what had felt so important in the moment could be discarded so quickly.

"It's going to be strange," Charles said. "Living without you."

"I know," Sam said. "But at least we lived well."

He opened his eyes. Jacob was singing and beating on his drum, and the vibrations of the drum made the whole room rattle and shake, and soon the rattling and shaking was inside Sam. *Get it out*, he thought. *How do I get it out?*

He had to keep going. *Deeper*, he thought, and the word was like a command, bringing him down into an inky darkness. Sam felt himself squirm on the floor, pushing his belly into the ground and arching his back in a slow, undulating motion, like he was trying to move the writhing mass inside of him, or more accurately, like the thing was moving within him—some great force that had to shake free of its home. He descended deeper into it. *Here we go*, he thought, like boarding a roller coaster knowing that the track was broken.

He was sitting in a dingy room. He squinted his eyes and recognized it: that meeting in Silverlake, where he had met Noah for the first time, two years later, two years after Charles and everything that happened in New York. Sam could see him standing at the podium, scruffy and lanky and kind, the way his eyes had lingered over Sam mischievously, and then they were having dinner and the conversation was so fluid, so easy, and Sam couldn't even believe how right it all felt—he was the anti-Charles, his laconic speech, the endless *whatever* of it all—and Sam had that feeling, that weight in his stomach, like, *Oh, this is gonna be a thing.* He hadn't felt that in so long; he hadn't even been sure he'd ever feel it again.

"Do you wanna get out of here?" Noah said and Sam looked around and said, "Yes."

And then they were on Sam's couch making out for the first time when Noah pulled away and there was some nervous thing in the corners of his mouth and he said—God, how had he said it?—was it quick and anxious or was it labored and deliberate like a heavy sigh, steeling himself for rejection?— "I have to tell you that I'm HIV positive."

It didn't surprise Sam; maybe he already knew that Noah was going to tell him this, on some level—so many of the men Sam knew in the rooms of twelve-step recovery, men who had spent their younger years blacked-out or sharing needles, were, and it never came as a surprise. Sam reached for Noah's hand.

"I'm negative," Sam said. "But that doesn't bother me, or freak me out."

"Okay," he said. "I'm undetectable."

"It's not a big deal," Sam said. Then he corrected himself: "To me."

"Okay."

"I'll get on PrEP," Sam said.

At the doctor's office, a young physician wrote him a prescription. "You should come back once every three months so we can test your kidney function, just to be sure," the doctor said. Then his face went a little funny. "You know, if the guy you're with is consistently undetectable, then you don't even really need to take this," he said. "But if it gives you an added level of security, so be it."

How quickly, Sam thought, the world had changed. He had been so terrified of contracting the virus just a few years earlier. Now there was a once-a-day pill to keep that from happening.

It felt unfair that it was just a matter of timing that now made it possible for him to stay negative when Noah had struggled through his diagnosis. It had been painful for him. Sam squinted. He remembered that conversation, on the way to Palm Springs. There he was in the passenger seat of Noah's car, on the 10, the strip malls of San Bernardino streaming past them in a tannish blur, when he told Sam the story of what had happened.

It was before Noah got sober, when he was still keeping it together. He didn't look like an addict; you'd never have known he was one, he said. This was always the gruesome shock of modern gay life: how often they don't look like tweakers at all, the men who do a little crystal meth on the weekend, so they can dance and feel free and then go back home to fuck without inhibition, to feel potent and virile and fearless. Sam remembered that high, too, the surges of euphoria, the sense of power and confidence, of his own desirability and arousal, of pleasure amplifying in radials like an underwater explosion. God, he had loved how it felt.

That was how it was for Noah. He would party on the

weekends, like so many other affluent London gays—"chemsex," they called it. And then weekends bled into weekdays and then he was missing work and his life was crumbling but he kept chasing the party, the sex and the darkness and the thrilling wrongness of it. Maybe all gay men are made to feel, at some point, that they are wrong in the eyes of God, aberrations whose desires are dirty and shameful, and there is no more perfect reinforcement of this message than to fuck on crystal meth. It is both the escape from the feeling and the confirmation of it.

The darkness took hold, Noah said. He had nothing left to lose. The shame of it. He started shooting up. He lost his flat. His job. Sam could see, so vividly, the look on Noah's face as he told this story. "It is still my greatest regret," he said.

Noah could be so taciturn, but he wasn't afraid to talk about this. The shame was radioactive. He had done the work. He had made his amends, after he got clean. But the shape of that shame still lived in him—it still occupied a space. Sam was grateful that Noah shared this story with him. He was grateful that he knew.

And Sam wasn't afraid of Noah. But he knew, on some level, that Noah was afraid of him. That he was afraid of doing to Sam what had been done to him.

No, Sam thought, and he rocked back and forth in his body. He hated all of this, hated thinking about it, hated the clinical way he had to consider viral loads and medications and risk factors, and the language that gay people used to talk about this—"clean," if they had no diseases, which was as ugly a slur as any Sam had ever heard. Noah's blood was not unclean. His blood was good. His semen was good. His spit. His hair. Sam loved it. It was as good as Sam's own. And when Sam felt Noah's heartbeat, the muscle that kept all that warm blood running through his body, he did not judge it or fear it.

Sam loved it instead, for keeping it alive when Noah did the same things he did—shooting up, fucking for money, trashing his body. He could not love his own body, but he could love Noah's. It had never seemed sick. It was perfect to him.

Risk—Charles had taught him about risk. There were so many things Sam hadn't known when he had fallen in love with Charles, when his heart was wide and open. When he was afraid of his own blood, his own semen. A cut in his mouth. A tear inside him. Would he get Charles sick? Was he sick in a way that was transmissible, or sick in a way that only existed within him, between his two ears, in his spirit?

Sam's body worked just fine. It was his brain that was broken. Only it didn't work fine, Sam suddenly remembered. It had stopped working that winter. After Vegas.

Sam gasped for air on the floor of Buck's den—he could not open his eyes, he was too deep—and in an instant he was back at urgent care, wheezing and gasping on the table as the doctor pulled up X-rays of his pneumonic lungs.

"When was the last time you had an HIV test?" the doctor said.

"A month ago," Sam croaked. He took a deep breath. "I take PrEP."

She shook her head. "I want you to take a rapid test," she said. "Just in case." And inside, Sam was fuming at this, at the likely homophobia of it—he showed up as a gay guy to an urgent care in West Hollywood and they just assumed that he had HIV—but he submitted anyway, chilled by the suggestion and in some strange way curious, dread forming in his belly. She pricked the point of his finger and let a daub of blood form on the test. He rocked back and forth and shook from fever, and for a moment he could not remember if he was shaking in his memory or shaking on the floor of Buck's house, but it didn't matter.

Why was she insisting on this when he was already so sick? Sam made his way to his feet and paced around the exam room. He steadied himself against a wall, wheezing. This was all so familiar. Nothing ever really changed.

A few minutes later, she came back into the room. "This test is positive," she said bluntly. And then, as if there was any confusion: "For HIV."

Sam looked at her dumbly. "But I'm on PrEP," he gasped. Then, it dawning on him, as if it hadn't even been a factor until just now: "My boyfriend is positive."

"Have you been taking your PrEP?" she asked.

"Yes," Sam said, and as soon as the word was out of his mouth he grew unsure. Had he been taking it? He had taken it in Vegas—he could see himself, standing in the bathroom, fishing it from his bag and swallowing it with a glass of water. Was it possible that he had missed a day, or even two? As he focused his attention on the memory, it seemed to grow blurrier in his mind's eye, as if he had imagined it instead of experiencing it firsthand, as if his body had never even been there.

"Well," she said, "this test is positive." She squinted at it. She showed it to Sam. "Do you want me to send it to the lab for confirmation?"

Sam shook his head. "No," he said. "I have to go to the hospital anyway, right?"

"Yes."

He pulled on his jacket. As he rose to his feet, all the feeling disappeared from his head. The air was being sucked out of the room. He choked.

Sick. He heard it in Charles's voice. *There's something wrong with you. You're sick.*

And then there were white curtains. A hospital bed. A thin institutional gown. Sam kept sweating through the sheets.

He was at Cedars. When they admitted him, he asked them

to test him for HIV. They drew blood, the familiar prick of a needle in his arm. Then there was a bag of fluid running through his veins.

They offered him painkillers. He took them gratefully. The fever rose and broke. Twice a day a nurse came by with a machine that looked like a pipe, and he held it to his mouth and inhaled a green medicinal smoke that was meant to heal the pneumonia. Pulling it into his lungs reminded him of smoking meth, but there was no speedy buzz, no shot of electric euphoria, just a heavy exhale.

He was alone. He slipped in and out of slumber, the television left murmuring in the background. He woke up and Noah was sitting by the side of the bed. "You came," Sam said, and then he remembered. This sickness made manifest, so handsome and seductive. Sam held his hand. He couldn't tell Noah. It would kill him.

"Of course I did," Noah said.

On the second day, Sam asked the nurse for the results of his blood work. "The HIV test," he said. She said she would come back with them. But hours passed and she never returned. Then it was another nurse. Sam looked to the window and saw that it was nighttime. How long had he been here, he wondered. Had it only been two days?

"My labs," he said.

"I'll get to the bottom of it," she said.

After she left, Sam thought about Noah. He was the first guy Sam had ever loved with whom he could have the kind of sex that he might have with someone he hated, which was a compliment. With so many of the guys Sam had dated, including Charles, the sex was connected and intimate and sometimes erotic but it was relationship sex, not porn sex. With someone Sam had no affection for, he could have more interesting, experimental sex—rougher, more aggressive, exploring the limits of one another's pleasure—but that was reserved for people Sam would hopefully never see again, certainly not for anyone who might stay until morning.

But Noah was rough. His hand wrapped around Sam's neck. He pinned Sam down. He spit in his mouth. He was verbal, assertive. To think of that now made Sam feel ashamed of his own desire.

Had Sam liked that Noah was positive? He returned to his body in ceremony, shifting uncomfortably, pressing his head into the floor, working his jaw.

It had made Noah realer, somehow. More dangerous, even if it posed no threat. What else had Sam liked about it? Maybe he respected the fact that Noah had been through something, that he had truly lived—so different from Charles, who had been so cloistered by his privilege. Maybe it was about Sam's own worth, about a desire to manifest within his body a sickness that he experienced in his mind and spirit. Or maybe it was about forging some connection to the person Sam had been when he was tweaking and having unprotected sex with strangers. Maybe it was about forgiving himself for how he'd endangered Charles, even though that risk had only ever existed in his head.

What was it—a moment that Sam was afraid to call up to the surface?

He smelled smoke and he wasn't sure if it was in the room or in his memory. Gold-striped wallpaper. Vegas. Their first night there. Noah was fucking him, pushing into Sam, grunting and heaving, sweat slick on his chest. He kissed Sam hard, and then Sam felt his mouth on his ear and Noah whispered, "You want this load, don't you?" And Sam had exhaled, and he'd said, "Yes, deeper," and they came together, so hard it felt like electricity rippling through them in glorious spasms.

Deeper. He turned over again. Shame. It was so sick. He had wanted it. He had wanted it all the time.

Sam tapped his head against the floor, feeling the pressure of the wood against his forehead. Jacob was beating a drum and singing again, but it sounded like there were many voices.

Maybe it was a relief. Now Sam wouldn't have to worry about getting it anymore. It had always felt like such an implausible miracle that he'd managed to avoid getting it while he was using. This was just karma catching up with him a few years late, he thought.

And Sam knew that he deserved it. He deserved it for wanting Noah in the ways that he had. He deserved it for being so greedy, so reckless, so demanding, for all the unfed desires that lived within him.

In the hospital bed, Sam rocked back and forth, shuddering as the fever took him again, and on the floor of Buck's house, he did the same, splitting himself into two, his past and present, shaking in unison.

And then Noah was there, in the hospital with him, sitting by the bench below the window. "Are you feeling any better?" he asked. It had been three days. Sam still hadn't told him.

Sam nodded. "I think the medicine is working," he said. *This will ruin your life*, he thought.

He intertwined his fingers and twisted them nervously.

"What is it?" Noah asked, and Sam felt himself crack open, seams ripping inside him, all the things he couldn't hold anymore.

"When I first went to urgent care," he said. He stopped. He couldn't get the words out. He started over. "When I first went to urgent care," Sam said again, "they tested me for HIV and it was positive."

Something flickered over Noah's face, some darkness.

"I'm still waiting on them to bring me my full blood work," Sam said. "I wanted to wait to tell you until I was sure."

Noah looked at Sam, his face a mask of something terrible.

"I'm okay," Sam said. "I think all my years of obsessing about whether I had it or not prepared me for this, on some level. I know all the facts. I mean, I took PrEP every day, right? Now I'll just…be taking something else every day. It's not that big of a deal." He believed this as he was saying it. He could almost will it to be true.

Noah was shaking his head. "Were you taking your PrEP?" he asked. "Is it possible that you missed a day?" He rubbed his eyes. "We had sex so many times in Vegas." He stood up. "It was Vegas, wasn't it?"

"I don't know," Sam said. "Yes, I was taking it. I don't know what happened. I don't—I don't even know how this is possible."

Noah sat back down. He took his baseball cap off and set it down next to him. "We'll sort it out," he said, suddenly resolved. "This will be all right."

"It will," Sam said forcefully.

And then they looked at each other, and Sam saw it in his eyes—that Noah knew that getting involved with him had been a mistake. At that moment Sam knew he'd lost him. There would be no coming back from this.

When Sam woke up again, Noah was gone and the doctor was in the room. *Finally.* "I'm sorry about the delays," he said. "For some reason your blood was never sent out when you first came in."

He sat down next to Sam at the computer and typed at the keyboard for a minute, then tilted the screen to show it to him. "Well, it's pneumonia," he said. "A really nasty case." He looked at Sam's charts. "You're doing better, though," he said. "You'll be ready to go home tomorrow."

"What about the HIV?" Sam said.

He looked at Sam. "What about it?" he said.

"They told me I have it," Sam said.

The doctor looked at the screen, tracing his finger down it. "No, you don't," he said.

"What?" Sam said. It was the second time that he'd been certain that he was positive. Only this time it hadn't been hypochondriacal anxiety—he'd had incontrovertible proof. Hadn't he?

The doctor pointed to the screen. Sam looked at it, squinting. There it was in plain English. He didn't understand. It didn't make sense.

"But at urgent care, they said I was," Sam said, hearing how stupid it was as it came out of his mouth—as if that made a difference now.

The doctor looked sympathetic. "Those tests are about 97 percent accurate," he said. "That's why they need to send it to the lab to be sure. But you're not."

"But the pneumonia," Sam said. "I thought that was an HIV thing."

He shook his head. "Just regular, run-of-the-mill pneumonia." He stood. "Seen a lot of it this year. You gotta be careful out there."

He left the room. Sam stared at the wall. He knew what he was supposed to be feeling—staggering relief, the shock of absolution. He was so lucky. He should have been grateful.

But instead he felt something bigger and stranger, a punch of loss in his belly.

He pulled out his phone and texted Noah: They just told me I'm negative. Sorry to stress you out. The smallness of it felt pathetic. He looked at the time. How many hours had it been since Noah had left the hospital? How many hours had he spent thinking that he'd given it to Sam? He wasn't sure. It was night now.

Sam gripped the thin cotton sheets under him and began to cry, big cracked dry sobs that stuck in his chest, and the force of it made his lungs ache, and he was so weak and afraid he felt like he could disappear.

What is it? He heard that question again, reverberating through his mind, and he knew the answer. This was it—the thing underneath it all, the thing Sam did not want to admit. When they'd told him he was positive, he was grateful. Because he thought it meant that now, Noah wouldn't be able to leave him. That he would have to stay with Sam out of guilt, out of some sense of responsibility. That it would link them together forever.

Permanence. That was all Sam had ever wanted, with anyone. Someone who wouldn't have the option of leaving him. Someone who would have no choice but to stay. Better to be bonded in pain than to be alone.

It wasn't good news. Not because he wanted to be sick, or maybe because he did, but mostly because he didn't want to be alone again.

The drumbeat grew louder in Sam's ears. He came back to his body. He touched his hands to his face; it was wet with tears, but he couldn't remember crying. He sank back into the memory.

They told him he was ready to go home a day or two later. Noah came to pick him up, waiting quietly by the side of his bed. Sam could see the weight of this responsibility on his face, his ticking clock. Deep in Sam's gut, he knew Noah was waiting for him to be well again so he could sever his ties with Sam, after what they had been through.

Sam winced as they pulled the IV from his arm. He staggered to his feet, tucking the folds of his hospital gown around him. It had been days since he'd stood and his feet felt strange and meaty on the cold linoleum, like they didn't belong there. Slowly he wobbled to the bathroom. He looked at himself in the mirror. His gown was bedraggled and his hair was matted but at least, he noticed, he was thinner than he'd been before he'd gotten sick. He studied his reflection.

A few weeks later, when Noah asked him if they could talk, Sam wasn't surprised. He had known this was coming. And it wasn't like he had ever really believed that Noah was the guy, that they would have a future together, that this would be about something more profound than desire.

"This all feels like a bit too much for me," Noah said in one rushed breath, like he was hurrying to get the words out. "I don't know that I can be what you need me to be."

"It's okay," Sam said.

"We'll see each other."

"I know."

"I'm sorry," Noah said. "It's all just been—kind of a lot, hasn't it?"

"Yeah," Sam said. "It has." Something bright flickered in him for a moment, not because he was happy, but because he was getting closer to the truth. "But it's always that way with me. Too much and not enough."

It had never been about Noah, anyway, not really. Sam understood that now. It had been about proving something to himself. He had used him, the way he used everyone. He had made it real, in his body, in the thing he hated most.

I'll show you how sick I can be.

Sam came back into his body. Jacob was singing again. He touched his fingers to his face. How strange this was, his ability to make things real. That he could will things into reality by believing them fiercely enough, that he could bend the world by the sheer force of his conviction. Wasn't that what he'd done—both with Noah and with Charles, in their own ways? The guy he'd been so sure he would make sick and the guy he'd been so sure would make him sick, the symmetry of this. The way he made himself sick, emotionally and physically, to force people to stay, or to make them leave—or both at the same time, pulling them closer to him and pushing them away.

There was something wrong with him. There always had been, something deep and intractable, something that he needed people to see and wanted urgently to hide, something that made him acutely lonely and desperate to connect, something that made him manifest sickness even as he pretended to be fighting to get better. He understood that now. But there was no anguish—only a deep sense of peace at beholding this now.

This, she whispered. *This is who you are. Your fear. Your shame. Your preoccupation with the way things look. Your need to make everything bad.*

I know, Sam said. *I know that now.*

You are the stories you tell yourself about how there's something wrong with you, she said. But she wasn't hostile. She was sad.

And her voice became the blinking white light over his left shoulder again that had been there the previous two nights, pulsating like a strobe, and in the strangest and quietest little way, it came to him, less like a realization and more like a memory, like running into an old friend who looks so different you don't recognize them at first: the white light was her, the spirit. He felt her presence, her weight, her femininity—it was a *her*, there was no mistaking that—and he felt her curious familiarity. There was no big moment of epiphany. Sam had known her already—he just hadn't recognized her—and her presence was as unimpeachable a fact as the air in his lungs.

Hey, Sam said to her, and he felt her beam back at him, acknowledging him, too, in this moment of recognition. Together they drifted through space for a little while, just the two of them, in an easy quiet.

And then deeper, deeper still, Sam descended, like he was disappearing into a darker corner of space, where the stars were brighter but the space between them was an inkier black, and as he felt this shift, he checked back in with his physical body, which he could still feel, lying on the floor of Buck's living room, on the surface of reality, as far away as that now seemed. Sam wriggled his toes. There was a blanket pulled over him. But it was just a vessel that he had traveled out of, and now he was somewhere very far away.

He didn't want to lose track of it entirely. He put his hands on his hips and squeezed the soft flesh around his pelvic bone, gripping it between his fingers. From a thousand miles away, which was exactly the right amount of distance, it suddenly struck him that perhaps this body was worth loving for no other reason than because it was his. *What a radical idea,* Sam thought. *I don't think I've ever had a thought like that before.* In this great detachment from his body, he felt suddenly tender toward it, as compassionate as he might have been toward a wounded animal.

Why do you want to be sick? he said to it, with genuine curiosity, and then it was almost hilarious, the amount of angst he'd been in about his body. He could feel the heavy, fleshy ordinariness of it. Just a body like anyone else's, a body that worked pretty well most of the time. What was it that made him hate it so much, anyway?

And then he was falling.

The air all rushed around him and everything collapsed. He was not in space. He was in his body—he felt it gasp—and he was infinitesimally small, the size of a single molecule, and he fell the distance from the crown of his head down to the base of his belly, very quickly and very far, a full theme-park-style drop. Down and down he plummeted into the deepest part of himself, somewhere in his core, and everything was blue-black, like he had fallen into a cave and was landing in the water, and through that water he descended deeper and deeper until he saw something that looked like the hull of a submarine. He couldn't see the full size of it, only the one piece directly in front of him, which was gray metal, with a round porthole. He floated closer to it to look inside. And as he approached the window, he suddenly knew where he was.

It was the room where he stored the belief that there was something wrong with him. It was as old as he was. It had been there forever, but he had never seen it before. It was astonishing to see this place up close, to know that it had always been, although it was his first time visiting it. But it was real.

Up on the surface, he could feel his physical body twisting and gawping, and the version of him that was up on the surface was watching the version of himself that was down in the room, and Sam felt something tearing within him as he assumed the shape of these two parts of him—the narrator-self and the character-self, splitting into two discrete wholes, those two "I"s that existed simultaneously and independently of one another.

Go! His character descended through the porthole and down into the room. It was white and sterile, with a long, orderly line of translucent plastic bins with flip-top lids. It was so well organized, so clinical. Sam had always believed that shame was a big dark ocean, a morass of emotion that couldn't be ordered or reasoned through, a snarl of intersecting traumas. But in fact it was as tidy as a bank vault.

His narrator couldn't help but laugh a little bit at how incredible this was, to see it all up close. That elemental sense of brokenness, of being wrong, of being bad—it all lived right here in this room, like a filing cabinet, where Sam compiled the experiences that proved there was something wrong with him. All of the memories associated with the reinforcement of this belief were stored in this place. It was an evidence room.

Floating above the first compartment, his narrator watched as his character looked down at it. Inside the compartment was a fine black powder, like silt in its texture. It was the Buck box. And when his character opened it, Sam felt a rushing, like a hot gust of wind blowing in his face, and there was the shame of Buck's rejection, his sense of not being good enough as he traveled through Buck's rarefied world, and it all felt so unimportant now. Buck—Buck who was always getting used by younger men. Maybe Sam had done that to him, too, even if he hadn't realized it. He'd taken advantage of him by coming along on this journey in the first place. That was his pattern, Sam's narrator realized—he was always looking for some guy to rescue him and to make everything better. But here, the shame of that admission was neutralized. He felt it and let it go. *I'm sorry, Buck*, his character said, and the box was empty.

Next his character turned to the second compartment, which, like the first, was partially filled with black powder. This box was for Brett, and as Sam's character opened it, he remembered what it had felt like to stand in the apartment in Yorkville for the first time with Brett, looking around it so proudly—those walls that, for a time, belonged to them— and the glittering synths of some pop song he'd forgotten that he used to love, and then that look on Brett's face the night Sam told him he was moving in with Charles, and he felt the full weight of it, how eager he had been to sell out his best friend, and he was ashamed but he knew that it was okay. He breathed in. He breathed out. *I'm sorry, Brett*, his character said, and the box was empty.

And then his character opened the next box, which was a little bit fuller, and as the lid came off, he realized it was the Noah box, and this one hurt more: the way he'd looked the night they met, and the taste of his mouth, and the expression on his face that day in the airport, and the prick of a needle in Sam's arm, and the hollowed-out shock in his eyes that day in the hospital. Maybe Noah had tried to love him and Sam just hadn't known how to accept it. Maybe Sam had loved Noah because loving Noah was so much safer than loving himself. And Sam felt it, more acutely than ever before, the shame of what he had wanted from Noah, and that was okay, too. *I'm sorry, Noah*, his character said, and then that box was empty, too.

The fourth box was full. His character opened the lid, eager to see what it contained. But as soon as it was open, he wanted to close it again, because it was the Charles box, and there was too much in there, too much.

All the memories came surging through him, all of them at once. His narrator could touch them all, not moment by moment but everything at the same time, the frames so fast and mighty they were concurrent, all of these characters inhabiting all of these different scenes, all of the different bad people he had been in all the places he had gone, the version of him that was cruel and the version of him that was a liar and the version of him that was wounded and the version of him that was afraid and the version of him that wanted to be loved but didn't know how to accept it. He hadn't been prepared. And now he didn't know how to stop it. His narrator wanted his character to close the box, to end this, but it was too late. Cobblestone streets. Billowing curtains. Breakfast in bed. Hollow of his chest. Sam's body gasped and clawed at the floor.

And there they were the first night they met, in that funny track jacket Charles was wearing that made him look like such a dork. And there they were in a taxi speeding back to Charles's apartment and Sam had his fingers out the window, feeling the air of the city on a cool summer night. And there they were, sitting on Sam's roof smoking cigarettes and Sam was telling him that he thought he was falling for him and Charles said, "Me, too." And there they were in Sam's bedroom and Sam was playing him songs he loved and Charles made a little "oh" noise when they got to his favorite verse in his favorite song and Charles had said later—what was it?—that it was then, in that moment, that he realized he was in love with Sam. And there they were watching *Real Housewives* together and Sam asked Charles what his tagline would be, and he said, "My personal time is the most precious commodity I trade," and then turned his head toward the camera theatrically like he was flipping his hair, and Sam was laughing so hard he thought he would pee his pants. And there they were, screaming at each other until their voices went hoarse, a hundred times at once. And there they were, standing in their apartment for the last time, surveying the empty space they'd made.

He felt all of these characters splitting and dispersing, moving across space and time, starting with the character down in the room and spreading to a dozen different places they had been, inhabiting each of them, the smell of the streets, the moisture in the air; he had characters in all of them at the same time. They had seen so much of the world together.

There they were in Cartagena, wearing tropical-printed shirts under a sultry Amazon moon, in a villa overlooking the old city, where Sam slept on the couch after they fought until he felt Charles's hands on his body in the middle of the night, and Sam followed him into bed, praying that the morning would be better. And then they were in Morocco, in a coastal town called Essaouira, where camels trundled gracelessly along the beach, but Charles slept funny on his back and woke up with stabbing pains, and so they were hurrying through the squalid alleyways to a chiropractor past beggars and street merchants hawking flip phones and spices, Charles murmuring in Arabic to him while Sam sat helplessly in the dark; and there they were making love in an ancient riad in the medina where rose petals were scattered everywhere, Sam's belly swollen from sweet mint tea, but he hated the way he looked in all the photographs Charles took and Sam was snapping at him, and he was seeing the hurt on his face turn to anger and in that moment Sam hated himself even more than Charles did, and his narrator was wondering—*why? Why was it so hard?* And then they were in Paris, in the middle of the night, running through the streets of the Marais, laughing, their sneakered feet slapping the ground, and Sam was thinking, *Please, let it stay this way*, but by morning the magic had gone, just evaporated like mist.

God, you took a lot of trips, his narrator said, and Sam thought about how spoiled he had been and for a minute all the characters felt lucky, so lucky to have had a life like that.

It was everything, the whole relationship, the entire world, and all of the other characters he had been—it was right there, and his body was aching and grieving, keening and grasping, and his narrator was reacting to the pain in his body, in heavy sobs, his chest quaking, his limbs spasming. *Why are you doing this?* his narrator called down to his character, but he wasn't listening to him now, too wonderstruck by all the memories to do it any differently.

Charles—oh God, Sam had loved him so much. He had loved his pigeon-toed walk and the feeling of his fingers intertwined in his own, the way his voice sounded when he answered the phone, the appendectomy scar on his belly, how much he cared about his mother, his goofy white-boy dancing, the way he looked at Sam with worry when he knew Sam was sad. And his narrator wished, so desperately, that Sam had fought harder to keep him, this boy who loved him and whom he loved back.

It was so clear now, down here, looking at all of it at once. The way Sam had tried to love Charles, when all the while, he had hated himself so much. The way he'd let all that money and stuff turn him into the worst version of himself. And these, the stories he'd gotten stuck in: the story he was writing, and the story he was living. And here, the story he'd been keeping inside himself.

You have to clear it, she said, and Sam's character looked down at the contents of the box, that silky black dust. He was ready to let it go.

And then he wasn't. *Don't let it go*, his narrator said. And he knew that this box was everything that still kept him connected to Charles. It was the only thing keeping Sam connected to Charles now; it was all of the memories that reinforced the belief that there was something wrong with him, and it was maybe the most vital thing here. And if he let it go, Charles would be gone forever.

And then she was there again, back over his shoulder. His narrator knew that she wanted him to let it go. *I can't*, he shouted silently at her. *I'm not ready.*

You are, she said. His narrator shook his head. Up on the

surface, he heard himself gasping for air. *You have to let it go*, she said. *I can't*, his narrator said again. He felt her pressing against his fear and resistance but he didn't care.

What do you need to keep? she asked.

Scrambling, his character looked around the room. He looked down at the black dust, but it was like a box full of sand. How could he sift through it, grain by grain? He had to let it all go. All of it at once.

And then he saw it—the box that it came in. The container. *That. That's what I need to keep*, his narrator said. *I have to keep the container.*

Okay, she said.

Up on the surface, in his physical body, Sam became aware that he had come to sit upright, cross-legged. He shook and wept. He touched his hands to his face. It was so wet with snot and tears and spit that it felt like amniotic fluid, like he was being born. Across from him, he could feel someone else sitting. Was it Jacob? It had to be. He was sitting so close to Sam that the heat of his body was radiating against him.

Faintly, down in the room, Sam's character could hear Jacob's singsong voice in some ancient prayer. And then, on the surface, Sam's narrator felt Jacob's breath, deep and deliberate and faster than normal, as if he were giving birth. His inhalations came fast and hard, like he was trying to suck the air in through his teeth. It was distracting.

Why is he doing that? Sam's narrator wondered, irritated. But when he turned his attention back down to the room, he realized what was happening.

Jacob was pulling on it. The contents of the container. The black dust. He was tugging at it with his breath. Sam felt the tension, the resistance, felt it dislodge from its cavity in the container and rise up out of the room. *No*, his narrator cried. *I'm not ready.* The blinking white light flashed faster and brighter. *I'm sorry, Charles*, he said. *I'm really sorry.*

Together, his narrator and his character watched transfixed as it rose up into the room, suspended in midair, this cloud of shimmering black dust, and as it moved, it began to assemble shape, all these little bits of data, until it resembled a sleeve, and then a collar, and then a zipper, and as the pieces of it found each other like shavings of metal manipulated by magnets, it became what it was, and what it had always been.

It was the black leather jacket that Charles used to wear.

On the surface Sam wept, rocking back and forth, pouring out his grief in sound.

And then as Jacob pulled in another big breath, the jacket dissolved again and it was just a pile of ash, and with one final, deliberate breath, like slurping an oyster from its shell, the whole thing tugged loose and Sam felt him pull it up and out of the room, and up it came out of Sam's mouth, the hot black energy of all that pain, and it was gone.

It was just gone.

Down in the room, Sam's character looked at the container. As promised, it was still there, but there was nothing inside. It was empty.

Sam's character and his narrator looked at each other. His narrator raised his palm in greeting to his character, and these two parts embraced and became one.

And then, just as swiftly as he had fallen, Sam felt himself ascend back up to the surface, shooting upward with dizzying velocity, traveling the length of his body like it was a thousand miles long, and everything was full of celestial light, like he was changing right there and then, in an instant, like his cells were regenerating, like he was being filled up and split open and turned over a thousand times, and then he opened his eyes and he was back there on the floor of Buck's house, lying in the dark.

It was eerily silent. Sam blinked. He felt her shift through him and out of him.

It was over.

Sam's body vibrated with the energy of what had just happened. He moved one finger, then two. He shook out his feet.

"Sam?" He heard Jacob whisper. "Are you still experiencing effects?"

"No," Sam whispered. "Maybe. I don't know."

He sat up and rubbed his eyes. His face was coated in snot.

"Are you ready to close the ceremony?"

"Yes," Sam said.

"Buck?"

Sam had forgotten all about Buck. Suddenly he felt him beside him. Buck rested a hand on Sam's shoulder. "You okay, buddy?" he said softly.

Sam nodded. And then it was all too much again. He didn't know what he was feeling—everything, maybe, all the anguish and joy and relief. It all lived there inside him for a minute, all of it at once. He curled up on his side in a fetal position and leaned into Buck, smelling the smoky musk of his cologne, twisting up his shirt in his hand, and Sam nestled his head in his collar and cried.

When he stopped crying a few minutes later, he rolled over and lay on his back, breathing fast, then slow. Then he sat up. Jacob looked at him expectantly. Sam felt his hands clasp in front of his body. He bowed his head.

"Thank you, spirit," Jacob said.

And Sam whispered, *Thank you.*

"Thank you for the gift of your medicine."

Thank you. When Sam looked up, the light of a candle

was illuminating the tower of selenite by his feet, making it sparkle.

Jacob looked at Sam. "How do you feel?" he asked.

Sam thought about it for a long moment, trying to find exactly the right word.

"Better," he said.

AFTER

Part Three

12

Integration

"There's something different about you," Brett said. He looked suspiciously at Sam. "Did you get Botox?"

Sam laughed. "No." He furrowed his brow. "Why, do you think I need it?"

"Open your mouth," Brett said. Sam obliged. "Did you bleach your teeth?"

"I have not altered my physical appearance in any way since the last time you saw me."

Brett shook his head. "No, you definitely fucked with something. You look so..." He groaned. "Healthy. Oh God. Is that just how people look out in California? You have that weird, smooth, glowy quality. Like a lifestyle influencer, or a person who takes a lot of supplements."

"I did go to yoga this morning," Sam said. "Namaste."

"Shit," Brett said. "I have to get out of New York."

They were having breakfast at a diner in Murray Hill. Sam had flown in to spend a few days working out of his office in New York. Mostly, though, he had wanted to see Brett.

"So what's been going on?" Brett said, picking at his corned beef hash. "I feel like I've hardly heard from you the last couple months. You've barely been tweeting."

"I dunno," Sam said. "I've been trying to spend less of my life staring at screens. Not in, like, a smug 'I don't even own a TV!' kind of way, just in a, like, my life is out here kind of way." He motioned around the restaurant. "I've even fallen behind on *Housewives*."

"LA has ruined you." Brett cocked his head, studying Sam as though he were an alien. "Are you, like…good, though?"

Sam settled back in his seat. "Yeah," he said. "I'm good. I'm really happy."

Brett pointed at him, circling his finger like he was making a bull's-eye. "This is fucking weird."

"Brett," Sam said. "What's going on with you?"

"Let's see," Brett said. "Well, obviously I took the news of Britney canceling her Vegas residency pretty hard, so that was a whole thing. Oh—you know how my apartment is right by the UN? I was fucking this hot ambassador I met on Grindr and then one day he just—poof!—disappeared. So I looked it up and I think his country just, like, doesn't exist anymore? I don't know. Maybe he got extradited. But to where? And—let's see, what else—yesterday a guy sat down next to me on the 6 train with a giant plastic garbage bag in his lap, and whatever was in the bag was moving. I think it was a raccoon. Or maybe a small child."

Sam was laughing. "I miss living here."

"You hated living here."

"I know. But I have so many tools now that I didn't have before."

"There are *plenty* of tools left in New York." Brett set down his knife and fork. "Speaking of, I saw Charles the other night."

"Oh?" Sam said. "Where?"

"I was DJing at Le Bain and he came in with a bunch of rich kids."

"How did he look?"

"Oh, fine," Brett said. "You know I always thought Charles was—well, you know."

"You never thought he was that interesting."

Brett considered it. "I guess the only truly interesting thing about Charles was how much he loved you." He pointed his fork at Sam. "That made him interesting."

"Did he love me that much?"

"Ugh, of course," Brett said. "And you were just such a fucking nightmare. All you talked about was furniture and how much you hated his friends." He paused. "Are you gonna see him while you're here?"

Sam shrugged. "I hadn't thought about it."

"Liar. You lied about getting Botox and you're lying about this!"

"I'm not!" Sam said. "I just don't think about him that much anymore."

"She's moved on."

"I guess," Sam said. "Or something."

"Let me know how you did it," Brett said, scowling. "I'm going to need your help. Unless there's a coup in Eastern Europe and my ambassador comes home to me." He mock swooned.

"Brett," Sam said. He cleared his throat. "You like your place, right?"

Brett looked momentarily uneasy. "What do you mean?" He blanched. "Oh God, are you here to tell me my building's going condo?"

"No! I just—" Sam looked down at his plate. "Sometimes I miss our apartment. And living with you. I feel like I cut it short. You know?"

Brett waved his fork dismissively. "Please! I've done much more impulsive things for dick. All good things must come to an end and all that."

"Right, well—I'm sorry. If that put you out." Sam looked at his friend. He had needed to get this out, to have this moment of honest reckoning, but now that he was here, Brett seemed so unbothered by it, it made him wonder if it had even been necessary. But then Brett straightened in his seat and looked Sam in the eyes.

"It's nice of you to say," Brett said. "But I like living in a studio. There's nobody to judge the boys I bring home. Well, except my doorman. Who probably thinks I'm a complete dumpster." He paused. "Anyway, when you're ready to drop the skincare regimen, let me know."

After breakfast, Sam decided to walk uptown. He didn't have a specific destination in mind, nor did he need one: the city was like that. In other cities, you moved through the streets as a means of getting to where you needed to go; in New York, the act of traveling through the city was its own worthwhile activity. He had only been gone for two years but it had been transformed already: old buildings that used to house bodegas and dive bars torn down and replaced with pharmacies and banks. Things could change so quickly, or maybe he just noticed different things now.

As he walked, the way the sunlight cascaded down in beams between buildings, all that light and shadow, made him think about Jacob, as he so often did, even now, two months after the ceremony. He closed his eyes and he was there again, in the guest bedroom of Buck's house, the first morning after it was over. The way it felt to stretch out his fingers and tighten them into fists, then hug himself. The way his body, which had always felt like a cage, suddenly felt a little more like a home. The way the hot water, when he stepped into the shower, made him laugh as it hit his skin. *His skin.* The way it felt to have a body.

Drying his hair with a towel that morning, Sam stepped in front of the mirror. He closed his eyes. He said a little prayer. *Please, let me love the person looking back at me. Please, let that part of me be healed.* He opened his eyes and looked at his naked body, as he had so many times before.

Some surface-level disappointment passed through him. It was still all wrong. There were the same hips that had been there yesterday, too wide. There was his belly, still round. There were his ribs, which stuck out like they belonged on the body of someone who was skinny, although he was not. There were his thighs, thick. It was all still there. He disliked it just as much as he ever had.

But as he looked at himself more closely, registering it, he waited for it—all of that chatter—to crystallize, to stick to him. Instead it just sort of dispersed. He looked at his body again. It was all so unremarkable, so no-big-deal. It was as if the tough cord that had connected that conversation to a more substantial sense of worth had been severed overnight. The pit in Sam's stomach that always formed when he looked at himself this way, and the choirs of inner monologue that began the moment he did were silent.

It was the first time he could remember that the way he looked had nothing to do with his value as a person. And it was strange to look at all his faults, acknowledge them and feel next to nothing about them—no shame, no discomfort, no self-consciousness. They just were.

Over breakfast that first morning, Sam told Buck and Jacob about what he had seen and felt down in the room. Jacob was dressed like a professor again. "It sounds so Jungian," he said. His expression was sphinxlike, but his eyes were playful.

"Did you know what you were doing down there, pulling it out of me?" Sam asked. "Except it wasn't you, though, right? You were just, like, the conduit. It was her."

Jacob didn't say anything.

Sam turned to Buck. "What happened for you, Buck?" he said, realizing suddenly that he had no idea whether Buck had experienced anything like what he had—or anything at all—and, stranger still, Sam realized that he cared, deeply, about whether Buck had found the healing that he, too, had sought. *Did you care this much yesterday?* he asked himself, and as much as he tried, he couldn't remember.

Buck turned his head to one side and a little half smile flickered across his face. "I don't know if I can describe it the way you can," he said. "So much of what I saw was beyond words, I guess."

"What did it feel like?"

Buck shook his head. He laughed. "I don't know," he said, and he laughed again. "I don't know. I felt…" He looked down. "I felt young and strong," he said finally. "I wasn't ashamed. She forgave me. And she connected me to everything. Does that make sense?"

"Does it make sense to you?" Jacob asked.

Buck nodded.

"Then that's all that matters."

Sam wanted to press Buck for more details, but he also knew that maybe it wasn't something that could be put into words.

Outside the house, in the driveway, the three men said goodbye. Sam hugged Jacob tightly, thanking him, promising to keep in touch.

"Be careful with your integration," Jacob said. "Drink a lot of water. Be gentle with yourself. Don't look at screens. Breathe."

Sam nodded. "I will," he said.

And then Jacob slung his duffel bag over his shoulder and walked through the gate, out onto the street, and Sam and Buck watched through the open door as he got into the Uber that would take him back to the airport, and for a second it was almost comical how normal he looked, just like anybody else, like any average traveler returning from a business trip, or headed somewhere completely ordinary. And then the car carrying the shaman sped away and he was gone.

Sam turned to Buck, his own bag at his feet. He gathered himself as best he could. "Buck," he said. "Thank you. For this. Whatever it turns out to be."

"Oh, don't mention it," Buck said. "Thanks for coming on the journey with me."

"I'm serious!" Sam said. "This—this whole thing—was just..." He closed his eyes and opened them again. "I feel really lucky."

Buck smiled, and he went crinkly around the eyes. "I can't imagine having done this with anyone else," he said.

And Sam wrapped his arms around Buck and squeezed him as fiercely as he could, and the gratitude was swelling within him, so buoyant it was almost suffocating, and there was no tension anymore, no awkwardness, no mystery of what existed between them to be solved. "I love you," Sam said.

"Love you, too, buddy," Buck said.

A few hours later, after Sam was home, he checked his phone to find a text from Buck. It said, I figured it out. Beneath it was a photograph of a handwritten note on a piece of stationery. Sam zoomed in so he could read it.

Scrawled in all caps, it read: THE FUNDAMENTAL AWARE-NESS OF BEING WORTHY OF LOVE.

Yes, Sam thought. *Exactly like that.*

He found himself noticing things that felt different, and in the beginning each one felt like an epiphany. The next night, dressing up for a cocktail party at Soho House, Sam found his favorite suit was a little snug, but it didn't bother him the way it should have—the way it always had before. And at the party, Sam ran into a television producer he'd been on a few dates with a year earlier; the guy had ghosted him, but Sam didn't care, and when the guy extended his hand for a hand-shake, Sam pulled him in for a hug instead. "It's so great to see you," Sam said, and it really was; he heard the warmth in his voice, the generosity of it, where he would have oth-erwise been chilly, or even ashamed, as though the ghosting had had anything to do with Sam, which he understood now, in a way that he never had before, it did not.

"It's nice to see you, too," the producer said, warily, as though Sam was behaving strangely, which, to be fair, he was.

They chatted for a minute, and then Sam excused himself to the restroom, and when he returned he saw the producer standing in a cluster of people, and Sam stood next to him for a moment, waiting for the producer to acknowledge him or introduce him to his friends, but that didn't happen.

Finally, Sam said, "Hey," and the producer turned and smiled faintly at him, then turned his back to continue his conversation, tacitly dismissing Sam, and for a split second Sam felt a pang of something—all those familiar waves of re-jection, anxiety and embarrassment—but then they passed, and so he shrugged and walked outside to get some air. It was the sort of subtle social slight that would have kneecapped him even a week earlier, triggering every bit of unworthiness and unbelonging that lived in him, but it didn't bother him anymore. *How weird*, Sam thought.

He wove past a pack of willowy male models, one of them impossibly tall and muscular with vaguely Scandinavian features, and his eyes brushed past Sam as if he wasn't there, and once again, Sam saw the outline of a dozen little thoughts, thoughts he'd had a thousand times, rapid-fire and so familiar that he had actually stopped noticing them, so integral were they to his consciousness: *I should look like that. I don't look like that. I am bad because I don't look like that. I am not enough.* But he didn't think the thoughts; he only saw their shape, like tracing something he knew from memory but could no longer see, and instead of settling somewhere in his brain, they just disappeared.

Instead, there was a louder thought, a thought Sam had never had before: *that is just another person existing in his body.* And it was true. That was all he was. It was so simple that it was almost maddening. How had it taken him so long to understand that? And more to the point, how much energy had he wasted trying to negotiate that insecurity with himself a thousand times a day—every time he walked down the street or opened Instagram? What could he do with that energy if he used it for something other than hating himself?

He stood on the balcony for a long minute, looking out at the Hollywood Hills. It was a cold night; he hugged his arms around himself, feeling the warmth of his body, feeling grateful for it. Then he heard his name.

He turned. It was Noah.

"It's you," Sam said, surprised that Noah would be here, but of course he was. He embraced Noah. "How are you?"

Noah lit a cigarette. "Good," he said. "Been good, yeah.

I've been meaning to call you, actually—I'm going back to England in a few weeks. Might be for a bit." He took a drag. "Well, might be for good, really."

"You're moving?" Sam said.

"Whole fucking visa thing," he said. "But I miss London, anyway." He paused. "And the people here—well, everyone's lovely, but they're a little self-obsessed, aren't they?"

Sam laughed. "I'll miss you," he said. He paused. He hadn't rehearsed this, but it had to be said. "You know, Noah, the thing that happened when I was in the hospital... I'm really sorry about that. That must have been awful for you."

"Oh, that?" Noah said, and his eyes were shiny and friendly.

"Yeah," Sam said. "That whole thing just weighs really heavy on me." He paused. "Or it used to, maybe. I don't really know yet."

"Really?" Noah said, as if he was considering it for the first time. "I hadn't given it a thought since it happened."

"But I thought that was such a big part of why, you know..."

"We split up?"

"Yeah."

"I just wanted to do my own thing for a while," Noah said. "And you can be, like, very intense." He raised his hands, as if to say, *Sorry.* "No offense."

"Oh my God," Sam said, and he laughed again, and the sound of his laughter wasn't snide—it was mirthful, even joyful. It felt like the punchline: to see now, so clearly, the way he had turned the people in his life into characters. He'd picked the narrative, then fit people, in his experience of them, to reinforce it. *What if you don't do that anymore?* he thought.

A taxi honked and pulled Sam out of his reverie. He reoriented himself—there was Central Park South, up ahead. He was almost to the Upper East Side. That was where he was going, although he hadn't realized it.

It wasn't all perfect. That was important, too, and in the days and weeks that followed the ceremony, Sam was struck by how easy it was to backslide into old behaviors, that progress wasn't linear, that he could still be the same version of himself he was trying to leave behind. A few weeks after ceremony, he binged again. It came on out of nowhere, like a blackout—he was driving home from a friend's house, after a perfectly pleasant night, and suddenly he was in the drive-through of a fast-food restaurant, ordering half the menu, and when he came back into awareness of what he was doing, he was already on the couch, surrounded by those greasy paper bags and his belly was swollen and he was so confused, like the promise had been broken, and he had this piercing, terrible thought: *Did it even fucking work? Have I changed at all?*

He ran to the bathroom and bent over the toilet, needing to get it out of him, so urgently—it had been years since he had purged like that, and he had to, even though he didn't want to—and he called out to her, the spirit, *Where are you now?*, staring down at the water, furious that he had ended up back here.

And then the hairs on his arms stood up on end and he felt her, like he'd felt her in ceremony, and he lay down on the tile floor and cried for a little while, then went to bed. The next morning he woke up early and went to a yoga class and on the floor, lying in savasana, he put his hand on his belly and whispered *I'm sorry* to his body and then, there, he felt her again, and he knew he was okay.

He had other grievances, too, of course—there was always traffic on Fountain and bills to be paid and emails marked urgent for no reason, and he still spent too much time thinking about his imperfect body and his stalled career and his financial insecurity and his lack of romantic prospects, but in a way that he couldn't quite articulate, it all felt manageable, when it used to be incapacitating, and the despair that had once threatened to swallow him whole just wasn't anywhere near as vast as it had been before, and on those nights where he felt lonely or sad, he just tried to wrap his arms around his body and be with himself instead of running from it, the way he always had before, and even when it rose to its highest intensity and the old and familiar monsters began to claw at his throat, it wasn't so acute.

And soon, so much sooner than he expected, that—*different*—felt normal. That was the worst part, the normalizing of it—what felt at first like a superpower becoming something that he took for granted, that he could talk to people without being deafened by the noise of his neuroses, that he could look at his own reflection without disgust, that he was rarely interested in fucking strangers or binge eating or any of the old fixes he used to resort to in order to get through the day, and even when he tried them, they didn't quite work anymore. Sometimes when he felt stressed or lonely or self-critical, he had to remind himself just how much better it was than it had been before. But there was a difference between remembering a feeling and feeling it, and he couldn't feel it anymore, that big empty. He only recalled it.

Still, he promised himself that he wouldn't forget how bad it had been before. He was grateful that she had let him keep the box that it came in, and if he turned his attention to his belly, he could feel it, the thing inside him that had once been emptiness, only now it felt different—less like emptiness and more like space.

And soon he realized that if he called out to her in those moments of crisis, she would visit him, descending down Sam's spine: a tingling that started in his head and spread through his shoulders. In those moments, he knew it was her, and that reminder, even a gentle one, that he was all right, was really all the solace he needed. Most of the time, anyway.

At some point, Sam figured, she would call him back to ceremony, and when she did, he would go. But he was unhurried. It was strange and divine enough to feel all these new forms of connection. Some clear evenings, walking back to his apartment, he felt the wind move in the palm trees and he knew that was her, too.

Was this how religious people felt? Not to have faith in something you hope exists, but to have actually felt the presence of something beyond this world. To know it was real. To be sure.

Thank you, he whispered out into the night. *Thank you*.

The other thing Sam found himself thinking about a lot in the days after he came out of the ceremony was what it had been like to get sober all those years earlier. He rarely thought about that time of his life anymore, maybe because he'd written it down already, and in so many ways the writing of that first book, his memoir, had been about being able to set it aside and put it away in the past, where it belonged— as though purging it from his memory onto the page made it a thing rather than his life, depersonalizing it in some crucial way. When he was writing the book, while he was with Charles, he'd had to think nonstop about what it had felt like to be a sick and broken drug addict in order to tell the story of it, and then once the book was over and done with, he'd stopped thinking about it altogether. Even when people asked him about it—like that first night at Buck's house, at the dinner party, when the woman with all the bracelets had pressed him for details—he resisted, reciting the same one-line elevator pitch to summarize his book, and accordingly, his life as a young addict, that he'd been using since it came out.

But suddenly he was thinking about it all the time, in a way that he hadn't in years, maybe because everything was new again, and he could finally remember it in a way that hadn't been in his book—to tell the story a different way.

And Sam remembered now, as he walked through the streets of New York, the way it had been when he had made that first decision, some morning in Boston when he was nineteen, hearing his mother's voice on the telephone: *Come home.* The way the words rang out, high and panicked, like two desperate notes. He stepped into the memory, now, but he wasn't afraid of what he would find there.

He had been nineteen and he was high all the time and he was walking then, too, away from his little apartment in Cambridge, where he'd crash-landed after rehab, but in the memory he was walking in a direction he'd never walked in before. How easy it was to get comfortable in certain routes, routes that began to feel as familiar as a favorite sweater; and after Sam had moved into that apartment in Cambridge, he only took one way home, walking from the train station at Davis Square through a little park down a winding foot-path where, occasionally, bicyclists would ride past, ringing their bright singsong bells, and from where the path ended at Massachusetts Avenue, Sam could see his apartment building standing across the street, the light in the window that he had left on during the day. There was a little convenience store on the corner where he would buy cigarettes and junk food. Down Mass Ave in one direction was Porter Square, and up the other was the nearest ATM, as Sam had discovered late one night when he had to pay a drug dealer, as well as a barber shop where one spring afternoon an old man with knobbed hands shaved his head.

But Sam had never walked south of Massachusetts Avenue in all the months he lived there, just had never had occasion to, and at that point in his life—frequently strung out on drugs, and terrified of everything—he wasn't the sort of person who would explore his neighborhood just for fun.

And yet, on that morning, or afternoon, whenever he woke up or came to, still buzzing from the drugs he had taken the night before, the crystal meth he had smoked or snorted still rippling through him, and the man who had come over to get high and lost in his body the way Sam needed to get lost in his still dozing in his bed, Sam felt adventurous, or curious, and he walked the other way, in the direction he had not visited before. And he would say *or* because he genuinely couldn't remember, both because memory was so flexible in the recounting of it and because of the way operating under the influence warps the surfaces of experiences. Remembering an altered state was a process of trying to impose logic onto that which was inherently illogical; how could he puzzle out the factual basics of what he did, let alone why he did it? He was always an unreliable narrator, if only to himself.

So Sam didn't know why he walked that way, but he did, and maybe there was a street with a row of beautiful old houses and it was spring—when did it become spring?—and maybe for a moment he couldn't believe that it had been here all along, just around the corner, if only he had thought to come here and see it. And at some point his phone must have vibrated in his pocket and so he would have looked at the screen and seen that it was his mother calling—and surely there would have been a moment where he debated, as he always did, whether to pick it up or let it go to voice mail—and when she asked him how he was, maybe he told her lies or maybe he made excuses. But he did not remember those things, not really.

He remembered only the sound of her voice, and for a moment all the static dropped out and he heard her, so clearly: *Come home. Come home and get clean.*

And this is how life goes: there will be times where you feel like nothing more than a patchwork quilt of all the worst parts of yourself, and then there will be times when the call to be better is just so lovely and clear, like a bell ringing at a frequency all the voices that keep you up at night can't hear. Maybe he had only had those calls twice in his life—the first, with his own mother, when she had called him to sobriety, and the second, with this one, the spirit of the medicine, when she had called him to healing. She'd been wanting him to come home, too. And he felt it now, the certainty of it. Perfect clarity, that rarest and most precious of things. Those were the moments worth remembering. Those were the moments worth recounting.

That chapter of his life, the years he'd spent as an addict—it didn't have to be some big story about what a shitty person he was. He could just remember it, acknowledge it and let it go.

This was the thing that he knew now, that he had never quite understood before: the way memory could be both the lock and the key, how easily it kept him in the bondage of old stories he didn't need anymore, and how easily, too, it could show him everything he needed to know about who he was.

He had been so afraid that he would feel like a fraud walking into twelve-step meetings after the ceremony, that no matter how useful it proved, having undergone this experiment with the shaman would somehow contaminate the integrity of his sobriety, but when he went to a meeting a few days after, he felt like he belonged more now than he had before. He looked around at the people in the room, and it all felt so human, so worthy, and he was warm and unguarded as he stacked chairs at the end, giving out his phone number and

telling newcomers to keep coming back, and in those moments he wasn't thinking about himself at all.

So it took a little while, but soon Sam felt like maybe this
was the person he was supposed to be, someone who woke up
early and meditated for a few minutes, someone who picked
up the phone when people called him, someone who made a
list of ten things he was grateful for every night before bed for
no reason other than that it made him feel good, and when
he fucked up, he just tried not to do it again. *Was it really that
simple?* he wondered sometimes. *And did I really need a shaman
to show me all that?*

He didn't talk about it, really, except with a few close
friends. It wasn't that he was ashamed of it, or secretive. It
was more that he wanted everyone else to get the call on their
own, the way he had, to find it if they were meant to find it
and in their own time.

Kat asked him once, "Do you ever wonder if it really
happened the way it felt like it did or if you were just super
fucked-up on ayahuasca? Like, was any of the magic stuff
real?"

Sam thought about it for a long moment. "It doesn't matter," he said. "It was real to me."

Sam turned the corner of East Sixty-Third Street toward
Second Avenue. He had arrived at the building where he'd
lived with Charles. He hadn't been back in two years, since
the morning he left for Los Angeles.

He sat down on the lip of the white brick planters that
lined the facade of the building a few yards away from the
awning. A doorman in a black suit helped a woman with her
shopping bags into the building, making small talk, both of
them laughing about something. Sam looked around him.
He hadn't remembered this little garden—was that new? The
flowers in it were in full bloom.

He'd half expected to cry, but he didn't. Instead he just sat there for a long while, thinking. Remembering. Not letting the memories constellate into a narrative, but just letting them pass through him, in and out, like breath.

13

The Whole Body

The next morning, Sam woke up to the sound of thunder, his eyes adjusting to the darkness. The neon lights of the clock on the nightstand told him it was just past 6:00 a.m. *Shit.* He looked around the hotel room, registering the economically sized desk and blackout curtains. New York. *You are back in New York and that is fine. You know what to do.*

He made a cup of coffee. He sat cross-legged on the hotel bed and put on a playlist of chants he had heard in the kundalini yoga class he went to some mornings in Los Angeles, ignoring the notifications that had rolled in overnight on his phone. He closed his eyes and sang aloud to himself in Gurmukhi: *Har har har gobinday. Ra ma da sa. Ek ong kar sat nam.* He did not look at his email inbox or unread text messages or Instagram or Twitter. He put on shorts, a tank top and a hooded rain slicker and headed out into the drizzly morning. He went to a class in Tribeca, where an instructor in cream tights and a cream crop top led him in an hour of movement, tapping heels that led into squats that became jumping jacks before giving way to unchoreographed flailing. "Get out of the fucking mirror and get back in your fucking body!" she yelled over the Maggie Rogers song that was thudding out of the speakers. He did push-ups back into child's pose, a set of four movements, each with a corresponding message, which he thought at his body in a clear internal voice: *Thank you. I love you. Forgive me. I'm sorry.* After it was over, he went back to the hotel and showered. He put a crystal around his neck, a chunk of clear quartz on a golden chain. And once all this was done, he felt the same way he'd felt right after ceremony: peaceful and embodied and alive, like he'd taken a different door into the same room.

In his office, he found that he kept touching the crystal, tugging at it, feeling the tension of its chain pulling around his neck. It brought him back to something.

That night, he dressed quietly in his hotel room. He slipped into blue jeans and a plain black T-shirt. He looked at himself in the mirror and took a deep breath. *You look fat*, a voice in his head said.

So what? a louder voice said.

He said out loud, "You're okay."

He felt better. He sat on the side of the bed and tied his shoes.

He took a cab to the Flatiron. It was dusk. He slipped through the curtained entryway of a new restaurant that had opened a few months earlier, everything gleaming and white. The hostess showed him to his table.

When Charles walked in, Sam almost didn't recognize

him. He looked exactly the same as he always had, wearing a shiny bomber jacket and designer loafers, as usual, his eyes bright blue and expressive, his mouth pink, a little scruff. But in Sam's mind, over the course of remembering him so many times, he had forgotten what his face actually looked like, the specificity of it. He had made Charles a character, one so vivid that he had ceased to be a person. Now here he was, in flesh and blood, and it was curious to behold him.

Charles smiled. "Hey," he said softly.

Sam stood up, coming around the side of the table. They embraced for a minute, and Sam inhaled the scent that lived at the nape of his neck, linen and oudh. It had been so long since he'd smelled it.

"I really missed you," Sam said.

"I missed you, too," Charles said.

They sat down. "How have you been?" Sam said, and as the words came out of his mouth, he realized he genuinely wanted to know how Charles was, not with an agenda—not because it would tell Sam something about himself, about his real or perceived value, about whether Charles was thriving or suffering without him now, two years later, but simply because he loved Charles and he cared how he was doing.

And so they talked for a while about Charles's job at the hedge fund and the shifts in the global market, about how his mother was considering buying a house in the Hamptons but couldn't find a property she liked, about the guy Charles had been dating who was nice but seemed a little too attached, about his family's upcoming holiday in Portofino, about how Eleanor's boyfriend had proposed and she was turning into a complete bridezilla, and Sam felt it all, the familiar rhythms of how they had talked to each other, the overlapping beats of their conversation, and it was as if no time had passed at all, and also as if a thousand years separated them instead of two, all that closeness and all that distance.

"Are you happy?" Sam asked.

"Yes," Charles said. Then he reconsidered. "I don't know. Most of the time, yeah—I am." He looked at Sam and the corners of his mouth turned down, like he was afraid. "Are you?"

Sam nodded. "Yeah," he said. "I am."

"Good," Charles said. He looked down, then back at Sam. "All my friends read your book," he said. "They all really liked it."

"That's really nice."

"It was a good book, Sam."

"Sure," Sam said. "I mean, whatever."

"You don't have to do that."

"No, I don't mean—it's just not about the book."

"You and me?"

"No," Sam said. "No, not that—I mean, all of it. I can't—I don't know how to explain it." He rubbed his face with his hands. "You know I only wrote that book because I thought it was going to fix me. To fill up the emptiness that had been inside me my entire life. And then it didn't work. It didn't fix anything. And I'd already lost you over it."

"You didn't lose me over the book," Charles said. "You were already too lost, by the end. I just couldn't keep trying to find you." He picked at his food. "You're happy now, though."

"I am."

"What changed?"

And so he told Charles the story of Jacob and the whole weekend, what he had remembered and what he had seen, and what had happened down in the room, and Charles's eyes widened when Sam got to the part about the leather jacket—"The Valentino?" he asked, and Sam laughed and said, "Yes, the Valentino."

"Why do you think you saw that?" he asked.

Sam thought about it. "The room," he said. "So that was the place where I stored all the evidence, right? And this is how I always moved through my life—trying to prove this thesis, collecting data to support my most deeply held belief, which was that I was bad. So I discarded the experiences that might disprove that theory, and hung on only to the memories of those that supported it. It was confirmation bias on the deepest level. And it just got worse and worse, the more proof I had that I was bad. And when you left me, I think, it was the ultimate confirmation I had been looking for." He shook his head. "It seems so obvious now. You, not being a complete fucking nightmare, basically understand that bad things happen to you because that is a part of life. But, Charles—I always believed, even if I couldn't articulate it, that bad things happen to me because I *am* bad. And so I needed everything to be bad so it would agree with the only thing I really knew about myself."

Sam sighed. "I wish I had known that then," he said. "I wish I had been able to accept how much misery is self-fulfilling." He felt tears well up in his eyes, then spill out down his cheeks. "But maybe I wouldn't have been able to love you the way I did if I had been any wiser," he said. "I really am sorry, Charles. I'm so sorry that I wasn't better."

"You were just so unhappy, by the end," Charles said. "I didn't know how to help you."

Sam laughed through his tears. "God, I was so uncomfortable," he said. "My body. My poor body. I hated it so much." He rested his hands on his thighs and squeezed them affectionately. "And I was so addicted to the stuff. To your lifestyle." He corrected himself. "Our lifestyle. Even though it wasn't making me happy." He looked down at his sneakers. "And now it all feels so dumb—I mean, none of it was really that important, but it mattered so much at the time, you know? I just didn't know how to be a person in the world."

"Being a person is hard," Charles said, and he looked sad. "Especially when you're complicated."

"It is but it isn't," Sam said. "I mean—even that. Why do I have to be complicated? Why do I have to be broken? Why can't the story be something else?"

"So you really think he healed you? The shaman?"

"Sort of?" Sam said. "Maybe he did. Or maybe I was just ready."

"Ready for what?"

"Change," Sam said. "To change. I mean, for so long I felt so sick and crazy. But maybe I was just healing in my own way. Slowly, and inelegantly."

"What do you mean?"

Sam closed his eyes. The hairs on his arms stood up on end. "Maybe you don't heal in a vacuum," Sam said. "Maybe you don't heal on the floor of somebody's house with a shaman blowing holy smoke in your face. Or maybe that's part of it, but it's not all of it, because the healing isn't just the part that looks like healing. You don't just get fixed in a weekend. You have to keep making the choice to fix yourself. Every time you choose to be nice to yourself instead of being unkind. Every time you decide to experience life fully in all its shades of joy and sorrow. Every time you participate in the boring drudgery of self-care. The whole thing was the healing—everything that came before and everything that's happened after. Not only what happened with the shaman. He just got me unstuck."

Sam looked at the door. The wind was moving in the curtain. It looked like it was dancing. "I go to this meditation class sometimes," he said.

"You're into meditation now?" Charles said in disbelief. "Oh God, you really do live in LA."

"Yeah," Sam laughed. "I do. Okay, so wait, listen—I go to this meditation class and at the very end, the teacher starts naming different parts of the body that you're supposed to draw your awareness to—like, she starts with your feet, and she says, 'The left big toe,' and you pay attention to your big toe, and she says, 'The left second toe,' and you pay attention to your second toe, and then it's your legs and your hips and each of your fingers, up to the crown of your head, and then she says, 'The whole body. The whole body. The whole body,' and it's like, all of a sudden I feel it, all of it, every cell and every molecule and all the life inside me, and they aren't different parts anymore. They're all connected."

Sam took a deep breath and exhaled it out through his teeth. "I guess that's what it's like. For so long all the things that happened to me were just these—these different parts, this jumble of disconnected incidents that didn't mean anything on their own. And now it feels like all those bones took shape and became a skeleton. Something assembled. It became a whole body." He looked down at his feet. "This entire story was just the story of my body. And how I had to hate it, because it was the thing that I came in. But the story is also its own body, and I can finally accept it, exactly as it is. So it's another memoir, I guess, because it's the things I remember about what happened to me, but it isn't, because it's all of me. And I can finally access everything. Does that make sense?"

"No," Charles said. He looked at Sam like he was speaking in another language. "Can you explain it another way?"

Sam started to laugh. "I don't know if I can," he said through gusts of laughter, and tears were streaming down his face again. "I guess what I'm saying is that it all had to happen in the body. You know? Like, I kept trying to get it out with my words—I was trying to tell a story. But that's what I was doing wrong all along. I thought the story was the medium. But the medium was the body."

"I have literally no fucking idea what you're talking about," Charles said.

"Shit," Sam said helplessly, and for a moment he was bowled over by the absurdity of it. "I'm one of those people!" He laughed. "I'm a crazy LA self-help person who talks in platitudes and metaphors and riddles!" He covered his face with his hands. "This is the worst!"

Charles reached across the table and gripped Sam's wrists. "Okay, but do you love yourself now?" he asked. There was an edge to his voice, something sharp and urgent, and it caught Sam off guard, to realize that Charles still cared about his happiness.

"Oh, no, I don't think so," Sam said. "But I hate myself so much less than I used to."

Outside on the street, they held each other for a long time. "I don't want to say goodbye," Charles whispered in his ear. He put his hand on the back of Sam's head.

"Me, either," Sam said.

But then he felt their bodies pulling away from one another.

So, one more time, Sam let him go.

And just like that, he was alone again.

Except he wasn't. Sam could feel her with him. Maybe she'd always been there, even when he hadn't known it. Or maybe she'd come to him in ceremony for the first time and now he had her, this funny sort of guardian. Something wise and ancient and true, something that was in him and around him, something that was real—realer than the clothes on his back or the shoes on his feet and realer even than Charles, whom he had loved so fiercely, long before he'd had any idea how to love himself.

What a thing—to love someone that much. And Sam was sad, but he was grateful, too, for each of the men who had showed him exactly what he needed to see; not only the spirit, who took no shape, but the way she moved in and out of people. He had loved them all, and been loved by them, in so many strange and nettling and incandescent ways, Brett and Noah and Buck and Jacob and Charles, these healers and teachers.

Maybe, Sam thought, he hadn't made a mess of anything. Maybe he had done it just right.

After Charles was gone, Sam walked through the city with her for a while. His legs were strong, and his heart beat fast. The streets were cool and dark, but the lights were bright above him. Everything was connected. And for a moment it seemed like magic that this body, the only body he would ever have, could take him anywhere.

★ ★ ★ ★ ★

ACKNOWLEDGMENTS

First: to Cait Hoyt, this book only exists because of your unwavering faith and encouragement. Thank you for shepherding this project forward with ferocity and grace. To Olivia Blaustein, thank you for being an extraordinary champion and friend for this story and all the others. To Kate Childs, Norris Brooks, Kelly Eichenholz, Jonas Brooks, Darian Lanzetta, Ben Levine and everyone else at CAA: I feel stupid lucky all the time to be blessed by your positivity, enthusiasm and hard work.

To John Glynn, I could not ask for a better editor and friend. I will never forget the way you fought for this story and believed in it from the beginning. To everyone at Hanover Square who worked tirelessly to help this book find a readership, I am so grateful to you: Peter Joseph, Laura Gianino, Roxanne Jones, Emer Flounders, Randy Chan, Linette Kim, Eden Church, Heather Connor, Margaret O'Neill Marbury,

Kristin Bowers, Jim Hankey, Gabe Barillas, and the people whose names I don't know who played roles both big and small in getting this into the hands of readers.

To Chase Lehner and Liz Mahoney, thank you for your passion, cheerleading and all-around brilliance.

To my wonderfully generous and supportive colleagues, particularly Kelly Conniff and Lucy Feldman, for your early reads, sharp notes and hand-holding, thank you.

To the authors who graciously said lovely things about this book when I was in a prepublication vulnerability vortex— Chloe Benjamin, Steven Rowley, Richard Lawson, Jamie Lee Curtis, Taylor Jenkins Reid, Garth Greenwell—I will always be in your debt.

To Taylor Swift, thank you for letting me nerd out over your lyrics in these pages and also for January 5.

To my family, sorry for writing another deeply personal thing and thank you for putting up with me. (I swear this is the last time.)

To my friends, too many to count, who read drafts, carried me while I was spiraling and buoyed my spirits at every step, thank you—I am especially grateful to Jill Gutowitz, Steph Stone, Debby Ryan, Dave Rocco, Carey O'Donnell, Tommy Dorfman, Kelly Stone, Jennifer Kaytin Robinson, Stacy Waronker, Bradley Stern and Ryan O'Connell for your collective humor, insight and kindness.

To the healers and teachers, both those I can name and those I can't, who inspired this story—thank you for all the lessons. Special thanks to wise women Taryn Toomey, Natalie Kuhn and Erin Rose Ward, for returning me to my body, as well as Maud Nadler, who taught me how to make it a home.